The Perfect Fraud

The Perfect Fraud

A Novel

Ellen LaCorte

HARPER LUXE

An Imprint of HarperCollinsPublishers

HarperCollins books may be purchased for educational, business, or sales promotional use. For information, please e-mail the Special Markets Department at SPsales@harpercollins.com.

FIRST HARPERLUXE EDITION

ISBN: 978-0-06-291155-1

HarperLuxe™ is a trademark of HarperCollins Publishers.

Library of Congress Cataloging-in-Publication Data is available upon request.

19 20 21 22 23   LSC   10 9 8 7 6 5 4 3 2 1

For Michael,
For Always

The Perfect Fraud

1
Claire

"Claire, your phone's buzzing. Again," yells Cal. I don't carry anything when we run, and my boyfriend, Cal, who whines about his role as my personal Sherpa, usually has his pockets stuffed with things like mints, tissues, and my phone, in addition to whatever he might need.

"Who is it?"

"Your mom."

"Decline, decline, decline," I shout over my shoulder.

At a minimum, conversations with my mother are stilted volleys of *how are you, I'm fine, how are you, fine, how's Dad, resting, that's good, okay, I better go, me too, bye, bye.*

Sometimes, though, because her natural resting state is worry—a condition exacerbated by my father's long-term illness—her phone calls are fueled by frenzied and unfounded concerns for me, their only child.

Since my mother is a psychic, as were her mother and her mother's mother, her twice-weekly calls are often peppered with messages from beyond: don't go near any green cars on the tenth; your great-great-grandmother says you should see a dentist about your back molar on the right side; toss your red pants (because of fire danger). I wasn't sure whether this last one really was predictive of disaster or because the pants on my five-foot-ten frame made me look like a clown tottering on garishly colored stilts. Obstinately, after that call, I wore those pants for six evenings straight, with every candle in our apartment lit, and met no catastrophic fate.

Miss Madeline, as my mother is known, is somewhat of a celebrity on the East Coast. She does it all: foretelling the future with tarot; channeling deceased spirits through mediumship; and medical intuitiveness, where she'll scan a body with her mind to identify areas of illness or disease. The only thing she can't or won't do is aura reading. She says all the electronic devices people have on or near them these days interfere with the energy fields and that this prevents her from accurately seeing the colors hovering around their heads.

Clients flock from every state and, not infrequently,

from other continents for an opportunity to sit across from her. It's not only to learn whether their deadbeat son-in-law will come through with the court-required child support payments so their equally feckless daughter and her two hyperactive sons will not have to live with them until their last opportunity expires to move to the west coast of Florida and have some peace at last, for God's sake. My mother is also a revered healer, having honed her skills in the opulent backyard herbal and medicinal garden of the suburban Philadelphia home where she still lives and practices. She can argue for hours about the virtues of goat's milk over cow's, or ferociously debate whether the benefits of a gluten-free existence are more fad than fact. So, besides offering assurance to Nanny and Pop-Pop that the universe predicts a move to warmer climes (and away from their wayward brood), my mother can also sell them kava kava root to steep, sip, and soothe their frazzled nerves.

Of course, as I have been told since I was old enough to comprehend, I am expected to carry forth the family gift.

Three days a week I read tarot and provide "psychic guidance" at Mystical Haven, the seventh or eighth— I've lost count—in a string of employers with names like Sandi's Spirit Spot, the Soul Center, and Psychic Circle. Before we moved to Sedona, Arizona, I worked at Tea and See, a store on Central Avenue in Phoenix, which specialized in leaf reading but was actually a front for the owner's thriving drug business featuring a whole different kind of leaves.

"I've pressed 'decline' six times, but she keeps calling back."

"Good. Do it again."

"Maybe it's important," Cal nudges.

"Press. 'Decline.' Please."

Since my mother keeps trying, I assume she's in one of her revved moods, and I refuse to spend what will be over an hour on the phone listening to her tell me about a vision she had where I was saved from quicksand by a fox or a hedgehog, she couldn't tell which, or to have her ask whether I'd read the article on "The Restorative Properties of Slippery Elm," which arrived in our mailbox earlier this week. She'd highlighted a paragraph—in neon purple—about "languid digestion." This was after I'd complained about a bellyache, although I was fairly certain my distress was from a spicy chicken enchilada and twice that in margaritas, details I'd neglected to mention.

I leap over a prickly pear, several of its pads half-mooned by javelina, a fact substantiated by the residual eye-watering stink. I figure they'd marked the area and breakfasted here, probably within the past hour or so, and I hope they'd moved on to forage through the neighborhood trash cans or doze under some mesquite shrubs.

Yards behind me, I hear Cal stumbling. He's all forward movement, little grace. I ran hurdles in high school, which trained me to gauge where to place my lead leg and to avoid stutter steps when facing an obstacle—like the agave that, judging by a string of curses, Cal flew into and not over.

"Watch out," I shout back, laughing.

This morning we're running on Little Horse, a trail most people avoid after a heavy rain, which I don't understand because it's precisely the time I want to be here. After the soaker last night, the dusty arroyos are overflowing, transforming the trail with glistening miniature waterfalls. It's a run we can squeeze in before work since we never take the side leg to Chicken Point because that's where the Pink Jeep tours deposit their customers. I get my fill of tourists in the store during the day, with their white sneakers, oversized glass "diamond" studs, and tacky sweatshirts pronouncing: DROVE HERE FROM BOBBIE'S BEANERY IN TOPEKA AND STILL HAVE GAS IN THE TANK.

Besides, I've heard the shtick from the Pink Jeep tour drivers so many times I could probably lead a group. First, they inch the Jeep back almost to the rim of the plateau so the women will scream, imagining themselves plummeting to their deaths. Then, after everyone hops down, the driver will shout, "Who wants a jumping picture?" and all the kids will line up. As he takes the photo, they'll leap as high as they can so it looks like they're hanging suspended in the air over a ravine. It's actually only ten or so yards down but it's an impressive shot to show the folks back in Minnesota.

A tiger whiptail lizard races across the path, his brownish-orange body nearly camouflaged by the puffs of red dust in his wake. He zips under a creosote bush at the base of a gnarled juniper pine.

Rounding the final bend of the trail, I nearly slam into a family hiking up. I can tell they belong together because of the matching red camp shirts with the white lettering on the front that reads: MALOVECKIO, LIVE THE ADVENTURE, 2018. Definitely not local. They're hatless, dressed in tank tops, and wearing flip-flops. The girl sports a sheer lace top, false eyelashes, earrings that dangle to her shoulders, and a deep brownish-colored lipstick. The older man (her father, I assume) is red-cheeked and sweaty, and his bald head shimmers like blacktop on a sweltering day. A woman (mom) and another, younger kid (son) struggle behind. I want to take the phone out of the daughter's hand, dial nine one one, and then return it to her. That way, she'll be prepared to save her father's life when he collapses with heat exhaustion.

"Phone, Claire. C'mon. She keeps calling back," Cal shouts, and then I hear him exchange pleasantries (*beautiful day for a hike; only another two miles to the top, cools down at night*) with the Maloveckios as he maneuvers around their caravan. Even though I'm always begging him to not engage, I've seen Cal have a fifteen-minute conversation with the guy who delivers our UPS packages. I observed this from the living room window and figured they were probably discussing the exorbitant expense of shipping. When I came out front to remind Cal we only had ten minutes to get to a movie, I interrupted the delivery guy's story about his daughter's attachment to her rabbit, which, at almost eleven years, had recently died, leaving his little girl brokenhearted. Nodding sympathetically, Cal said that was a pretty long life for a rabbit and he hoped his daughter would feel better soon. He also advised the guy not to replace the bunny quite yet, to allow for a period of grieving.

"Fine," I yell to him. "I'll call her when I get to the store. Let's finish this, okay? You sound like you're about to collapse." I glance back to confirm what I knew I'd see: Cal, scarlet-faced and puffing, navy

T-shirt plastered to his chest. The little engine that tries and tries and almost can't.

"Only another half mile," I say in a voice I hope sounds liltingly encouraging but suspect comes off as condescendingly disapproving.

A grunt from behind.

We skid into the gravel parking lot, and Cal bends over to clutch his knees and gulp air. From here, there is a clear view of the sky, which is an unblemished turquoise except for a jet plume streak of white.

"Good run," he huffs and grins. He means it sincerely, even though it will take another twenty minutes for his breathing to stabilize, and tonight he'll be limping from a strain in one or both calves. He means it because he knows I love to run and because he loves me.

Five things about Cal:

One, Calloway Parker Reinberg is the name on his birth certificate, a reflection of his parents' love of jazz, particularly scat and bebop.

Two, Cal was born circumcised, a rare occurrence, which in the Jewish religion indicates the baby boy will be blessed with unlimited potential. His parents gasped in joy when presented with their foreskin-less baby. At the time, since they possessed both optimism and creativity, they were certain this child, favored with a sparkling future and sporting the initials CPR, would somehow revive their crumbling marriage. He didn't.

Three, Cal dreamed of becoming a psychologist and had just started a master's program at UCLA before he ran into me five years ago at Taste of the Maze, a beer and wine sampling event held on seven acres of corn. There are probably inebriated attendees still wandering around in the labyrinth, searching for the exit.

Four, Cal is more generous, kind, and understanding than I can ever pretend to be.

"Let's go, Oz. Those cards aren't going to read themselves, you know," he says now, grinning and pushing me toward the car.

It's a nickname—Oz, sometimes Ozzie—he gave me after we smashed into each other at the drunken maze event. This was during fall break my sophomore year at the University of California, Berkeley. I drove north to visit a friend, who adamantly refused to go into the maze with me. "I get lost in the mall," she whined.

I had rounded a corner I was certain was the same one I had passed three times already and hurtling toward me was a blur that only registered to me in the dark as "man, tall and wide." We collided and as we untangled limbs and exchanged *Are you okay?*s he extracted a toy-sized flashlight from his pocket—sub-fact about

Cal: he's always prepared—and directed it toward my face. He introduced himself and declared my eyes were so incredibly green they reminded him of the Emerald City of Oz. He then took my hand and, illuminating the turns ahead of us, led us to freedom within three minutes.

The fifth thing about Cal is that he knows I can read tea leaves only if the bag is clearly marked Lipton. That the tarot deck means nothing to me except that the pictures are pretty. And that any psychic visions I have are likely the result of a terrible hangover.

Only Cal knows that Claire Hathaway is a complete fraud.

2
Rena

"Yeah, they want to keep her some more in the hospital," I tell my sister. Squeezing the phone between my shoulder and my ear, I count out underwear. "And I still have to finish this stupid packing."

"How's that going?" Janet asks.

"Pain in the ass."

"They giving you a hard time?"

"Like you would not believe. Listen, I gotta go, okay?"

"Sure, bye."

A "hard time"—that's a laugh. When Gary and me were first married, our cat got stuck inside a birdhouse. One of those ones on a pole. I'm washing dishes that afternoon and there's this black tail waving back and forth from the hole. Gary had a hell of a time getting that dumb cat out. Still has the scars to show for it too.

Trying to get Stephanie, my little girl, discharged from the hospital has been like that.

Moving her from New Jersey to a new doctor in Arizona was my idea. Of course, Gary's mad. He sells spiral staircases, and his territory is the southeast. He said, "I can't be expected to just pick up and leave, you know."

No, he can't. But I have to do anything and everything to help my baby.

I really don't know how much more her tiny body can take. It started when she was six weeks old. She'd throw up and scream all the time. I took Steph to Dr. Grant, her first pediatrician. He tested for anemia. He checked her heart and her lungs, and after a million more tests, he says to me she's a "failure-to-thrive baby." I just busted out crying when he said that. It felt like what he was really saying was I was a failure as a mommy. He told me that wasn't true and that some kids just needed more food.

No shit, but anything I fed her came right up or went right out. The doctor says to me, "Just keep up the calorie intake any way you can."

That's when I switched her to an all-organic diet, but it didn't seem to help much. Her stomach was still a fucking mess. *I* was a fucking mess. I couldn't sleep. I stayed up all night long, listening to see if she was in pain or needed anything.

I really thought Dr. Grant was great at first. He was always nice. Once, he even complimented me on the way I was holding Steph because it calmed her right down. But when he told me to just feed her more, it felt like he was totally blowing me off. I mean, wasn't I the one at home with her all the time? Gary and me, we could see how sick she was. The doctor, he says, "Rena, overall, she's a healthy little girl, just small for her age." He told me to try changing formulas. Oh, sure, like finding another organic formula was so easy. And he said to feed her a lot of small meals during the day.

I followed all his advice, I really did. She'd still scream for hours, and this was after only a stupid spoonful or two of mashed potatoes. What the hell? What's easier to digest than mashed potatoes? Sometimes when things got too bad, I'd have to take her to the emergency room. I swear, we've been to every single ER in the five hospitals around where we live in northern New Jersey. She's been examined by physician's assistants, interns, residents, and nurses. And she's had more CT and PET scans than I can count on all my fingers and toes. They keep checking for things like missing stomach enzymes, cystic fibrosis, celiac disease, allergies, and congenital heart defects.

Nothing's ever found. I've been bugging Gary to go to the doctor because he's had a horrible stomach ever since him and me have been together. Maybe it's a genetic thing? Who knows? We need to look at every possibility. We have to figure this out.

When Steph and me go to a new doctor, I always say this little prayer right before the appointment: "Please, God, let this doctor figure out what's going on so my baby can get the help she needs." And I'm always so sad and disappointed when it doesn't turn out that way.

Where is Gary all this time? On the road selling curving steps. It's been me doing what I needed to do when I needed to do it. The doctors here don't seem to know shit about what's going on with my baby, so I spent hours and hours on the computer to find the best pediatric gastroenterologist in the nation. Gary's pissed, but is it my fault that Dr. Riley Norton's practice is in Phoenix?

Gary and me split when Stephanie was only one. As part of the divorce, we coparent. On paper, this means he lives in the next town over and is supposed to have Steph every other weekend. But since he's on the road at least three weeks out of every month, I take care of most everything, including all the medical stuff. Really, he only sees her on holidays, usually at my house. He said he'd try to get to Arizona sometime during the six months I think I'll need to stay. I don't care how long it takes. Six months or six years—I'm not leaving until someone can finally tell me what's wrong with her. Gary's right about making sure he keeps his job. He definitely cannot do anything to screw up our health insurance, which he carries. This was part of the divorce settlement too.

As I probably could have guessed, Stephanie's current specialist, Dr. Rondolski, has been an absolute asshole about me taking this step. But if he can't cure her, what the hell does he expect me to do? Sit by her bed, hold her little hand, and watch her slowly die?

I'm luckier than other moms with sick kids. I had three years of nursing school, and I'm still amazed at how much I remember. During my third year I got pregnant with Stephanie, but before that, I was studying hard and getting ready to start my clinical training in the community hospital. Shock all around and a quick wedding. Of course, I quit school the month before she was born.

But I know a lot of the medical terms and can understand the tests and what the results mean. To most people, it's like a foreign language. That's why, when Steph's in the hospital, I'll go room to room to talk to the other parents. Sometimes they're confused about what's happening to their kid, and I can translate the scary medical words into plain old English. I swear ancient doctors did this on purpose. I mean, what better way to get patients to do whatever they're told? Just make the language totally impossible to understand.

I was really hopeful about Dr. Rondolski. He was highly recommended by my daughter's fourth pediatrician, who said after treating her for almost two years, "I'm not sure what else I can do." At first, Dr. Rondolski was so wonderful. He was really on top of things. Of course, he ran every kind of test, including some new ones, but mostly repeats. At least fifty blood tests, lots of CT scans and MRIs, a breath hydrogen evaluation to check for lactose intolerance, and also an endoscopy and colonoscopy to try to find out why Stephanie almost always has the shits. And he would actually listen to me when I told him about her symptoms. In the beginning, he even said that my nursing background was a huge bonus since I could understand what he was saying to me. I thought, great, we were partners, and together, we would figure this out.

But that isn't what happened. It started to take a really long time for him to return my phone calls, or sometimes he never called back at all, and I had to call again. Of course, I knew he was busy. It took months to get in for that first appointment. But I began to wonder whether his dipshit front office person was screening my calls and telling him whether or not I actually needed to speak to him. It was so frustrating.

The final straw was in the emergency room, six weeks ago. Stephanie had been doing so good for a few days. No vomiting, no diarrhea. And she was actually eating. Not a lot but a couple of bites here and there. I thought maybe, finally, she was getting better. Then, that night, we're sitting on the couch watching *Frosty the Snowman*. I taped it for her last Christmas. Out of nowhere, Steph begins to ask me all sorts of crazy questions. Like what was the snowman's name and why was that little girl going with him on the train to the North Pole? Stephanie had Frosty practically memorized by the time she was three and could sing the whole song, without screwing up any of the words. But that night, she was all confused and couldn't get it right.

She asked me for a drink of water and then for another one. She gulped these down so fast I wasn't surprised when she grabbed her stomach and threw up all over the couch. I ran to get a towel, and when I came back, she was on the floor. Her back was arched, and her arms and legs were twitching. I recognized a seizure when I saw one, so I threw her in the car and drove like a maniac to the emergency room.

They called Dr. Rondolski, and he met us there. He asked me if Stephanie fell that day, thinking maybe she had a head injury. He asked me if she had been running a fever. He was looking for anything to explain why she was having seizures.

After eight horrible hours in the ER, he finally told me what was going on. He said that Stephanie had hypernatremia, which was too much sodium in her system. He said normal serum sodium levels are 135, or maybe 145. Hers was almost 170. They gave her fluids to get down the level of sodium, and eventually, the seizures stopped. Dr. Rondolski wanted to keep her in the hospital for a while to see if he could find out why her sodium level was so high.

But it's been six weeks and he still doesn't know what the hell's going on. He ran all the same tests all over again, and it feels like we're no closer to an answer. We still don't know what's wrong with her stomach or why her sodium level went nuts. I feel like I'm just standing by and watching her go downhill every day. I'm scared out of my mind. I decided that, even if it meant moving to another state, I had to find someone who could finally figure out what's going on with my daughter. Now I just have to get her discharged so we can leave.

Getting ready for the trip is driving me nuts. I'm

only taking two suitcases. I roll pajamas to squeeze in next to our sandals. I'm thinking we'll probably need sneakers too. When I kneel down to lift up the dust ruffle, I feel the pain in my knee. I had a bad fall off a bike when I was a kid. What was I thinking anyway, trying a wheelie like the cool girls? The nineteen pounds I put on the past five years don't help either. Even though I'm only thirty-two, I know I need to get knee replacement surgery. But it will have to wait. Stephanie is first. Stephanie is always first.

No sneakers under the bed. I hold on to the side of the mattress and pull myself up. The sheets smell like cheese, and there's a cup with day- (or week-?) old coffee on the night table. Piles and piles of pages of printed Internet articles about kids' stomach issues are all over the floor, the chair, and the top of my makeup table. Every drawer in my bureau is open, and stuff is falling out onto the rug, which still has a piss stain on it from Maxie. That poor cat is always ignored when I have to stay at the hospital all one day and into the next. It looks like the house was attacked by robbers who didn't have a fucking clue what they wanted to steal.

I shut my eyes and try to take a deep breath, but it feels like the air only makes it as far as my collarbone. When I open one eye, I see the toe of Stephanie's pink

Ked sticking out from under my jeans on the floor in the corner. This is at least half a success, but I'm too tired to keep looking for the other sneaker. I head into the kitchen. It's only slightly less gross in here. I fix coffee that's old and probably tastes like shit, but so what? It's caffeine. I shove the mug in the microwave and sniff the half-and-half. There's an open package of powdered-sugar miniature donuts in the cabinet. Stale, but I don't care. I eat two, and white powder falls all over the front of my T-shirt.

Out the back window, I can see Mrs. Manfield's head above the fence between our yards. She looks over and waves, and I wave back. It's a nice neighborhood with medium-sized houses that were built in the early eighties. Some people have lived on this same street for over twenty years. We're the newbies, only three years, but everyone's been really great. They know what's going on with Stephanie and bring over lasagna and meat loaf to help me out.

I open the kitchen door a crack, letting in the soggy air, and yell, "Hey, thanks for the snickerdoodles. They were yummy. And your tomatoes are looking amazing."

"Oh, you're so welcome, honey. I'll give you some when they're ripe. How's that baby doll of yours?"

"Hanging in. Might get her discharged real soon."

"Bless you both." She blows me a kiss.

Heaving myself onto the stool at the counter, I open up my laptop to check comments on my post from last night. I started Stephanie's Battle Blog about a month after she was born. I thought if I talked about what was going on with me, maybe I could help other moms with real sick kids.

Marti in California wrote: Hi Rena, Your most certainley right-sometimes the docs and hospitals make everything so much more dificult. I had to go to the ER again last week because of Brians asthma. I thought my boy was dying. It was awful and they kept him for two days and pumped him filled with drugs. I need someone to figure out why Bri can't breathe. Keep up the fight!!! please for all of us.

From Lizkitty: Have you tried apple cider vinegar? It's great for tummy aches—full of good enzymes. Just 1–2 tablespoons a day does it. But you MUST get RAW, UNFILTERED, ORGANIC. Hope this helps [smiley cat face blowing kisses]

And one from Barbara T: As always, you and your little girl are in my thoughts and prayers. I know Jesus will guide you to the right care.

Only three responses so far, but it's still early.

I take a sip of the coffee and gag. Two black-capped chickadees are pushing each other around on the bird feeder. There's not much seed to fight over, since I don't have any time to keep filling it. I try to sit quietly and pay close attention to every movement and each sound, letting the experience fill my brain and body. That's what Ricki, my Madness to Mindfulness instructor at the community college, said to do. I try to focus on their teeny hops and their peeping sounds. I think I'm doing this mindfulness shit right but then, the birds get pushed away as pictures of medication drip bags, IV tubes, infusion pumps, and my little girl's pale, sweet face take over my brain.

Maybe it's relaxing for some, but I'm pretty sure mindfulness is for people who have plenty of time to waste.

I look at my watch. Shit. My appointment with Dr. Rondolski isn't until one, but since I took so much time forcing myself to watch the stupid birds, now I won't be able to wash my hair or even shower. I run back to the bedroom, grab wrinkled khakis from the dirty laundry and one of Gary's old shirts. I put that on over the Giants sleep T-shirt I'm wearing, which has not only the powdered sugar but also last night's BBQ sauce on it. I wipe at the sugar and manage to smear the white across the front. My hair is a disaster. I pat down the blond frizz in front and fluff up the squashed pieces on the sides. I move my part back and forth a couple of times to try and cover the black roots. It's like cleaning the bathtub after the rest of your house blows away in a hurricane—nice try, but forget about it. I spit on some tissue and rub at the black smudges of mascara under my eyes. Nothing I can do about the dark circles and huge bags there, unless somehow I can go to sleep for about four days straight. Yeah right. I smear pink gloss across my chapped lips.

Slamming the door behind me, I jump into the Toyota and screech backward onto our street. Late again, but Dr. Rondolski will just have to wait. I need to check up on Steph first. Maybe I can get her to take some broth, just a spoonful or two.

It starts to rain as I park the car, and the dark hospital lobby feels even gloomier than usual. St. Theresa's has been updated many times since the 1850s, when it was built, but it still feels like somewhere in here there's a doctor with dirty fingernails taking out an appendix with a hacksaw. As always, I try to make small talk with the guard. And as always, he mumbles something I can't understand and points to the visitor's log. I write my name and clip a plastic badge to my shirt.

This place was definitely not my first choice, but it is close by, two parkway exits north of us, so I can get here in less than thirty minutes when traffic's not a mess, which it usually is.

Stephanie's room is dark, and the shade is pulled down. The television is turned on, but the sound is low—just like I instructed the nurses. In my heart, I know Steph feels better in this kind of environment, like she's in a cocoon, all warm and snuggly. A mother's hug, when I can't be with her. I can hear my baby. She's snoring softly.

There's a tap on the doorjamb, and I wave at Marsha, one of my favorite nurses. I smooth the hair back from Steph's damp forehead and walk into the hall.

"How was her night?" I ask.

"Hard, very hard, Miss Rena." Marsha is from Jamaica, and with that accent, even bad news sounds a little better. "She up all night, restless like. Say her stomach hurt something awful."

I look back into the room, where Stephanie is curled up tight. She looks like a tiny sleeping shrimp. The blankets are tucked around her, which I'm sure Marsha did. She's the only nurse who always follows the instructions I typed and had laminated, and then taped to the wall above the bed.

"Poor baby," I whisper, giving Marsha's fat upper arm a squeeze. "Thanks for everything you do. I don't know how Steph and me could stand it here without you."

"Of course. Now, Miss Rena, don't you worry. I'm

sure she'll be better real soon. That doctor you going to, she good, right?"

"Here's hoping. Before we go, I'll make you that fudge you like. I'll leave it at the desk, but you be sure to share, okay?"

"Maybe I will and maybe I won't," she says. She laughs and follows me back into the room.

I sit on the edge of the bed, listening to my daughter's hoarse breathing. Stretching out next to her, I carefully push my hands through the IV tubing and hug her damp body close to me.

"Okay, good mama, you girls have a little nap, now," Marsha says.

Someone shakes my shoulder.

Standing above me is the shift charge nurse, Betsy. My shirt bunched up while I was asleep, and she's staring at the tattoo (a heart with the letter *S* inside it) on my lower back. Her arms are folded over her uniform, and she looks like she just sucked a lemon.

"He's waiting for you, Mrs. Cole."

"Huh?"

"Your appointment . . . with Dr. Rondolski. He's waiting for you in his office. Number three-oh-four. That's on the third floor," she adds. Hospitals should really screen their staff for bitchiness.

It takes me a minute to untangle myself from Steph. I sit up and rub my eyes. "Wow, how long did I sleep?"

"I really couldn't say. I just told him I would tell you he's waiting." She looks at her watch.

"Fine. I'm going. And Stephanie needs a fresh pillowcase. It's on the schedule," I say, pointing to the wall. Nurse Bitch thinks I don't notice, but as she turns around, I see her roll her eyes. The sooner I get my child out of this shithole, the better. Kissing Stephanie on top of her head, I whisper that I'll be back.

I take the elevator to the third floor and knock on the office door.

There's a muffled, "Come in."

Dr. Rondolski is sitting on a big leather chair behind a huge desk. He doesn't even look at me when I enter.

"Please, take a seat." He waves at the chair across from the desk.

I've never been in his office before. All our other conversations have been in the ER or in Stephanie's hospital room. Not exactly conversations, mostly him talking at me, blabbing about his latest theory. Crohn's, inflammatory bowel disorder, GERD. My baby's on the floor screaming her tummy hurts, and he thinks it's acid reflux? Are you shitting me? Lately, every time we talk, it's ended in a fight, with him trying to convince me to keep Steph here.

I sit down.

On the wall behind him is his doctor's certificate. It's from Yale, and it's in a dark wood frame that takes up most of the wall. Fine, we get it. You're a hotshot doctor. Probably have a teeny red convertible—and a dick to match.

Dr. Rondolski starts tapping the fingers of his right hand on the top of the desk. With his other hand, he pulls a file folder from his drawer. I see Stephanie's name on the tab. He takes his time flipping through the papers, still tapping—*tap, tap* (pause), *tap, tap, tap.*

I start to say, "Hey, I need to get back down to my daughter, so if we—" when he cuts me off, not moving his eyes up from the file.

"Thank you for coming to see me." He finally looks at me. "I know it's been a difficult time for Stephanie, and for you. Her case has been, to say the least, challenging." He stops talking. I'm not sure if he expects me to say something like *yes, it is challenging, and, of course, I know you've done everything you could.*

"Yeah, the whole situation stinks" is all he gets from me. Then I add, "Which is why I'm taking her somewhere else."

He stares at me for so long, I think maybe my lip gloss must be smudged, so I wipe at the sides of my mouth with my fingers.

"As you know, I'm concerned moving her now could compromise her already delicate health," he says. He scratches behind his ear and then rubs the back of his neck. His face is so pasty, it looks like he hasn't seen the sun in about ten years.

Then, he coughs into his palm. Gross and very un-sanitary for a doctor who should know better. I tell myself to remember not to shake his hand if he offers it when this is over.

He sighs and says, "I wanted to try one more time to dissuade you from taking this step. Your daughter is a very sick little girl, and until we can fully get a sense of what's going on, we feel any change right now could have serious negative ramifications for her health."

That does it. The mama bear starts to rise up in me. All the fear and frustration from the past six weeks—Jesus, from the past four years. I don't want to, but I just lose it.

"Serious negative ramifications?" I sputter. "Until you can get a sense of what's going on?" My teeth are grinding together so much, my jaw hurts. "Are you kidding me with this? Exactly how long did you think I was going to leave my baby here while you torture her with all your tests and even after almost two months, you still don't have a single clue what's wrong? You think I won't do anything I can to get her the best care with the best doctor? Well, then . . . you've got the wrong mother." I stand and push the chair back so hard it crashes over.

"Mrs. Cole, please sit down so we can talk about this rationally," he says.

"No way. Not a chance," I shout. I'm shaking as I march to the door. He stands and holds up his hand. What is he, the crossing guard at the elementary school?

"This is a bad idea. She's too weak right now. Please, in my opinion, moving Stephanie at this time is a very bad idea."

"Hey, guess where you can shove your opinions and all the rest of your worthless medical advice." I yank open the door and it bangs against the wall.

"Won't you at least tell me where you're taking her?"

I don't turn around. I don't want him to see the tears running down my cheeks.

"To Wisconsin," I say. "There's a fantastic doctor there who specializes in kids' stomach problems."

3
Claire

Cal and I lie in bed, having exhausted ourselves with the run and the shower sex. Glancing at the bedside clock, I zip through the catalog in my mind for a reason I haven't used in the past two weeks to explain why I'll be late for work—again. I can't think of anything, but I'm in such a state of delicious inertia that I'm sure, even if I tried very hard, I couldn't come up with one reason why I'd want to get out of this bed.

Cal snorts and rolls over onto his stomach. I've never known anyone who can sleep like Cal. One time we went camping in Mendocino, and since we arrived late, we got the last site, which had a beautiful view of the Pacific but was situated on a forty-five-degree decline.

Even though we angled our sleeping bags so our

heads were above our feet, the pull of gravity interrupted my sleep throughout the night. When I did
finally doze off, I dreamed I had been working on a
roof when somebody removed the ladder, and since
the person was relocating to study the mating habits
of horseshoe crabs in China, I knew I'd have to live on
that roof for the rest of my life. Cal—he was asleep as
soon as he zipped himself in and woke the next day,
alert and refreshed, shouting for me to get up and see
the amazing pods of dolphins crossing below us.

He's like that, how excited he gets about . . . well,
everything.

Like the first time he proposed. It was barely eight
months after our corn maze collision. We both happened to be free on a Tuesday, an unusual occurrence,
since we were both working retail at the time and our
schedules hardly ever meshed. I discovered later this
was more collusion than coincidence as he had contacted my boss and asked her to give me the day off.

We headed to Disneyland, which we figured wouldn't
be too busy on a weekday in early fall. Except we didn't
count on it being some random school holiday—a
teacher's in-service training day or something—and
there were actually crossing guards at the park's street
intersections, coordinating the mob flow. Forget about
Splash Mountain. The line circled around itself five

times. Same with the Matterhorn. We broke from the herd, shared a churro and a lemonade, and considered our options, which is how we ended up on the slightly less jammed Peter Pan ride. As Peter's ship was heading from the Darlings' house in miniature London to Neverland with the yawning mouth of the ticking alligator semisubmerged in the blue water below, Cal turned to me. Not easy to do as he was trapped under the safety bar. He took my hands in his and began, "Claire, will you . . . ," but I cut him off with, "Oh, look, there's Wendy walking the plank."

His face, once we disembarked, was that of the most lost of any of the lost boys.

"Why?" he asked. I told him I wanted to graduate college first. I had eighteen more months until I would get my completely useless degree in English Literature. Despite my mother's disappointment that I had no plans to go into the psychic and herbal business, and even after my father and mother pleaded that I at least learn something where I could earn a living, I refused to get the necessary credits for a teaching degree.

I read some wonderful novels, though. And I got as far away from Pennsylvania as I could, while still staying within the contiguous United States. Of course, I found it was impossible to get a job after graduation with just an English Literature degree, and I needed to eat and pay bills, so I ended up doing what I thought I never would—working as a psychic.

It was a good excuse, wanting to graduate first, but had the disadvantage of a hard expiration date. The day after the graduation ceremony, which I blew off (another parental disappointment), Cal took me to the most expensive restaurant in town. Over chocolate mousse, he bent down on one knee and presented me with a small black velvet box. Very discreetly, I looked into his hopeful face and mouthed *No*, then pretended I had dropped my napkin and made a show of letting Cal help me retrieve it. The couple next to us observed everything that happened or didn't happen, but at least I saved Cal the embarrassment of having the whole restaurant watch me reject him. Later, as we were driving back to our apartment, I told him I loved him but I wanted us to first get established in our careers before taking the next step. He was crushed but, at the time, accepted my rationale.

I often imagine the reason he hangs on when another man would have bolted in frustration long before is that, in some way, he believes I need rescuing. That somehow after he failed to save his parents' marriage, he thinks he can redeem himself with me. On an intellectual level, this makes little sense, but is it possible that Cal and I are drawn to each other relative to both failing at our intended destinies? That we were both overwhelmed by the responsibilities we thought were given to us—me to continue on the path of generations of psychics and him to save a marriage that had less chance of surviving than a snowflake during a heat wave? Could it be Cal and I both opted to swing our life pendulums as far as possible away from our presumed genetic predispositions? The crown rests heavy on the head of the person who doesn't want it or feels it's undeserved.

Of course, I know this isn't the only reason why we work as a couple. Our likes (hiking, movies, Indian food, historical fiction, cats in theory but not in the house) on balance far outweigh our differences, which include political stances (he's wrong), museums (I want to scream while he reads each and every placard beneath each and every painting), and clean sheets (at least once a week, which Cal declares unnecessary. Yes, if you live in an all-boys' dormitory).

Cal turns onto his back again and yawns. He opens his eyes, stretches his arms wide, and pulls me on top of him. I brush over his chest hairs with my palm. They're springy and damp from the shower. It's still a surprise to me that I'm with someone like Cal—mostly because of packaging. He's not the swarthy, wiry guy with the piercing black eyes I saw beside me, or on top of me, in my fantasies. Instead, Cal's skin burns when he walks to the mailbox. He tends toward doughy, which his height mostly camouflages. None of that matters. I love his hands, how his touch can slow my heartbeat. I love how he looks right at the clerk when he checks out at the grocery store around the corner from us. He wants the guy to know he sees him and honestly appreciates the service. How he'll stop and give the homeless man on the street a few dollars every time he passes him and even took the time to learn his name (Jerry). He'll listen to his story—and really, anybody's story— but doesn't actually need a reason to be kind—he just is. And I love his eyes, the depth of understanding there, even, and especially during those times when I don't understand myself and the things I think or say or do. They are grayish blue or bluish gray, depending on his mood. This morning, they're mostly blue, which tells me he's serene and satisfied.

I hate to ruin that.

"Cal, have you thought any more about what we discussed? About going back to school?" I ask, sliding from him and pivoting off the bed. I walk to the bathroom and grab my toothbrush and paste.

"Cal?" He's slung an arm over his eyes.

Walking back, I lift his arm. He reaches to pull me down beside him, but I curl out of his grasp.

"No kidding," I say. "Did you call the admissions office?"

He throws me a look that might as well have been reinforced by a bubble above his head with LEAVE IT THE HELL ALONE, CLAIRE written inside it. Untangling himself from the sheets, he opens the closet and pulls on a navy-blue short-sleeved jersey sports shirt with the Mountain and Stream Superstore logo preprinted above the right pocket. The regulation khaki slacks and a pair of sneakers follow.

Standing behind me while I brush my teeth, he meets my eyes in the bathroom mirror, smiles, and says, "I think the real question here, Ozzie, is why it matters so much to you if I go back to school or not." He kisses my neck and leaves. I hear the front door close behind him and the sound of the key in the lock.

Late already and having decided on an excuse I haven't used for some time (car wouldn't start, had to call AAA), I stop for an iced tea on the way to the store.

Taking out my phone, which I had muted once we got home, I see my mother called seven more times, but never left a message. I don't want to call her from this noisy place, so I fill the waiting time thinking about what Cal said.

His parting comment to me this morning is still on a loop through my brain. Why is it so important to me that he go back to school? After all, he works steadily, merging his meager earnings with mine. It's not a lot, but we don't need or use much. Hiking is free, meals out (at least where we go) are cheap, and neither of us covets driving anything other than what I refer to as "basic white underwear" cars. Nothing fancy, no need for the Victoria's Secret upgrade. You have to have a way to get from here to there so you buy used, cheap, and sturdy, which explains my 2001 Honda and his 2003 Jeep.

Cal works as a sales associate in an upscale outdoor activities store, selling hiking supplies like moisture-wicking socks, tents, and propane stoves. Naturally endowed with an abundance of sincere charm—as opposed to the always transparent and oily sycophancy of most salespeople—Cal's truly good at what he does. He's patient and sweet and willing to spend thirty-plus minutes with the geriatric who can't decide between low- and high-top hiking boots. Systematically reviewing the pros and cons of each, he'll eventually suggest the high-top because they have more support, without directly mentioning that, at her age, her bones are probably dried kindling held in place by sheets of parchment and the more support, the less likely a shattered ankle.

He's been a top performer for the past six months, and the company's been wooing him to move into a management position, but he's not the least bit interested. Cal's that rare person who is happy in the now, never regretting the past or anticipating the future. Maybe I do both on his behalf because I don't believe selling venom extractor pump kits and disposable personal urinals is what he wants or is supposed to do, that his mind and his heart yearn elsewhere—perhaps as the psychologist he intended to become before he met me.

For certain, I am not that woman who needs her man to be in a status job. Even in my fantasies, my swarthy, wiry, piercing-eyes guy is wearing sandals, not a white lab coat and stethoscope. I don't care what Cal does professionally or if he does anything having a title attached to it. We only need to be able to afford the fundamentals, and so far, we have.

Same with Cal. If it would make me happy, he doesn't care if I'm a brain or a tree surgeon or if I decide my life's goal is to pick coffee beans in Brazil. He certainly didn't give a damn when I told him early on in our relationship my psychic skills were bogus.

Two months after we met, while we were sharing samosas on the outside patio at an Indian dive we'd discovered, I told Cal I make up most of what I tell my clients.

"How?" he asked. Not, *How could you fool them that way?* or *That's cool because I knew psychics were big fakes all along.*

No, he was actually interested in the process, so I explained.

"You get a certain feel for what answer the client is looking for. I mean, I studied all of the cards, so I do know what each one means. Then I try to figure out how to interpret them based on what someone wants to hear. Happy customers mean bigger tips and return business."

Cal responded that he bet I had a lot of happy customers and then he told me for the first time he loved me. With yogurt-mint dip dripping down my chin, I asked, "Why?"

He looked surprised, laughed, and responded, "Do I need a reason?"

It was the dearest thing anybody had ever said to me. That he didn't need a justification to love me, and that I wasn't to be measured for worthiness was liberating and exhilarating.

Can't I offer him that same totality of acceptance? Why do I want him to be other than he is, and why do I keep nagging him about school?

Within a year after we escaped the maze, Cal quit his master's in psychology program and moved south to be near me. We, or at least I, had discussed the possibility of a long-distance relationship. After all, six hours of driving wasn't an insurmountable hurdle. I suggested he transfer credits, enroll at Berkeley, and continue in his program. Not interested in this option, instead, he got a job as a stocker at Mountain and Stream, eventually moving up in rank.

Whether we're watching a vapid TV rerun, or strolling through a Van Gogh exhibit at the museum (while I tap my feet as he reads about the paintings), or shopping for a new bath mat, or sitting and talking in our shoebox living room, or eating Chinese from boxes, it doesn't matter if we go or not go anywhere—"I love you, Claire. Nothing else matters, just you." I believe him. I believe he loves me for who I am, not for what I do or don't do.

"Claire? Claire? Green tea for Claire?" I'm startled by the barista shouting my name into the din.

I pay, tip, take a straw, and get in my car.

Maybe it's guilt, the reason I keep urging Cal to return to college. Maybe I feel in some way I'm responsible for truncating what Cal was going to be and short-circuiting the trajectory of where his dreams seemed to have been leading him. That would certainly be a positive spin on what, in my heart, feels like the true reason—that I want Cal to pursue goals not related solely to being with me because I suspect Cal is overly dependent on me for his happiness. And that this dependency will inevitably lead to marriage and probably, children, makes my heart seize in terror.

The reality is I cannot be responsible for anyone else's happiness. I'm simply not reliable enough.

4

Rena

I'm still shaking after the meeting with Dr. Rondolski. I check in on Stephanie, but just real quick, because I don't want her to get upset too. On the way home, I stop at Jake's Juice.

Jake's name is actually Stanley, but Stanley's Juice didn't sound as good. This is what he told me the first time I went to his store a year or so before Stephanie was born. I didn't know hardly anything about nutrition and healthy eating then. There was only one nutrition course required for my nursing program, and it was pretty lame. But thanks to Stan, I know enough now that I even have a nutrition advice section in Stephanie's Battle Blog. It's called Rena's Way to Well: Feed Your Kid Right. I put recommendations in there for food and supplements moms can give their sick children. I'm absolutely disgusted by what some parents will let their kids eat.

"Hey, Rena," Stan yells. It's really noisy because he's got the juicer going. He pushes some more wheatgrass in. A guy in a red bandanna pays for the green drink.

One time, my sister and me went with my mother to a local farm. There were these goats there, and you could pay a quarter for corn kernels to feed them. But I wouldn't do it because the week before, in Sunday school, we had a lesson about evil. Those goats, with the horns and that black line through their freaky yellow eyes, looked too much like the picture of the devil Miss Chambers taped to the wall. She said, "Children, if you do bad things, you'll be visited by him." It was enough to scare me off goats . . . and corn for a very long time. Besides that, what I remember most about the day was the smell. Stan's store smells like that farm, minus the goat shit. A mixture of dirt and grass, clean but not sweet.

Bandanna boy leaves. I climb up on one of the four bar stools next to the butcher-block counter. It's stained from the vegetables and fruits Stan uses for his juices and smoothies. Lots of red, I'm guessing from the beets.

He leans over the counter and kisses my cheek. It never went anywhere, Stan and me. The first time I came to his store was after one of my asshole teachers at nursing school said I should take something for anxiety because I lost it (her opinion) during a gynecology lab, knocked over an exam tray, and had to resterilize the speculum, cervical scraper, and specimen slide. I tried to tell her what happened, that my idiot lab partner didn't have a clue where everything needed to go for the most efficiency. Sure, I know it was only a fake vag, but it should still have been done right anyway.

I don't do drugs. I've always been against that shit. Stan agreed, and that first day, he talked to me about how the brain works and then handed me a bottle of organic valerian root capsules. I asked him how much, but he said just try them and if they worked, promise to come back.

Those capsules were un-fucking-believable, especially for when I couldn't sleep, which was pretty much every damn night, and I've gone to Stan's store ever since. At least twice a week, I come by for his homemade oatmeal-and-flaxseed cookies. He gives me advice on all kinds of stuff, like last week, he told me how to prevent bug bites without using poison (lemon eucalyptus oil and witch hazel). The few times we fucked in the back room were just a friendly thank-you for all his help.

After I got pregnant, I wanted to make sure my

baby had the best care possible, in or out of me. Stan recommended magnesium supplements to prevent preeclampsia. In my third trimester, he said to try red raspberry leaf tea. This was supposed to make contractions stronger but without increasing the pain. Uh, really? I was in labor hell for forty-six hours and it hurt like a son-of-a-bitch.

Okay, but most of the time, he's given me really good advice. When Stephanie was a baby, at first the doctors were sure she had colic. They all said put her in a warm bath and swaddle her up tight. But she'd still scream for ten hours straight. I was seriously losing my mind. Stan made up this mixture he found out about when he went to India. There were at least ten things in it, like ginger, turmeric, and garlic (those were the only ones I could pronounce). But it was an honest-to-God real miracle. After a teeny, tiny amount of this paste on her tongue, no lie, she finally, finally fell asleep.

Stephanie and me went into the store all the time, and Stan was just nuts about her. He even has this special corner with those wooden toys from Sweden or someplace and lots of stuffed animals—all different types of dogs, because one time, Stephanie told Stan she really wanted a puppy. He would give her snacks of carrots and hummus, and peanut butter and apples, and he would sit on the floor and read her a story from a book of fairy tales he kept special for her.

"I was just thinking about Stephanie," Stan says, wiping the counter. "Some guy brought his puppy into the store this morning, and I was remembering how she'd line up all her stuffed dogs and pretend she was the teacher." He laughs. "She'd put them in rows, making sure the short ones were in front so they could all see and then quiz them on their colors and numbers. She told me I was her assistant and my job was to pass out treats to everyone. I remember, she used to lay them down and, real gently, cover them with the blanket. Then she'd kiss each one on the head and sing them a lullaby, with made-up words." He stares past me out the window, where a silver convertible turns into the parking lot. "I really wish I'd taped that, her singing." He walks around the counter, sits on the stool next to me, and asks, "So, how's the little princess doing?"

"Really shitty. Damn doctor doesn't want to release her, but also has no clue what's wrong with her." I could feel the stupid tears starting again.

"Geez, poor little thing," Stan says, shaking his head. "And you too—this is really rough on you, I know."

I take a napkin from a pile on the counter. I blow my nose and wipe at my eyes and say, "But no way am

I keeping her there. And after, when I get her out, I know I have to build her strength back up."

"Stomach still the issue?"

"Definitely. Always in horrible pain."

"You tried the peppermint tea I suggested?"

"Yeah, but not since she was admitted. It helped her a lot, but you know how in the hospital they won't give her anything but those synthetic crap chemicals."

"True." Stroking his beard, he slides off the stool, saying, "I have something that recently came in you might try once you have her home." He walks over to a narrow shelf along the wall and moves around some dark bottles with black rubber stoppers. He pulls out one labeled TENDER TUMMY. I check the ingredients: lemon balm, chamomile, spearmint, fennel, and catnip.

"You need to shake it," he says. "Use five to ten drops on her tongue, up to three times a day. I had someone else in here last week who said it helped her son a lot."

"Great, I'll give it a try."

"As far as building back her strength, you pretty much know the drill. Fruit, vegetables, whole grains— all organic. Lots of sleep and, especially, fresh air, since she's been basically on recycled stuff for a long time. Make sure she keeps up with those probiotic supplements I gave you. And absolutely no sugar—that junk'll kill you."

I reach into my wallet, but he says, "On the house. Just bring her in to see me when she's up to it."

"Sure."

Helping me off the stool, Stan squeezes my shoulder and says, "There should be more moms like you, as interested in what goes in their kids as the sports they play or the grades they make."

"Thanks, but sometimes I feel like I'm going crazy."

"I bet. Just keep doing what you're doing though. I don't know, but I still think it might be allergies? Maybe something she'll grow out of. That's at least half of what people come in here for. And you know what? Most of the time, the allergies are from toxins in the foods they're feeding their kids. They need to get to the source. Like what you're doing."

We walk to the door.

"I'll let you know how this works out." I hold up the bag.

Opening the screen door for me, he says, "I really miss seeing her, Rena."

Yeah, I've noticed how Stan looks at her, especially her eyes, the color and the long dark lashes, like his. Maybe he's calculating her age and counting backward to the dates we screwed around. Is she his kid? Honestly, his guess is as good as mine. What it came down to was medical coverage for me and my baby. Stan didn't have that; Gary did.

Hugging Stan, I say, "We'll visit as soon as she's stronger. Promise."

An old man with a limp comes up the steps and I wave goodbye. I get in my car and head to Whole Foods, thinking about everything I need to buy for my daughter.

5
Claire

It didn't start out this way.

I never intended to con my clients. I never doubted their sincerity, their abject neediness: Should I sell my house to pay off my sister's gambling debts? Could my brother's cancer be cured? When will my husband get home from overseas? Can I get pregnant? Will I ever find true love? Will my dog come home?

I have this recurring dream. Clients are in straight lines, eight across and eight down, all on their knees, moving toward me from miles away. Supplicants in pilgrimage. They progress slowly, and it's obvious they're in pain. Finally, they halt before me, kneeling in formation, their heads bent as if in prayer, each with a gaping hole in their chest where the heart should be. I am the only one who can help. I wake up, choking and sucking for air.

It all started out so promising.

My parents swore that at birth I had "the gift," a particular look in my eyes projecting, according to them, a sense I was gazing not only outward but inward as well. As evidence, they said I would never cry but would just lie on my back as an infant in the crib, or sit upright, when that skill became available to me—and patiently wait for one of them to come into my room. They said it was as if I knew they would be there shortly and found no compelling reason to fuss. When my mother was breast-feeding, they've also told me, many times I would whip my mouth away from her to stare at the phone, which would then ring. Frankly, I think I was just the winning ticket in the baby lottery: a serene, nonwailing infant. What more could you ask for?

But it's what happened on my third birthday that, according to my parents, provided solid evidence of my future psychic acumen.

It was a small party: only family and two kids and their parents from the neighborhood. My mother asked everyone to sit in a circle and plunked me in the center while she handed me presents to open. She selected a package from the small pile and held it out to me, but before I'd even touched it, I clapped my hands and shouted, "A Mickey Mouse ball."

True, this wasn't overly impressive. Although the red foil paper adequately disguised it, the gift was clearly round. A few chuckles from the group and some passing questions on how I could have guessed the ball had Mickey on it. Then, as my mother was passing me a square box wrapped in purple striped paper with a gold bow, I shouted, "Baby-doll clothes." I opened it and the adults exchanged perplexed looks. This too could have been discounted as I had for weeks been pleading for new dolly outfits. Everyone started commenting about apples not falling far from trees.

Even at three, I felt I owed my audience a grand finale, which I delivered with a flourish. My mother grasped the last present—a standard nine-by-eleven gift box, wrapped, as she's told me, in Strawberry Shortcake paper—and brandished it above her head. A hush fell over the assembled and, in the lull, a picture of the package's contents slid smoothly into my brain, encompassing the space behind my eyes. Springing to my feet, I twirled twice and shouted, "Ballerina pajamas!" I ripped open the box and held up the pink pajamas with the ballerina in a tutu on the front. Shrieks of amazement and furious clapping ensued.

With that, my stellar prescience abilities were solidly confirmed, and a lifetime of unfulfilled promise opened before me.

Because, after that day, as far as I remember, I was never able to fully recapture the skills or the magic or whatever it was that had produced such adulation. Yes, occasionally, I would still point to the phone a full minute before it rang and one time, when I was about seven, my mom and I were in the mall, and I was behind a woman at the pizza place in the food court and told her that her father was truly sorry he took her allowance to buy drugs when she was a kid. The woman turned around so quickly she spilled her soda on my shoes. She then shook my mother's arms, screaming and pointing at me, "How does she know? That bastard's been dead twenty-two years. How could she know?" It took a security guard to pull her away.

Even though my mother worked with me daily—in ten-minute blocks when I was a toddler with a limited attention span, and longer as I matured—I couldn't correctly identify whether it was a picture of a cow or a pig, or whether it was the number nine or the letter C on the back of the blank cards she'd hold before my face. At least not with any accuracy greater than what would be statistically anticipated in the general population. Sometimes, though, I did guess right, and my mom would whoop and press an animal cracker—and later, a quarter—into my palm. Her pleasure at what I saw as my "trick" was the greater reward.

Since I became an adult, I've never wanted to diminish her joy by telling her that I'm actually a fake.

My father was an amateur photographer and had a full darkroom in our basement. Spending hours on weekend afternoons, he'd take black-and-white shots, which he thought were going to be amazing pictures of the herbs and flowers in my mother's garden. He'd rush to the basement to develop them. Many times, he'd be disappointed when, as he pulled the paper from the final bath, the photographs weren't nearly as brilliant or as unusual as he'd expected.

I felt like that: a photo taken that didn't develop into the anticipated masterpiece.

Even so, surprisingly, over the years, I've actually been moderately successful in my readings. Like the return client who hugged me and whispered, "How did you know our daughter was using cocaine?" Since, in her first visit, she'd told me her kid was acting paranoid and had recurrent nosebleeds, advising her to check her daughter's room for small bags of white powder was less paranormal than predictive of what could be considered normal—although stupid—behavior for some sixteen-year-olds. Another time, I flipped over the Nine of Swords in a tarot reading and told the guy he was carrying around a lot of guilt and shame. He jumped up, backed away from me, and ran out the door, screaming, "I didn't mean to do it." After he left, when I looked back at the card, I realized that, as it was upside down—giving it a whole different meaning—what I should have told him was something like, "You've been losing sight of the situation you're in and worrying unnecessarily."

As the saying goes, even a blind squirrel will occasionally find a nut. And if that means a child can be saved from drug abuse or a guy may be prompted to unload an uncomfortable secret, then perhaps what I do isn't entirely without redemption. This is what I tell myself anyway.

Of course, I've been wrong more than right and, in those situations, have to dig around—cue the squirrel imagery again—until I get closer. It's often simply a game of thrust and parry.

ME: "I see a person who's crossed over, a female, someone like a mother figure."

CLIENT: "Well, my mother's still alive and kicking, so maybe it's my aunt?"

ME: "Someone with dark hair and a huge smile."

CLIENT: "Aunt Connie. Sounds like her, always joking."

ME: "Oh, I can see that. She's dancing too."

CLIENT: "Dancing? That's odd. She was in a wheelchair most of her life. Car accident."

ME: (Pausing to listen.) "Now, it makes sense. She would dream of dancing when she was in the wheelchair, and she wants you to know that she's dancing now."

CLIENT: (Smiling.) "That's so good to hear. She was a wonderful lady."

Of course, there have been many times when a client has left in disgust, even though I try to explain that sometimes the information doesn't come through clearly enough for me to correctly interpret it. Translation: I am either too tired or too annoyed to dig. A few years ago, I decided to begin all my sessions with a caveat explaining the idiosyncrasies of spirit—that often the loved one the client really wants to hear from won't "come through," and that sometimes the information offered could be of the most banal type: "Your father says, 'Don't forget to check the air in the Chevy's tires.'"

Most clients, though, will find some way to link whatever information I tell them to something they feel is relevant to their lives. Give some people a room full of poop, and they'll surely look to find the pony.

The funk of patchouli incense engulfs me as I enter Mystical Haven. I know it's to create ambiance, but no matter how often I spray room freshener at home or wash my clothes, that pungently cloying smell clings to and around me. I'd taken to wearing the same black T-shirt and leggings to the store and then washing them in hot water and putting them in a plastic bag in the closet until the next time I'm scheduled. It helps a little.

I wave to Mindi, the owner, who's manning the front desk. A petite woman with bovine brown eyes and a perky ponytail leafs through a binder splayed on the counter.

"Boy, I can't decide," the woman says to Mindi.

"I have something that might help," responds Mindi, directing her to a display of crystal pendulums.

In the cramped space behind the front desk, I lean against the wall to watch what I'm certain will be an interesting piece of up-selling.

People off the street usually don't know which psychic to choose. Mindi, or whoever is at the front, will show them the binder of plastic sleeves with our photos and résumés. My picture is an eight-by-ten glossy of me gazing in wonder—that was the goal anyway—at the magnificent sandstone spire on Cathedral Rock. If you look closely, you can almost see my lips forming the words *Take the damn picture already*. Cal was attempting to capture a sense of sight beyond sight-ness. I was trying to get to Taco Loco in time for happy hour.

"Oh, heck, maybe it doesn't matter. I'll just see whoever you recommend," says the woman, fiddling with her hair tie. "I'm only here for the weekend, and my husband went to the ice cream place across the street, and I thought, *Well, why not, I'll have a tarot reading.*"

"Selecting a psychic is an extremely personal decision," says Mindi in her *everything will be all right; I'll help you through this* voice. "It's important to be matched correctly so you can get the most out of your session. Only you can make this decision." She glides her fingers through the crystals dangling on long chains and asks, "Do any of these speak to you?"

Mindi thoroughly believes in what she's saying. She hears messages everywhere, primarily from inanimate objects. She'll occasionally take on clients for readings, but mostly she runs the retail operation.

"Speak to me about what?" The woman unties her ponytail, redoes it, and looks ready to bolt and join her husband for a root beer float.

"Let your mind relax, and you will likely be drawn to one."

The woman closes and opens her eyes, inches closer

to the display, and then points to a cone-shaped blue crystal hanging from a silver-link chain. On the opposite end of the chain is a dragonfly pendant.

"Opalite. Great choice. Good for purifying the blood and kidneys and for building strong relationships. And the dragonfly symbolizes change." The woman nods vigorously while Mindi extracts the pendulum from the tangle of chains around it.

"You know what's weird?" the woman asks. "I'm actually getting over a very bad urinary tract infection. Maybe that's why I picked this one." She giggles.

"There's less chance to these selections than you'd think," Mindi says, nodding. "The next step is for you to determine your *yes* and *no*."

"Huh?"

"How this works is that the crystal merges the person's intuition with the universe's energy. That's how it can help you with any question that can be answered with a *yes* or *no*."

"Oh, I get it now."

"Hold the chain above the counter and say 'Show me *yes*.'" The woman does, and the crystal swings slightly to the right. "Now," Mindi instructs, "say 'Show me *no*.'" She does and the crystal moves left.

"There you go. For your crystal, *yes* is right, *no* is left. Now you're ready to find your psychic."

They return to the binder, and when the woman suspends the pendulum aloft for the first seven pages, it shifts to the left. Finally, over Cynthia's photo and résumé—"I'm a native Sedonian and believe the vibrations from the red rocks of our beautiful area have infused me with the ability to help others find their true balance of body and mind, which assists them on the road in their journey to inner peace. Specialties include: tarot, psychometry, and mediumship for beloved pets that have crossed the Rainbow Bridge"—the pendulum waves to the right.

The woman draws a shaky breath and stares at Mindi. Her huge eyes dampen and she says, "Now, I know why." She sniffs, and reaches for a tissue in her purse. "I know why this doohickey thing led me to Cynthia. I have a cat. I *had* a cat." Tears plink on the counter and she blots them with her tissue. "He died last month. A twisted bowel. It was hor—(hiccup)—ri—(hiccup)—ble."

Mindi reaches over the counter and touches the woman's elbow. "Like I said, less chance than you'd think. Let me call Cynthia and tell her she's got a client. Would you like to purchase the pendulum?"

"Absolutely," the woman says, palming the crystal. "I can see how this will be helpful in my everyday life. All kinds of little decisions. And, I bet, the big ones too."

Mindi turns to me. "Claire, would you mind ringing up the pendulum, please?"

"Sure thing." I step to the register. "With tax, that'll be $34.78. You can pay for your visit after."

The woman probably could have chosen her psychic without the benefit of the all-knowing pendulum, and I don't think Mindi realizes what she's done is what any shrewd business owner should—capitalize on one sale with another related purchase. Or maybe she does, but feels guilty about it, and that's why I'm the one collecting the money.

After Cynthia greets and takes the woman upstairs to her cubicle, I check the schedule. I have two clients who want to be read together, but they're not due for another fifteen minutes.

"Mindi, I need to make a phone call, okay?"

"Sure." She's dusting and rearranging Buddha figurines and humming something atonal and dirgy.

Outside, a breeze tousles the Tibetan prayer flags draped along the fence surrounding the parking lot. The sun glares off the white stucco building across from us. It's empty, and the windows are covered with white paper. It was a bakery, then a tae kwon do studio, and I hear the new renters are planning one of those paint-your-own-pottery places. I perch on the edge of the concrete planter by the side of our store, careful to avoid the cigarette butts snuffed around the cactus planted there.

I hit my mother's number and Aunt Frannie, my mother's best friend for decades, answers on the first ring.

"Oh, thank God, Claire. What took you so long?"

"Aunt Frannie? Why are you answering Mom's phone?"

"It's crazy around here, that's why. Oh, honey, I hate to be the one to tell you this, but your dad's in a bad way."

"Bad? How? When? What happened?" The questions squeeze through the growing constriction in my throat.

"Another stroke, sweetie. Early this morning. Came on so sudden. We've been trying to reach you for hours."

My dad. My sweet, brave father. His fifth stroke. How much more could his poor body take?

"I'm sorry. I'm so sorry. I was running and didn't answer my phone. How's he doing now?"

"They've got him pretty sedated. We'll know more this afternoon. And your mom . . ." Aunt Frannie clears her throat, sniffs and then blows her nose. "Well, you know."

I do. I do know. I feel the familiar tightening in and around my head. It's as if the barometric pressure has dropped in anticipation of a storm, and my skull feels like it's about to explode. I look up, surprised to see the clear sun-washed sky when my mind anticipated low-slung massive gray cloud cover. A lizard navigates through weeds and scuttles under one of the angel statues flanking the entrance. I want to follow him. I want to still be on the trail this morning, running with Cal. I want to be anywhere else but in this moment, being sucked back in.

"Claire, you need to come home," says my aunt. "Today, if possible."

I tell her I'll text my flight information, and disconnect.

The lizard peeks out from under the statue, stares at me, whips his tail, and darts up the wall, vanishing into the purple bougainvillea.

Standing, I can already feel the heaviness, as if I have lifted a backpack of granite to carry with me back east.

6

Rena

STEPHANIE'S BATTLE BLOG

Posted on July 7 by Stephanie's Mommy

I'm so, so sad. Stephanie and me are <u>still</u> here, in New Jersey. As you can see in this pic, she's still in the hospital, knocked out and getting hydration in her IV.

I am to say the least PISSED. I almost did it—I almost got her out. Yesterday, I was soooooo upset after meeting with Steph's doctor. He told me it wasn't safe to move her and I told him I needed to get her somewhere else because she wasn't getting better. Afterwards, I checked on her again and left. That night I was packing for our trip and I get this call from a nurse who says Steph is in a COMMA!!!!

WTF. I saw her not even five and a half hours earlier and of course, she was as weak as ever. But she opened her eyes and gave me this little smile and whispered Hi mama. I was so happy when I left.

I made the 30 minute trip back to the hospital in 10. Screw any cop who tried to pull me over.

I ran to her room and there was this big crowd around her. They kept holding me back and I was screaming let me see my baby, I need to see my baby. Finally I got through and there she was, as pale as could be. It was awful.

The doctor says to me that when the nurse checked on her, Steph said she felt like she was going to throw up. The nurse left to get something for her tummy and when she comes back, Stephanie was unconscious, laid there, with all her muscles twitching. Then they called me.

I am so, so scared. Things are just getting worse and worse.

They ran tests. AGAIN! All the same tests as LAST time. They took blood to check her hormones to make sure there's no pituitary tumor or something called Diabetes Inspitus because both of these can cause kidney problems. They checked to see if her hippothalamus was working since that controls thirst. They checked for a urinary track blockage—anything to explain what was happening, why my little angel has SO MUCH SODIUM in her system.

Yes—that's right! It's HYPERNATREMIA—AGAIN. The <u>exact same condition</u> she had when she was first admitted! What the fuck is going on? This is like one huge nightmare.

As you know from my other posts two much sodium is EXTREMELY dangerous. Brain damage, seizures, coma. She could even DIE from it.

Sorry, I have to get back to the hospital. Going to spend the night next to her but no way I be sleping.

Rena's Way to Well: Feed Your Kid Right

Stop feeding youre kids canned fruits. They're filled with high fructose corn sirup and the cans are lined with a chemical perservative—NOT GOOD

Peel a clementine instead—YUMMY

7

Claire

I tell Mindi what's happening, that I have to leave and don't know how long I'll be gone. She opens her arms to hug me. I pat her on the back and then slip out of the embrace, my mind on the details of leaving.

When I get to our apartment, I open the refrigerator. We have only one jar in there, with one olive in it. Which I can see will have to be tossed as the olive has sprouted a tail of slime.

I'm hot, and the coolness helps, although being inside what most households would consider a source of food only reminds me of how much I hate to cook.

All the annoying details: Should we have salmon or flounder for dinner? Is that papaya ripe enough to use tonight? Do I stir-fry vegetables in coconut or olive oil?

And . . . you have to buy it and wash it and store it and then clean up after it.

After Cal and I moved in together, every Sunday, I'd scan the computer for recipes and compile a list of ingredients, which I taped to my steering wheel as a reminder to food shop after work on Monday. And maybe, once a month, I'd actually make it to the store, only to return with items like a supersized jar of Vicks VapoRub and a pad of rainbow-colored sticky notes.

Then, because we were hungry, and because Cal is completely inept in the kitchen, we'd head to Burrito Betty's or the Tamed Pony.

Because a restaurant is an emotionally neutral territory.

Some nameless, faceless cook is paid to toss your penne pasta, and the waitress pockets a bigger tip because of her dimple. It's the quid pro quo of gastronomy, eliminating any of the emotions underpinning the feeding of another person.

That, I suspect, is the biggest reason I hate to cook. Because it propels me back to my teens, when my mother was so distraught, so completely depleted by my father's medical situation, that if I didn't cook, we didn't eat. Many times, even after I prepared the meal, I ate alone because she would be seeing clients or tending to my father, who was in bed most of the time.

At first, I admit, I was proud my parents trusted and needed me to do something so adult and necessary. I did my best to fulfill this role, just as I tried to assist my father as he struggled from the bed to the bathroom and back again, and to be patient and understanding when I was the frequent target of my mother's emotional stew of anger and misery at what she saw as the injustice of the situation, of what was lost and could never be. I tried to adjust to months and then years of what felt like solitary confinement where my parents and I would orbit around one another but never seem to make landing. I'm not sure that my mother and father also sensed this isolation. Illness seemed only to solidify the existing exclusiveness of their relationship. It wasn't new for me to experience the feeling that the two of them belonged to a private club of which I was not a member.

Over the years, pride morphed into resentment. I often wonder if there are lifetime limits on being responsible and whether the wellspring of nurturing can ultimately become parched.

I slam shut the refrigerator door and turn to see Cal.

"Hey, Oz. Any ideas about dinner?" he asks, kissing me.

"My dad's had another stroke. I have to go there. I don't want to."

He wraps his arms around me and says, "I'll come with you. I can take off work, no problem."

"I need to make reservations," I say.

"Did you hear me? I'll go with you."

"I know," I say, untangling myself to move to the couch, where I open the laptop.

Kneeling in front of me, he closes the computer screen and takes both my hands in his.

"I . . . want . . . to . . . help . . . you." He enunciates each word. "Claire, please, let me help you."

"Don't," I say. "Not now. I have so much to do."

I pull my hands away and walk to the bedroom. At the doorway, I turn to see him still sitting on the rug, head slumped forward onto his chest, eyes closed.

"Cal, I'm sorry. I have to make calls, start packing."

He nods.

8
Rena

"I can't believe I had to find out our daughter's in a coma through your blog, Rena."

"What the hell did you expect me to do, Gary? I'm at the hospital day and night since it happened."

I just walked through the door. The trip home from the hospital was awful. Thunder and lightning and two times I almost slid into the other lane. I'm shivering and dripping, and all I want is a damn nap. Fifteen minutes to lie down and try to get rid of this fucking headache.

"You could have dialed the phone, sent me a text, something, anything. Tell me what's going on with my daughter, for Christ's sake. You obviously had time to type your stupid blog but not a second to let her father know?"

"Yeah, well, you weren't there," I shout. "You're

never there, are you? Do you have any idea what I'm going through? Do you even know what drugs your kid's taking? Do you know the tests she's had? No, I didn't think so. Because you are not here. You didn't get the phone call from the hospital and then see your baby all tied up in tubes. You didn't have to sleep there in a stupid plastic chair all night long." I rub at the side of my head, but it doesn't help.

I can hear what sounds like huge trucks, and I'm guessing Gary is calling from a stop somewhere in Raleigh or Atlanta or Tuscaloosa or wherever the hell he's heading to or coming from this time.

"Still, there's no excuse for this. I'm her father, dammit." He sounds only a little calmer.

When Gary calls and yells at me like this, it really pisses me off. He's always bitching about wanting to see Stephanie more, but he's never home. I try my best to keep him updated on everything that goes on with her, but sometimes it happens so fast I just don't have the time to give him all the details. He has zero medical background, so he wouldn't understand them anyway. I try to make things sound positive. So the news sucks this time. Is that my fault?

"Rena," he says. "All I ask is that I get told things before those idiots who read your blog."

"Are you kidding me with this? I'm here trying everything I can, looking everywhere possible to find out what's wrong with our daughter. And doing it for four years, all by myself."

"Hey, I wanted to be there, remember? You were the one who pushed for the divorce. I never wanted it. You know that." He's screaming now, and I just can't fucking take it.

I start to cry. "Gary, I'm so tired, and I'm really, really scared. I don't know what to do anymore."

"Listen, I'm sorry," he says. "I know it's not easy for you. It's just I feel terrible about what's happening to Steph." He's finally starting to settle down some.

"Yeah, fine, but don't take it out on me. It's tough enough without you loading shit on me too."

"So, what now? What's going on?"

"She's finally out of the coma, and there's no permanent damage, thank God."

I walk into the bathroom and reach for a towel that's stiff and smells terrible. But it's dry and I'm not.

"How did this happen? Do they know why her sodium levels shot up like that?"

"Of course not," I yell. "You just don't get it, do you? They don't know what the hell's going on with her. That's why I have to get her out of there now before something else happens." I drop the towel on the floor and sniff my arm. It smells moldy.

"Okay, okay. But maybe they need more time to figure things out."

I hold the phone away from my face and stare at it.

"I can't believe you just said that," I tell him. "Your daughter, the one you say you're so concerned about, is dying in that place. You hear me, Gary? She's dying, and she needs to get the hell out of there." I spit out each word. Maxie rubs up against my leg, probably because his food and water dishes are empty again. I swipe at him with my foot, and he hisses.

I hear the car engine start and then Gary says, "Fill it up, please—premium."

"Hey, I'm sorry," I say. "I'm under a shitload of pressure here. I'm not sleeping and barely eating." Opening the bathroom cabinet, I look for Excedrin and flip three into my palm.

"And Stephanie? How's she handling all this?" he asks. "Poor little girl. Maybe when she's discharged, she can spend the weekend with me? I'll be home as soon as I can finish up here."

"She ate a little bit this morning, but I think she doesn't really get a lot of what's going on."

"I guess that's a good thing. You know what? I can probably be back there by the end of this week. I'll have to cut my sales trip short. I can always make it to Summerville the next time I go to . . ."

"No, you don't have to rush back," I say.

"But I want to see her soon, so let's work something out, okay?" he asks.

"Sure. Call me when you get home." But I know there's no way I'll let my daughter spend a whole night away from me, at least not yet. What if something happened? What if she woke up in pain and I wasn't there? "Hey, did you call the doctor for the appointment?" I ask.

"Yeah, but he can't get me in until next month."

"That long? Shit. How's your stomach been doing?"

"Not so great. Man, I'll really feel guilty if I passed my horrible stomach problems on to Steph."

"But at least then we would know what's going on."

"That's true. Are you still planning to take her to that doctor in Arizona?" he asks.

"After all this, what do you think?"

"Yeah, I guess so," he says. "I better go. Long drive ahead. You were going to send me that doctor's name so I could look her up?"

"Oh, I'm sorry. I forgot, but yeah, I will."

"Thanks. And I'm sorry I yelled. You're doing a great job, Rena. You've always done a great job with Stephanie, taking care of all of the medical things. I'm worried is all. Keep me informed, okay? Will you do that?"

"Sure." I hang up, pour a glass of water, take the pills, collapse on the living room couch, and cry until I finally fall asleep.

9

Claire

C al is mad. Worse, Cal is hurt.

There are no flights from the Sedona airport into Philadelphia and the soonest I can get to the East Coast is through a multistop flight out of Phoenix that, unfortunately, lands in Atlantic City, about an hour from Philly. Since it departs tomorrow morning at three, I decide the best option is to drive to Phoenix tonight and catch a few hours of sleep at some cheap hotel near the airport. I pack a few things and the essential toiletries, make the flight reservation, and text Aunt Frannie the information. It's not optimum that she has to trek to Atlantic City to pick me up, but it's the best I can do with such short notice.

"Cal?"

"Over here," he answers from the back patio. *Patio*

is an exaggeration, since it's only a concrete slab, maybe six feet square, with barely enough room for the peeling Adirondack chair we hauled there from the curb of a neighbor's house.

Squeezing through the screen door, I wedge myself between the block wall and the chair and bend down to kiss Cal, who is sprawled sideways, his long legs draped over the arm. His forehead is damp from the midday heat.

"I'll call you when I get there and let you know what's happening," I say, brushing back his bangs, which have fallen over his eyes. He needs a haircut.

Circling my wrist with his hand, he pulls me to him.

"Stay for a little longer?" he asks.

"I can't. I should get going so I don't get caught in commuter traffic."

"Claire . . ."

"Listen, I know. I know what you're going to say, but I can't talk about it now."

"Why, though? Why do you always think you have to handle these things alone? I love you. You love me. Aren't we supposed to help each other through times like this?"

We've had this conversation so often, the lines feel as if they've been extracted from a long-running play. We've memorized and delivered them flawlessly, utilizing nearly the same emphasis each time on those words we want stressed (*need, dependence, fear, marriage*) and accenting passages to make the points critical to our argument: the gentle probe ("Tell me what I can do to help"), the forceful pushback ("I can't be what you want"), the impassioned plea ("You know we belong together").

The same show, time after time, with the same anticipated dramatic arc ("You could if you tried") and semisatisfying denouement ("I will. I promise, I will. Give me more time, please"). The curtain closes and ushers move in to clean up the trash.

I lean over to kiss him again, but he turns his face from me and says, "Claire, I don't want to make things any harder for you . . ."

"Cal? What?"

He unfolds himself from the chair and stands to face me.

"Nothing. I guess I'm saying nothing, except . . ."

"Except what?" I ask

"Except . . . nothing." He shakes his head, hugs me loosely, and turns to go back into the apartment.

It's funny how often the performers are not aware the show may be closing.

The next morning, I make it through the serpentine security line, flash my boarding pass, and buckle my seat belt. Because of the last-minute reservation, I'm sitting within six inches of the toilets, a good excuse to close my eyes and direct my mind to the roaring from the engines as the plane accelerates.

It doesn't take long for me to zone out, a skill I've honed to perfection. When I was growing up, we had a neighbor with a narcoleptic dachshund, apparently a condition to which this breed is predisposed. Whenever Mischka became overstimulated in some way (that pesky cat invaded his yard again), he'd suddenly drop to the ground—fortunately, a short trip—roll onto his side, and seemingly fall into a deep sleep.

It's actually a very handy trick, the ability to remove oneself. Sleep deprivation, anxiety about my dad, and the upsetting conversation with Cal, combined with the mechanical drone, almost lull me into a state of nothingness.

But not quite. Yesterday's interaction with Cal is on replay, running over and over through my brain. He wasn't wrong. Especially in a situation like this, I should be able to accept help from the man I love. And I do love Cal, but I couldn't blame him if he finally decided to walk away. It's got to be impossible for him to be on the receiving end of me always simultaneously pulling him in and pushing him away.

I try to open my ears to all the noises around me,

concentrating solely on sound—the couple next to me discussing their plans to see the Degas exhibit at the Philadelphia Museum of Art; the flight attendants in the galley, opening and closing compartments, preparing for beverage service; the kid whining that if he doesn't get in the bathroom soon, it will be too late. Finally, it works. These individual pieces slowly meld together. It's as if I've placed a pillow around my ears and soon everything muffles to a softened murmur.

Into this self-imposed cocoon seeps a memory.

I'm back in ninth-grade biology, and Mrs. Kemple is droning on about symbiosis. It's spring, three days before the end of school. The window next to my desk is cracked open enough to entice with the fragrance of impending summer, a mixture of bees, lilacs, and clover. I'm barely listening to the lecture but infiltrating my it's-almost-vacation haze, the real truth about symbiosis floats into my consciousness, gels, and solidifies there.

Here's what I figured out. No matter whether it's a symbiotic relationship that's mutualistic, where the blind shrimp digs a burrow for the goby fish because that fish can warn the shrimp of predators, or whether it's parasitic, where the tick feeds on the blood of its host—it all sounded like love to me.

Another memory: one night, when I was almost nine,

as I was brushing my teeth, I overheard my mother say to my father, "I couldn't live without you," and his reply, "I hope we die in each other's arms at exactly the same moment."

What I understood then about symbiosis of any kind was that, at its core, it's a desperate, life-sustaining, and imperative connection but at best a precarious link. Because what if the goby fish deserts the blind shrimp or the tick infects its host, which then dies of Lyme disease?

What I concluded about love was that it was steeped in the ever-present potential of pain and loss and imbued with a suffocating sense of responsibility, and the fear of being subsumed. I've spent most of my nearly thirty years running from it.

Until Cal. With him, I occasionally slow down and allow my heart the benefit of his soothing voice, his full understanding and . . . shock . . . acceptance of me. For a moment, I think, perhaps this too is love. It feels pure and light and joyful. And terrifying.

I must have slept, because as I open my eyes, the captain is saying, "Ladies and gentlemen, we are beginning our descent into Atlantic City International Airport. It's currently seventy-three degrees and drizzling."

10
Rena

My headache's only a little better when I wake up. I feed the cat and scrape his crap off the den rug. In the last few weeks, he stopped using the litter pan. But why the hell can't he at least shit in the same spot in the same room instead of trashing every rug in every room? I shove a load of whites into the washer and call my mother.

She picks up on the first ring. "Yeah?"

"Hi, Mom, it's me."

"Oh . . . Rena."

"Yeah. You expecting another call?"

"No, no. It's fine. Your sister, she was supposed to call me this morning."

Of course. Janet.

"I can hang up if you want."

"No, I have a few minutes. What's going on?"

What's going on? Her only granddaughter is in the hospital, nearly dying, and she never even bothered to visit her, and she asks me this question?

"Stephanie's better. Out of the coma. That was pretty scary."

I hear her flick the lighter. I know exactly where she's at, sitting by the picture window, in the wooden rocker with the smashed and ripped cushion. I hear her take a puff of her cigarette, and then cough.

"When are they releasing her?"

"Soon, I hope, but I don't really know. They might run more tests." I reach for the bleach. Some of it splashes onto the front of my shirt. Fuck. I grab a dish towel from the kitchen to wipe at the three huge white circles. But, of course, it's too late.

"I thought we'd come see you, you know, before Stephanie and me leave?"

She shouts, "Don't pick the red box, you moron. It's never the red box. Stupid jerk." I should have known better than to call when *The Price Is Right* is on.

"Mom, did you hear me? We're coming to see you, okay?"

"There's my other line," she says. "I better get it. Yeah, come over. Call first." Click.

I throw the phone at the wall and knock off the calendar hanging there. I step over it on my way to the laundry room to rearrange the wash. The piece-of-crap machine is unbalanced and moving all over the tile floor.

Later, when I get to Steph's room, Dr. Rondolski and three nurses are standing around her bed.

"Hey," I shout. "What's going on? What's wrong?" They turn around and the nurses leave.

"Mrs. Cole, I'm glad you're here. I wanted to talk to you," says Dr. Rondolski.

I give Stephanie a kiss on her cheek and hug her. There's an applesauce stain on her pajama top. "Look, sweetie, your shirt's all dirty. I brought your favorite from home, the one with the penguins?" I reach into my bag for the shirt and take off her dirty top. I slip the clean one over her bony shoulders.

"Oh, honey, I'm sorry. Did I get lipstick on you?" I rub at her cheek with my finger.

She pushes my hand away and whines, "Stop, Mama."

Pulling the blanket up to her chin, I say, "Well, you're in a mood today. That's okay, sweetie." I give her another kiss and say, "Let the doctor and me talk a teeny bit, and then I'll be right back."

Dr. Rondolski pats Stephanie on the arm and says, "You feel better, kiddo, okay?" She looks at him with those sad puppy-dog eyes and nods her head.

We walk into the hallway. The overhead lights make Dr. Rondolski's skin look kind of green. His glasses are full of greasy smudges.

He says to me, "We're still having difficulty figuring out what caused the problem with Stephanie's sodium levels. Fortunately, today, they're almost normal, but, without any basis for why they spiked, we can't be certain they'll stay that way."

I look down at my cuticles, which are a mess, all torn up. I pull at one until it bleeds. "When can I get her out of here?" I ask.

One of the nurses at the desk calls to him that Mrs. Fatel in room 3-C wants to see him. He says he'll be there in a moment.

He's frowning when he turns back to me and says, "I'm not sure. Like I said to you the other day, I think we should run more tests."

I find a tissue in my jeans pocket and wrap it around my bleeding finger.

I ask him, "Yeah, but, is there some reason she absolutely can't be released?"

His glasses slide down his nose, and he pushes them

back up. With his other hand, he jiggles the change in the pocket of his khakis.

"No, I think it's safe, at least relatively so, to move her now. But as I said, I can't promise the sodium issue will not reoccur, especially since we still don't know what caused it."

I look him straight in the eye. "Well, that's the problem right there, isn't it?"

I'm about to walk back to Stephanie's room when he says, "Mrs. Cole, there's one more thing." I turn around.

"Yeah?"

"Something Stephanie told one of the nurses this morning," he says.

"What's that?"

Rubbing his forehead with his palm, he says, "She said you scared her."

"Scared her? How? When?"

"Last week. After you and I talked in my office."

I think for a minute.

"Oh yeah." I pause. "It must have been the night I brought her the giraffe."

Another nurse is waving at him, trying to get his attention. She mouths, *I need a signature.* He waves back at her.

I tell him, "I came back to the hospital that night because I wanted to bring this stuffed toy she's been begging me for. It was dark in her room when I got there. I wanted to surprise her, so I stuck the giraffe through a crack in her door and said in this silly voice, something like, 'Hi, cutie,' and she gave out a little scream. Poor thing. I felt so bad. But I told her I was really, really sorry, and she was fine." I smile up at him. "And I took that stupid giraffe right home so she wouldn't be scared of it again."

The nurse is walking toward us, holding a folder and a pen. Dr. Rondolski looks at me and says, "Yes, I guess that was it," and turns away to sign a paper.

I walk into my daughter's room and shut the door behind me.

11
Claire

Aunt Frannie pulls to the curb outside the terminal, and it seems she loops around the car and hugs me before even coming to a full stop. Squeezing my upper arms, she steps back to get a better view, dark eyes flashing and cocoa curls frizzing in the damp air.

"How beautiful you look. You get more beautiful every time I see you. Which isn't often enough. And your hair. It's growing out. I like it this length, but I also loved it short like it was last summer too. You looked like a woodland nymph."

"Not exactly what I was going for, but thanks anyway," I say, lifting my carry-on into the trunk and sliding into the front seat.

She puts the key in the ignition and then turns to stare at me until I start to squirm.

"What?"

"Nothing," she says. "It's just, with your hair longer, I can't believe how much you look like your mother. Except maybe a few more freckles." She reaches across the gearshift and cups my cheek in her hand.

"How is . . . ?"

A minivan blares a horn behind us. Aunt Frannie pats my knee, pivots the car away from the curb, but doesn't answer immediately.

Finally, "Not good, honey. Things are a little dicey right now."

I wipe my palms across my eyes and she reaches over me into the glove compartment to grab a handful of tissues, causing the car to swerve right. A driver revs past us, flashing my aunt the universal sign of road disgust.

"Dicey?"

"Your dad's going into surgery, probably tomorrow, assuming he remains stable through the night. Like I told you on the phone, they're keeping him sedated."

"But what . . . ?"

"I don't know. We don't know anything yet."

"But what are they saying about the operation?"

"Unfortunately, what we don't know is much greater than what we do. Listen, you must be beat. It's a long drive to the hospital. Why don't you lie back and sleep for a bit? I'll wake you up when we get there."

I start to ask another question, but Aunt Frannie gently presses my forehead back onto the headrest and says, "Sleep, Claire."

Somehow I do. Exhaustion trumps anxiety, and I drift off as a scientist in a singsong voice on NPR discusses how whales might be the link to understanding human longevity. When I open my eyes, the sun is out. We're pulling into the parking lot of the public beach in Drift Point, a town where two weeks every summer when I was a kid, we rented a house with Aunt Frannie and my Uncle Ted.

"I decided to break the trip in half. Besides, I thought we could take a little time to talk," my aunt says in answer to my questioning expression. "Don't worry. We'll get there before visiting hours are over."

After she turns off the car, we sit for a moment as the engine pings, and look at the ocean. I'm guessing the earlier cloudy weather kept people away, because the beach is deserted except for seagulls squatting like tea cozies in the sand. As we watch, the sun breaks through.

For the first time in two days, I inhale deeply.

We get out, slip off our shoes, and Aunt Frannie pulls me by the hand toward the shoreline. As waves pass over them, mussel shells cascade, a percussion section of miniature castanets. Frenetic sanderlings prance and peck, darting in and out of the surf, hunting their unseen delicacies. When we can no longer feel our toes, we retreat several yards and lie on our backs. It's my favorite time of day, late afternoon, when the sunlight sluices diagonally across the beach, illuminating the jetties in a citrine glow.

"Know what I'm thinking about?" asks my aunt.

"No, what?" I'm playing the cloud game and spot one that looks exactly like a cow, if a cow had five legs.

"The summer you were twelve and we played miniature golf in that horrible storm? We were racing around the course, shooting balls all over the place because your mom refused to leave until we got our money's worth," says my aunt.

"Yeah, gave a whole new meaning to a lightning round."

"That was a good day," she says.

What she means but doesn't say is what we're both thinking: that was the last good day.

Soaked, we ran off the course, promising ourselves we'd come back the next day to finish. But it rained for the rest of the week, forcing us to stay inside the small house, eating popcorn and playing multiple rounds of gin rummy.

Finally, on the following Monday, we ventured into a day that started out clear but, as we drove back to the miniature golf course, began to cloud over. Laughing about our bad weather luck, we decided to persist anyway. It began to pour when we were at the last hole, a metal windmill where the challenge was to maneuver the ball between rotations of the blades. The storm grew exponentially. Uncle Ted hit a ball, which flew off the green, bounced against the fence, blew back to the other side of the course, and then into the traffic on Ocean Boulevard, narrowly missing the windshield of one of the cars. Gusts tilted the windmill sideways, rain pelted us from what felt like every direction, and a boom of thunder seemed to climb through my club and shake my shoulders. My mother shrieked and laughed and shouted that someone needed to sink a hole in one so we could get the free game and go around again. That was my mom—before everything changed.

"She's bad, Claire, your mom," Aunt Frannie says now, interrupting my memory. "I've never seen her quite this bad." She hoists herself onto her elbow and flips toward me. I study a seagull executing a graceful flyby before it swoops in to investigate an empty potato chip bag.

"Claire?"

"I heard you."

"Maybe you did, but I don't think you understand. And I need you to."

I sit up, hug my knees to my chest, and lower my

head. "It's always the same. She's a mess and I don't know how to help and besides, whatever I do won't make any difference," I mumble.

Nobody aced the last shot that stormy day. We drove through flooded streets to the beach house and waited our turns for hot showers in the only bathroom. Finishing mine, I opened the door wrapped in a towel, and as the steam cleared, I could see my father lying on the floor in the hallway. One part of his mouth was yanked to the side as if pulled by an invisible fishhook. My aunt, who as a nurse must have recognized the symptoms, was saying, "Mark, I need you to repeat this sentence: 'Today I played golf.' Try, okay?" My mother was screaming our address into the phone. I ran to her and asked what was wrong with Daddy, but she pushed me away so hard I fell to the floor and the towel slipped off. I grabbed it and tried to cover myself.

She was inconsolable when the EMTs moved him, rain drenching his exposed face. As they carried him outside, she reached for his glasses, cleaned and replaced them, carefully pinning the temple frames behind his ears, only to repeat this three more times before the EMTs slid the stretcher into the ambulance.

After, my mother became unreachable. She was solidly barricaded, captive within her grief, and the unremitting stress sapped every ounce of her energy, emotional and physical. She'd move through the hours, zombielike, expressionless, no glint of connection in her eyes. Late into the night and early in the morning, I could hear her sobbing in her room. Eventually, she'd emerge, her face blotchy and wan. There was simply nothing left in her for me. No matter how hard I tried, I couldn't break through her grief.

All I wanted was for her to let me experience the pain with her. Eventually, I gave up trying.

"She's not easy, I'll give you that. And I know, I do, that the years after your dad got sick were terrible for all of you. But, you're too hard on her. You can't turn your back on your mother," my aunt says, pushing sand into small hills and then smoothing them flat again. She touches my arm and continues, "I will be honest with you, Claire, I'm afraid you're becoming a very hard person, overall."

I think about Cal. How he offered to come here with me. All he wanted to do was help me. And I wouldn't, couldn't let him.

After I don't reply, she continues, "It was particularly tough for you. I know that. You had to handle things nobody so young should have to. Your mom and dad, they had . . . have something remarkable. The whole destiny thing they believe about their relationship. Who's to say there isn't something to that? Honey, look at me. Please?"

I raise my head and stare out to a sea that, with the sun moving to the horizon, has turned silver. The air is chilly, and I shiver. My aunt wraps her arm around my shoulders.

"What I'm saying," she continues, "is, yes, you've suffered, but she's suffered even more. Your dad's been sick for such a long time. You can't blame her for being terrified she'll lose this person who, she'll tell you, shares her heart."

Finally, I look at Aunt Frannie. "That's the problem, isn't it? There's simply no room in her heart for me." I can feel tears hot against my eyelids and I'm immediately transported back to my awkward, preteen self: powerless, sad, angry, forgotten.

"It seems that way, I know," my aunt says. "But she loves you so much and always has. She did the best she could under the circumstances, but here's something about your mother you need to understand. She's fragile, Claire, and she always has been. Even when I met her, when I moved into town and we were in the same eighth-grade class, you could tell there was something, oh, I don't know, otherworldly about her. It wasn't only her psychic abilities. It was like she was almost transparent." Aunt Frannie gives a chuckle. "Or like an amoeba. Not a sharp edge anywhere on her. Life flows in and out of her, and it's as if she has no ability to filter it. Like that time some butterflies got trapped in the garage during a heat wave and they all died. Remember, she collapsed in a heap on the floor, wailing?"

I nod.

Aunt Frannie turns my face toward her. A brown curl whips across her cheek. She yanks it away and gathers her hair into a sloppy bun at the back of her neck. "See, she's not nearly as strong as you are. You're tough, probably because of how you were forced to grow up fast. And you're independent, and those are both great qualities. But sometimes, those traits . . . well, they can take over. And that's not good."

I sniff and she reaches into the pocket of her sweatshirt and hands me a few crumbled tissues.

I press them to my eyes and whisper, "I'm not sure what I can do to help."

"Here's what I think. I want you to continue to be strong, but I also want you to soften your heart," says my aunt. "I know I'm asking a lot, but you need to find a way to forgive her for whatever she did or didn't do in the past. Do what you can to help her through this. Your mom probably doesn't even know what she needs, but, see, as the stronger one, this means it's up to you to try to figure out a way to help her, however you can and in whatever way she'll let you."

I put my head back down on my knees, close my eyes, and remember: the dance recitals with the empty seat where she wasn't; the time I broke a glass and she threw a broom at me, shouting, "Like I don't have enough to worry about around here"; me in the emergency room with the school nurse, my arm broken after a fall from the monkey bars, while she tries to reach my mother to get permission to have the doctor put on the cast. Picture after picture of me, alone, facing what had to be faced, good or bad, by myself. It wasn't that I didn't know where she was: it was always one of two places, either at home helping my father or working in the shop. But that didn't make the absences any easier to handle.

The disconnect between my mother and me eventually became intractable, the bricks in her barricade laid so close, mortar filling every crack, that there was no way to break through—for either of us—and, over the years, I feel like I've lost the ability to even guess how to try. And, worse, like I've lost the desire to even want to try. I've been pushed so far away for so long that I'm not sure, even if I wanted to, how to bridge the gap.

My aunt stands, looks down at me and says, "Listen, I know you're still mad and upset about what you had to take on as a kid, and I don't blame you at all. But, Claire, you're not that child anymore. You can't continue to blame her for what she couldn't help." She stretches out her hand.

Grabbing it, I stand.

"How?" I ask, trying to stop tears that have soaked through the tissues. "How do I do this?"

Aunt Frannie pulls me in for a hug. Her words are muffled by the wind, which has shifted and strengthened, pummeling our ankles with sparks of sand.

"Forgive her for what she wasn't able to give you and forgive yourself for what you think you didn't or couldn't do right."

I lean away from her and say, "Who are you, Dr. Phil?"

We start to giggle and she says, "Learn to love her so you can love yourself and can then truly give your heart to someone else."

"Got any more clichés in there I need to hear?" I say, laughing and grabbing her arm to run to the car, sand pelting our backs.

Aunt Frannie stops and stares at me. "No kidding, Claire. Maybe take the first step and the rest will come? You'll figure it out. I know you will."

I look at my aunt whose face I've known my whole life, who, to my knowledge, has never told me anything but the truth. I'm almost a foot taller than the twelve-year-old of that long-ago summer, so I need to bend down a bit to kiss her cheek, and as I do, I can feel the first sliver of brick begin to chip and fall away.

"I'll try," I say.

12
Rena

STEPHANIE'S BATTLE BLOG
Posted on July 18 by Stephanie's Mommy

THANK YOU, THANK YOU, THANK YOU GUYS FOR THE PRAYERS!!!

THEY WORKED!

It's true! Stephanie will finally be coming home ... but not for too long. Me and her will be out of here SOON to go to the doctor I know/pray can help her. YAYYYYYYYY!

Of course, I'l keep everyone unformed on my journey to cure my little girl.

Keep those prayers coming. Really—this makes miracles happen.

I'm sure of it!!!!!!!

Rena's Way to Well: Feed Your Kid Right

You all know I believe in making your childs gut bacteria better.

Probiotics are good but for a more natural way, try sauerkraut.

I got three 24-ounce bottles of Orley's Organic Kraut for Steph—the best!

She's not crazy about the taste but its soooooo good for her tummy.

And, so is playing in the dirt, specialy in bare feet!

13
Claire

When we arrive at the hospital my father is asleep. From above the stiff white hospital sheets, my father's face looks waxy, like plastic fruit. His eyelids flutter slightly when I touch his cheek and whisper, "Daddy?"

"I'll give you some time," says Aunt Frannie.

"Okay. Where do you think Mom is?"

"Don't know. Maybe the cafeteria? I'll check and come back."

Left alone with the beeps and clicks and whines of the ICU machines pushing in or taking out whatever's necessary, I can't think of anything to say to my father. I'd watched enough made-for-TV movies to know what you're supposed to say in this kind of situation (*You are strong, Dad. I know you can pull through this. I love you very much. Please don't leave me and Mom. Dad, please don't die. Please don't die. Please don't die.*), but they all seem too pat, these reheated lines.

Instead, I start to simply talk to him, the way I used to, when I lived at home, when he wasn't too sick or weak to listen. Back then, even when his eyelids would drift shut and I knew he'd been carried gently into some medicated half slumber, I would continue talking to him because always, I could imagine what his responses would be. It wasn't the same as a real conversation, but it was close enough.

"So, Dad," I say now. "This is quite a pickle you've got yourself in, right? I come all this way to see you and what are you doing . . . sleeping?" I smooth the blanket over his arm, running my hand down the length of it. The covering can't hide the boniness of what's beneath.

"Hey, remember when you taught me how to use a compass? Remember that day when we went hiking and got lost in the forest and you had me use the compass all by myself to get us home? Wow, that was something, wasn't it? How old was I? Eight? No, maybe nine. Yeah, I think I was nine."

His chest rises and falls, and a gentle whoosh of air escapes his lips, and one of the machines switches from short beeps to an extended high tone.

"Dad? You okay?"

A nurse rustles into the room, gives me a small smile, adjusts one of the clear bags above the bed, and says, "Sorry, but ten more minutes until visiting hours are over."

I nod and she leaves, closing the door quietly behind her.

"Anyway, Dad. That was some day. Being lost and then you trusting me to get us home. And I did it." I reach under the blanket and the sheet and squeeze his hand, which feels artificially warm, as if the heat is generated only from outside his body.

I lean toward his ear. "I'm scared, Daddy. See, if you go, I'm not sure . . . I don't know what she'll do . . . what I'll do . . . I'll be lost, for sure."

I kiss him on the cheek, my tears dampening his skin.

I find my mother and Aunt Frannie in the hospital chapel, huddled together in the pew behind the only other occupant, an older man who is sobbing openly, a white hankie smashed against his mouth.

I slide next to my mother, who looks up with red-rimmed eyes but doesn't immediately seem to recognize me. Then she pats my hand, mumbles "Claire," and collapses forward, weeping.

I say, "I saw Dad."

My mother straightens and stares at me, her eyes raw and pleading. "What do you think? How do you think he's doing? Do you think he'll be able to handle the surgery?"

"I don't know, Mom." She begins to cry again.

"But this is a great hospital. And the doctors here are supposed to be excellent. Right, Aunt Frannie?"

Placing her arm around my mother's trembling shoulders, Aunt Frannie says, "The best."

My mother calms slightly, and we're quiet for a moment, listening to the man, whose sobs have now downgraded to sniffles.

The chapel is small, a blank space that could just as well have been a conference area or an employee break room. The ceiling lights are dimmed, which only adds to the gloom but does nothing to impart any sense of serenity or warmth. The room feels stark and clinical, an extraction of its environment. Electric candles burn from within the musty silk flower arrangements placed throughout. Even with the faint nondenominational music pumping through speakers set high on the beige walls, I can feel the hum of the medical system, an undercurrent of machines, blood labs, fear, and grief.

"Mom, let's go home, okay? Visiting hours are over,

and there's nothing else we can do here tonight. What do you say?"

She nods weakly, and Aunt Frannie and I help her stand.

After I transfer my carry-on bag from her car, Aunt Frannie hugs my mother and then me and says she'll meet us at the hospital tomorrow morning before the surgery.

"What time's the operation?" I ask my mother as she maneuvers the car out of the parking lot.

Adjusting the rearview mirror, she says, "As long as he remains stable during the night, they're planning for eight thirty."

"Early. That's good."

She nods and asks, "Flight okay?"

"Slept most of the way."

"That's good."

When did this stiltedness between us become entrenched? Unless my mother is unloading her anxiety on me via psychic vision or through nutritional advice—more of a monologue on her part than a two-way exchange—our conversations are mostly superficial and perfunctory. It feels like we both have to carefully consider what we're going to say, as if we were strangers who'd met in the grocery line, marking time until our turns at the register by discussing the pros and cons of firm or extra-firm tofu.

After that day at the beach when my father had his first stroke, we were all hopeful it was a one-time terrible event, that if he followed a regimen of basic good living and took the multiple medications the doctors recommended, he would be fine. After all, nobody, certainly not us, believed a man in his early forties—especially someone like my father, who played tennis weekly, ate with enthusiasm the vegan meals my mother prepared, and didn't smoke or drink—should worry needlessly about death. He looked good, and all of his doctors praised him as their model patient, the poster boy of stroke recovery. Our naïveté took on a whiff of hubris that first year.

Over the next six years, both pride and hope diminished as we experienced the unbridled vengeance of genetics.

My father's father, a bitter man who had vigorously disapproved of his son—a promising medical student at the time—becoming involved with a "woo-woo nutcase," and who demanded a paternity test before he would even see me, was as ill as he was nasty. After multiple strokes, he eventually died of a final one when I was nine. Even so, when we compared my grandfather's lifestyle of cigars, booze, and nearly constant acts of venomous retribution, we refused to believe that my clean-living, gentle father could have been splashed with even a drop from that particularly fetid DNA pool.

It wasn't until after Dad's third stroke in as many years, where his right arm hung limply at his side and when it took him fifteen minutes to remember the names of the bones in the wrist (something he could once do in seconds without using the mnemonic "She Looks Too Pretty Try To Catch Her") that we began to imagine a future that was more drearily realistic and less optimistically rosy. The following year, yet another stroke left him unable to do more than release the occasional incoherent garble and, then too, the humiliation of incontinency.

It was too much for him. It was too much for everyone.

Using her own vast knowledge of alternative treatments, and tapping the collective wisdom of her far-flung holistic community, my mother tried everything: bilberry to lower his cholesterol, ginkgo to improve the blood flow to his brain, and a series of exercises she performed on his mostly lifeless limbs with the rigor and consistency of a drill sergeant, straining along with him as they attempted to uncurl toes spastically frozen in pain.

Besides caring for my father, my mother also shouldered the sole financial burden for the family. As his health deteriorated, Dad could no longer work and the other doctors in his practice absorbed his patient load. Mom began working extra hours, taking on private holistic care clients in the evenings and weekends. In desperation, she even began to offer group psychic readings at birthday and bachelorette parties. I'd heard her once tell Aunt Frannie she felt she was prostituting herself but simply did not know what else to do. She'd come home late in the evening, her eyes sunken with fatigue, ask me how my father had been, and then go to his room to check for herself.

We were shift nurses exchanging information about a particularly difficult patient. There was no time, no energy to trade familial niceties or to even inquire about the routine matters of each other's day. We knew what they were: I went to school and she worked and we both took care of my father. Once we lost that sense of ease, of effortlessly chatting back and forth about the most mundane of matters, we couldn't seem to find it again.

As we drive home from the hospital, I look across at my mother, her face a jigsaw of light from oncoming traffic. It's begun to mist outside, and she doesn't seem to notice that the inside of the windshield has fogged in the humidity.

"Mom, can you see okay?" I ask. She doesn't answer, so I reach over and flip on the front defroster.

It's as if I've slipped back in time, that I've again donned my cloak of super responsibility. I'm the one who's supposed to watch over things and make sure everything's okay. It's worse than that—again, I'm the one who has to save my mother from drowning in the murk of her fear and grief. But here's the question: Who will help me?

I think about the talk on the beach with Aunt Frannie and what she said about me taking the first step and wonder how I can even begin.

14
Rena

STEPHANIE'S BATTLE BLOG
Posted on July 20 by Stephanie's Mommy

SHE'S HOME!

Finally—my baby is back where she belongs. Of course, she was pretty droopy at first. But I gave her a lot of good organic food and she slept in her own cozy bed (she really missed her stufed animals). She looks so much better now. The first night she was home, I slept on the floor next to her bed. I just had to be near her. I know all you mommies understand that!

Ginny P: We're with you, Stephanie's Mommy. Keep up the good fight. Get your baby where she can have the treatment she needs. Ur in our thoughts and prayers . . . always.

THE PERFECT FRAUD • 113

Yolandathegreat: Stay strong. She's lucky to have you as her mama. Pls keep us posted on this.

Krisiblue: we mums have quite the job, don't we? Consider using wheat germ. I swear by it and my little guy has never been healthier

MartinaQ: Let us know where you are when you get settled and could you please post that recipe again for the quinoa pancakes? They were terrific!

It takes forever for my mother to answer the door. I ring the bell and knock again.

The house hasn't changed a bit since I was here the last time, about six months ago. The lawn is all brown spots, weeds, and dandelions. The Cape Cod is falling down on both sides so it looks like a melting birthday cake. Brown grocery bags cover the two front windows and taped to the front door is a ripped piece of cardboard. My mother wrote on it: I AIN'T BUYING WHATEVER YOUR SELLING SO GET LOST.

Finally, the television shuts off. I can hear her mumbling. "Give me a second, will ya?"

When Mom answers the door, Stephanie runs up the steps and grabs her around the waist.

"Gram, Gram," she says.

"How you feeling, bunny girl?" Mom asks.

Stephanie looks at me and then back at my mom. She says, "Good."

"Speak up, Stephanie. Gram can hardly hear you," I say.

"Well, you look tip-top," my mom says. Turning to me, she repeats, "Tip-top. Hardly would know she's been sick at all," and motions for us to get in the house.

As always, the inside smells like stale smoke and mold, mixed with oil of wintergreen. That's from the arthritis liniment she rubs into her joints all day long.

Prince, her fifteen-year-old beagle, walks into the room. His stomach drags on the stained carpet. My eyes start to water from old dog stink. But Stephanie gets right down next to him and pushes her nose into Prince's neck. She squeals, "I missed you so much. I was in the hospital, did you know that?"

"Come away from that dog, Steph. I don't want you getting sick again," I say, taking her arm.

"Leave the child be," my mother snaps. "There's no germ she can get from Prince that she probably already didn't get from the hospital."

Stephanie skips over to my mother. She takes each of my mother's swollen fingers, slowly moves them back and forth, and tells her, "Gram, guess what? I was in the hospital, and I was so sick. I couldn't hardly eat nothing. But the doctor, Dr. Ron, that's what he says his name is, was so nice to me. He said I was his bestest patient. He smells funny, though."

"Smells funny, huh?" my mother says. She signals for Stephanie to jump up a little so she can lift her onto her lap.

"Yeah, like medicine."

My mother laughs and says, "Well, I guess that makes sense, him being a doctor and all." Steph nods. I'm thinking, *She notices how the doctor smells like medicine but the disgusting dog odor doesn't bother her at all?*

"And guess what he has around his neck?"

"What's that, sweetie pie?" my mother asks.

"A stekapope. He can hear what my heart says with it."

"Stethoscope, Stephanie," I say.

"Well, isn't that amazing?" My mom hugs Stephanie to her. "You sure are one smart cookie."

"And you know what else? He said my heart was the sweetest one he'd ever heard."

"I can believe that, baby girl."

"Gram, do you have anything to eat?" Stephanie asks. She hops down to give Prince another hug.

"Course I do. How 'bout your favorite? Grilled cheese and bacon."

"No crusts?" She's jumping up and down.

"Not a one," my mother says, walking to the kitchen and leaning over to reach for the dented frying pan. She gives me a look before I can even tell her that a cheese-and-bacon sandwich is crap food. She says to Stephanie, "I pulled out some dolls your mother had when she was little. They were in the basement. Why don't you go play with them?" She points to a box in the corner of the living room. Stephanie skips over to check it out.

I start, "I don't think—"

"Rena, I feed that child this sandwich every single time she's over, and she eats it every single time, and never, not once, did she get sick." She puts the bacon on a paper towel and slides it into the filthy microwave. Then she plops two huge lumps of butter into the pan.

I say, "Steph and me leave tomorrow. The flight's at seven forty in the morning. I guess we need to get there lots earlier, though, because of security and all that crap."

The microwave bings, and she takes out the bacon. She lays the strips over a piece of orange cheese and between two slices of white bread (without crusts), and then puts the sandwich into the sizzling butter. As she flips it, cheese oozes from the sides and smokes. Her hands look all lumpy and veiny.

I ask, "Do you at least have milk for her?"

She points to the refrigerator. There are about twenty

kitten magnets on it. They hold up a rate increase notice from the electric company, an appointment card for a dentist appointment that was five weeks ago, and seven pictures of my sister, Janet.

"Have you seen Janet lately?" I ask. I straighten a shot of my sister sitting on the grass wearing an Easter bonnet. She's got colored eggs in her skirt and all around her. I take out the milk and go to the cabinet for a smudged glass.

Mom slaps the sandwich onto a paper plate and yells, "Stephanie, lunch." She pulls out a chair and groans as she sits down. She says, "Every day. Your sister comes over every afternoon."

I use a napkin from the plastic holder on the table to try and wipe off some grease from the top of the sandwich.

"Stop fussing, for God's sake," my mother says. "It's fine."

Stephanie runs into the kitchen, hugging a doll. It has no clothes, the hair is hacked off, and it's missing a leg and two fingers.

"Why the hell would you keep that?" I ask.

I used to love my dolls, especially one called "Little Peanut." She looked exactly like a real baby. I saved up my allowances and Christmas and birthday money for over a year to buy her. You could press two fingers to her tummy, and it was like she was actually breathing. She even had a heartbeat and would "coo." I wasn't sure how she could do this. I guess some kind of mechanical shit set up inside her that turned on when I touched her—it was amazing. I took that doll with me everywhere. I remember I even had a regular-sized stroller and I'd roll her through the park. Old ladies would stop and look inside. A lot of times, they'd think she was actually real. One lady even told me what a great sister I was, taking such good care of my baby sister.

Stephanie hands the doll to my mother and climbs onto the chair. She takes a bite of her sandwich and oil runs all over her chin.

"You were always rough on your dolls," my mother says. "I was just saying that to your sister yesterday. How rough you were on your dolls. When you first got them, you'd love them all to bits, changing them into their pretty outfits, feeding them those bottles that looked like they had juice in them but didn't. You'd spend hours and hours giving them baths and putting them to bed."

I try to wipe the grease off Stephanie's face, but she turns away from me.

"But, then, always," Mom continues, "after a while, we'd find one of the dolls in a closet, missing an eye or some such thing."

The red plastic clock above the table clicks to twelve noon, a full hour and fifteen minutes earlier than it actually is. That clock never has been right, even when I was living here. The window is open, and I can hear the neighborhood sounds of Mr. Patterson's lawn mower and his dog (probably the son of the son of the dog) barking. That stupid dog yapped all day and all night long when I was little.

"How's Janet feeling?" I ask. "I talked to her a few days ago but forgot to check."

Stephanie says, "All done." She hops down from her chair.

My mother takes away Stephanie's plate and tosses it into the trash can, which is overflowing with garbage. Some eggshells fall on the floor.

"She's fine, I guess. I'm not sure you can ever really be healthy after what she went through as a kid." She looks at me. "You know, the females in our family have always been kind of sickly." I nod.

When Janet was five, she began having these fevers for days at a time. Then her joints would get all stiff and achy. At first, my mom thought it was the flu. But even after six months, she was still really sick. I'd come home from third grade and there would be Janet in the dark, under a quilt, barely blinking. She'd be watching whatever soap opera my mother had on.

My father was long gone, which was actually better for me than when he was living at home. But Janet missed him a lot. Well, that's because she was his favorite. On the other hand, he always told me I was the one Kleenex that ruined the load of wash. Like him, Janet, and my mom would have been so goddamn perfect, except for me? Yeah right. He went to every single one of Janet's meets when she could still swim. He'd be there standing in the bleachers and yelling like a maniac. I was a Girl Scout for about six months and made this little quilt for a merit badge. I was trying to show it to him one night, but he kept telling me to move so he could watch some stupid football game. So I waited for the commercial. When he finally looked at it, he told me, "Those stiches are all crooked." Mostly, though, he just ignored me. I was actually happy when my mom and him finally got divorced and he moved the hell out.

My dad would still show up at Janet's meets, but I can count on three fingers the times I saw him after he left. Not for lack of me trying. This one time, I had a small part in my ninth-grade play. Nothing big at all, but I did have a couple of lines. I fibbed and told him I was the lead and that the acting teacher said I had this natural talent and that he should come see me on opening night. He didn't make any of the shows.

Another time, I called and told him I broke my ankle when I fell down the basement stairs. I thought he'd come racing over to the house to make sure I was okay. It was a lie. Not the broken ankle—that was cracked in two places and I was in a boot cast for three months. But it wasn't so much that I fell as that I threw myself down the cement stairs. When she finally got home, my mom took me to the emergency room, and my bastard of a father never did come to the house. I cried all afternoon.

Without my dad around, it was totally up to my mother to take Janet to the doctor and to specialist after specialist. They thought it might be lupus, but that diagnosis was thrown out. Same with juvenile rheumatoid arthritis and Lyme disease.

Then, after about a year, she began to feel better. Slowly, at first. But by her seventh birthday, she was running all over the park, playing on the swings and slides with her friends.

It didn't last long. Ten months later, she was sick all over again. In fact, she was even sicker than before. More doctor appointments and treatments that never worked. My mother was a wreck. She was putting in thirty-five hours a week cleaning rooms in a hotel. My jerk of a father sent money at first, but then that stopped. The neighbors helped. Mrs. Malone, who still lives two doors down, took Janet to some of her doctors' appointments. And at least once a week, the Harris sisters, the old twins (dead now, for sure) from the hospital league, brought over brownies or Rice Krispies treats. Those were Janet's favorites, and sometimes she shared them with me. Every day, it seemed like my mother would bring home something for my sister: a comic book, crayons, and one time, a kitten. I would hold him at home when she was at the lab having a blood test or in the hospital for X-rays.

This went on until I was twelve and Janet was ten. Then it all stopped. She never got sick again. Not like that anyway. She'd have some colds, and one time she sprained her wrist, but nothing like when she was really young.

I look at my watch and say, "Stephanie, it's time to go. We still have a shitload of packing to do before tomorrow."

She's sitting on the floor, hugging another one of my old dolls. This one has only one foot and streaks of red and purple paint over her chest and butt. I take the doll from Steph and throw it back into the box.

Her bottom lip starts to curl and she says, "Please, please, can I stay a little longer with Gram?"

I say, "Now. No whining. We have to go."

She walks over to my mother who grabs the edge of the table to pull herself up.

"Give me a kiss, girly." My mother bends down to hug Stephanie. "I'm going to miss you a whole bunch."

Stephanie kisses her twice on the cheek.

"I'll let you know where we're staying once we get there," I say.

My mother says "Fine" and shuts the door behind us.

I hear *General Hospital* on the TV before we're even down the steps.

15
Claire

No lights are on in or outside the house, so we maneuver our way carefully over the broken flagstone stairs my parents have planned to fix for all the years they've lived here. My mother rummages through her purse for her house key, opens the front door, and flips on the porch light. Moths dive toward the illumination, and she quickly turns it off.

It smells like home, a combination of eucalyptus and rosemary, my mother's proprietary blend of essential oils she spritzes everywhere. It's a big seller in the shop.

Feeling our way through the front room, we switch on the desk lamp and those on the tables near the sofa, casting pools of light, one of which catches our dog, Sammie, curled in the corner of the sofa. I scratch her behind the ears, and her lips turn up in a doggy grin.

"Why don't you try to get some sleep, Mom?"

She gives me a blank look. I'm not sure she heard me. "Mom?"

"I can't, Claire, not right now. Maybe in a little bit."

Lifting my suitcase, I'm about to walk upstairs to my old bedroom when she asks, "Want to sit outside? Not for long. Just until we get sleepy?"

I nod, although I'm fairly sure all I need to fall asleep right now is a pillow.

The night's turned muggy, but she gathers wood, sticks, and paper and lights a fire in the pit that sits on the bricked back porch. From here, under a red-tinted full moon, I can almost make out the silhouettes of the herbs and flowers in her eight raised box gardens. As always, I'm amazed at what my mother can accomplish in such a small space.

"How are your crops doing this year?" I ask, taking the glass of red wine she offers me. I sip and hope I can remain awake for her answer.

"Not bad, considering."

"Considering?"

"That I haven't had time to give everything the attention it needs."

Fireflies hover and flit above the grass and within the bushes.

"I miss them," I say, pointing to the tiny sparks.

"You know, we have them out west, but they don't light up."

"Really?" My mother has finished half her wine and stares ahead without blinking.

"Seems like a waste to me," I continue even though I sense she's not attuned at this moment to the variants of lighting and nonlighting beetles.

"Yes, such a waste," she murmurs.

A breeze ruffles the tips of the tallest plants, which, guessing by the fragrance blowing toward us, are lavender. I'm instantly thrown back to a summer so many years ago—I can only guess I was seven, based on the image in my mind of me sporting pigtails and a blue-checked cotton shirt knotted at the waist. It was one of those days when sunshine made everything look pristinely outlined and the sunflowers had golden halos surrounding their prehistoric-sized petals. I was spread-eagle on warm dirt in the herb garden, lying between the lavender and dill, each fighting for scent supremacy within my nasal passages. From that vantage point, I could see the undersides of the butterflies and hummingbirds landing to feast. Then, above me was my father who shouts, "Maddie, here she is. I found her," and he's laughing and holding a basket, and my mother comes to him with a sweating pitcher of lemonade. We have a picnic right there of roasted chicken, homemade biscuits, and chilled asparagus spears.

I turn to my mother now and begin, "Hey, Mom, remember when we had that picnic . . . ," but I'm stopped by the sight of her wet cheeks.

Still looking forward, she says, "I'm so frightened. I don't know what I'll do if he dies. I truly don't."

"He won't. The surgery will go fine, and he'll be home soon." Even I'm not convinced as I say this, my voice trembling. My father looked so pale and weak, I can't even imagine him swallowing water, much less surviving a major operation.

Her face is striated by flames flickering from the pit.

"I know he's in bad shape. Worse than he's ever been," she says, wiping at her cheek with the back of her hand. "I need to face the reality that this may be it. Part of me, the unselfish part, wants him to be done with his agony."

I nod my head and feel tears pulse behind my lids.

Reaching for the bottom of my T-shirt, I press the fabric to my face.

"We are so different, your father and me, but it didn't matter. A doctor and a psychic herbal healer? Who in a million years would have thought that match should happen?" She chuckles softly. "Even we didn't at first. We both tried our best not to be together."

"Really?" I ask, even though I'd heard this story many times before.

"Absolutely. Your dad, as you know, is so . . . rigid."

I laugh. "Did you ever find the oregano after it wasn't next to the paprika?"

"Yeah, finally. Turns out he decided to wipe off all the jars and, by mistake, stuck it next to the cumin."

"Ah, another spice catastrophe averted."

We giggle together. Maybe it's the wine, but I don't care. We're talking, like a real conversation, and that hasn't happened in so long. I feel, even under these horrible circumstances, a tiny spark of hope. But I quickly talk myself down from even that modulated level of optimism because I know from experience how disappointing the drop will be when everything goes back to what it's always been.

"Anyway," she says, twisting to face me, "we were such opposites, and his parents absolutely hated the match."

"His father was an awful man," I say.

"He was, and the mother was no prize either. Do you know his mother never called, not even after I told her how sick he was? And his sister, she's no better. After his mother died, there was absolutely no contact with us. We tried to reach out, but after getting snubbed so many times, we gave up. Sure, at first, Dad was hurt, but we had each other, and you." Her eyes drift upward to where the moon has started to move behind a shelf of gray clouds. She says, "Even though at first everything seemed to work against us, the universe had other plans."

I know I need to ask the question. "Do you really believe that? That the universe wanted you two to be together, that you and Dad are part of some great cosmic design?" It came out snarkier than I wanted, but either she didn't notice or didn't care.

"Yes. Yes, I do." She starts to droop, not only her eyelids, which flutter, but her whole body softens into the chair and her head drops to one side, resting on her shoulder. I'm thinking she probably hasn't slept for almost two days now.

The neighborhood is quiet except for the trees, which are swishing, and the air is tinged with the pungent ozone smell of oncoming rain. I watch the twinkling of the night's few remaining fireflies and remember my father telling me the females will lurk in the bushes and watch the males' illumination patterns, trying to find the superior suitor. It's last call now at the firefly bar, and I silently wish the ladies good luck in finding their perfect match.

Certain my mother's asleep, I'm about to touch her arm and suggest she go upstairs, but then she suddenly says, "So many times I truly would not have made it without him. He accepts me for exactly who I am. That's very important. You know that, right?"

I think about Cal and nod, but her eyes are closed and she doesn't notice.

"And then those tough periods. Everyone goes through them. Don't kid yourself. Don't look at other people and think they're having an easy, breezy time of it. And Mark . . . ," she says, and I know I'm not here for her right now, ". . . there's no one better to have with you than that man. He's strong and methodical and doesn't overreact. In other words, he's nothing like me."

Pulling herself upright, she stares into my face.

"On September eleventh, especially in the early hours, people thought this was it, that since we lived on the East Coast between two major cities, we would, without a doubt, be bombed into oblivion. But not Mark. Not your dad. He didn't have any inside knowledge or anything like that, but he knew panicking wouldn't help. He came home from the office immediately after the first plane hit the tower and found me cowering under the granny square blanket. You know the one my aunt crocheted?"

"Sure."

"I had it over my head and was staring at the TV

through the holes. He walked over, sat down next to me, and gently took it off. He said, 'I don't know what will happen, but I know it will be fine in the end,' and then we talked about escape routes and where we could go and whether we should cover the windows with plastic. But it was those words, the assurance things would work out, even when it seemed as if the world was shattering. That's what he did for me. He comforted me and made me feel safe. He's the kind of person you want with you at the end of the world. All the other stuff, his taste in music, the way he dresses, his need to have his socks rolled a certain way . . . none of it matters."

Sammie is scratching and whining at the back screen door, wanting to join us. I think again about Cal. How last summer, when I twisted an ankle during a run, he set me up on the couch, foot elevated with an ice pack wrapped in a dish towel. He raced to the store and returned with Advil, three different kinds of gossip magazines, dark chocolate, and the movie *Love Actually*. It didn't matter that it was a holiday movie and it was August. He knew it was my favorite.

My mom reaches over and grasps my arm. She pulls me closer to her so that she's looking directly into my eyes and says, "Claire, this is what I want for you. I want more than anything else for you to find someone who . . ." My arm smarts under her wrench-like grip.

"Mom, it's okay. I'm okay."

"It's just, it's just . . ." Letting go of my arm, she falters and draws a raspy breath before continuing, ". . . he's always been here. I feel like there wasn't anything before him. That I was, I don't know, somehow untethered before we met," she says, floating her hand up into the air. "I'm so afraid, terrified, to feel that way again. That I'll simply blow away."

Her sobs hurt my heart, and I know patting her arm and cooing sympathetic sounds are no salve for the wretchedness of this pain. Again, I'm filled with an old remorse, faced with suffering that I still don't know how to help. Finally, her crying subsides, diminished to gulps and sniffling. There's a rustling in the hydrangea bushes along the fence, and my mother points to a rabbit hopping across the open space next to the flower garden. Sammie, sensing the interloper, begins barking in high-pitched staccatos.

"Hush," I shout to her, not lowering my voice, figuring the dog's likely already woken up most of our neighbors.

"I should shoo that bunny away, but I don't have the strength," my mother says, hiccupping. I push out of my chair and walk toward the rabbit, who crosshatches his way through the flowers and then the herbs until he reaches the rows of lettuces, where he takes a delicate nibble and then perches on his hind legs to dine.

Mom gestures a *forget about it* wave, and when I return she's slouched in the chair, her eyes shut, one arm draped over her head.

I think she's sleeping, but then she mutters, "You're closed off. I know that. You don't open yourself up, and it's not only with me." I start to comment, but she looks at me, reaches over, and rubs her hand gently down my arm.

"It's true," she says. "I sense it, and you do too—I know you do. The thing is, that's not good. It's not good to be so closed off. Sure, you shut out the pain, the disappointment—and people, they'll always disappoint you—but it's the other part," she says mushily. "You get so good at keeping things out that everything stays out, even the wonderful stuff. Like love." I sit down.

"Well . . ."

I don't want to cry, but it's like trying to keep the rising tide from washing away the sand castle you just built. Even though you may have dug a moat around it, it's inevitable the water will come in and destroy it.

"Honey? What is it? I'm sorry," she says, bending awkwardly in her chair to wrap her arm around my heaving shoulders. "I'm sorry. I didn't mean to upset you. Please, Claire, don't cry."

"No, Mom, it's fine. It's just . . ." And then I tell her about what happened with Cal and me before I left. I spill it all, how I can't seem to settle into the relationship, how it always feels as if I'm standing outside myself, unable to break through to truly connect with him the way I want to and the way he deserves.

Finally, I run out of words, out of energy.

"I'm so sorry to dump this on you, especially right now."

My mother is silent for a long time. Then she pulls me to her, kisses the side of my head, and says, "This was such a gift. You talking to me this way. It's what I've wanted for so long. Now, let me ask you three questions, okay?"

"Okay."

"Does Cal know everything about you and love you anyway? Is he kind and generous? Do you have interesting conversations and fun together?"

I giggle and say, "That's actually six questions squished into three."

"Don't be so technical. Just answer."

I mull over what she's asked me and say, "Yes, yes, yes, yes, and yes."

She then takes both of my hands in hers.

"Maybe you don't know this, but it's not easy to find a *yes* answer to all those questions."

She squints at me and says, "Aunt Frannie told me about your talk at the beach today."

I fiddle with the rim of the glass, moving my finger around and around the top until a soft squeal emits. In the diminished glow from the fire, I see the spooked rabbit race back into the hydrangeas.

"I won't say I'm surprised," she continues. "And I won't lie and say that I didn't know what was going on at the time, that I had no idea you were hurting too."

"It's okay," I mumble, fixing my eyes on the hem of my jeans and pulling at the fraying threads.

"No, it's not. But the truth is I probably couldn't have done anything different. I know it doesn't change what happened. I know it doesn't take away your pain or give you back your childhood, but I need to tell you, I want to tell you, how very sorry I am. You shouldn't have had to take on what you did. And I wasn't there when you needed me. But know this . . . I loved you then, more than you can possibly know, that I truly appreciated everything you did for me and for your father. And that I love you now."

I slide off the chair, kneel, and place my head in her lap, breathing in the smell of her, earthy and sweet. I start to sob again.

And it's before. It's before the first stroke, before all the roles shifted, before I lost both my parents. I'm the child I was before, and as my mother strokes my hair, I feel the love, coming into me and going out from me. It's a start. I know it'll take time and trust to build up from where we've been, but it's a start.

"I love you too."

The fire sputters and smokes as giant raindrops splatter over us.

"I'm guessing I won't be sleeping much tonight, but still, a few hours are probably a good idea," she says as we stand.

"I think so."

Inside, at the base of the stairs, we hug and say our good nights. As I turn and place my foot on the first step, the house phone rings.

16
Rena

We have to take a really early flight out of Phila-delphia, so at five a.m. I drop Maxie off at Janet's. She answers the door in her bathrobe. I'm not sure who's less happy: Janet, who already has two cats, or Maxie, who hasn't ever been in a house with another animal before. I feel sort of guilty leaving him, but now I know he'll at least get some food on a regular basis.

"Thanks again for doing this," I say. I hand my sister the plastic grocery bag of canned food and a gallon jug of kitty litter. Steph brings in a box of dry food, and I pick up Maxie's carrier and take him into the house.

"No problem," she says, but I notice her eyes don't exactly match what's coming out of her mouth. Janet's life is super orderly, and an extra cat (or, an extra anything) doesn't really fit into it.

She taps her finger on the nylon netting at the front of the carrier, and Maxie hisses. "What time's your flight?"

"Seven forty." I peek into the carrier and unzip the front. I try to give Maxie a rub on the side of his neck, but he backs away and growls.

Janet says, "Running a little late, aren't you?"

"Little Miss Dawdle here couldn't get her act together so we could walk out the door. Isn't that right?" I bend down to kiss Stephanie on the top of her head.

Stephanie's sitting on the foyer floor, petting Janet's cats, Mewy and Flounder. They're huge, twenty-pound Maine Coons, and Steph looks even tinier next to them. They crawl into her lap and over her shoulders. It's like she's being attacked by a hairy python.

"Stephanie, honey, get up and let me brush you off. You're completely covered with cat hair." Pouting, she pushes the cats away and stands up. From out of the corner of my eye, I see a flash of black that is Maxie escaping from the carrier.

"Got any tape?" I ask Janet.

I follow her into the kitchen. As always, it's perfect. There's a three-foot-tall ceramic rooster on the corner of her white granite countertop. There are two framed prints on the wall of roosters eating corn, rooster dish towels, and even measuring cups and spoons with rooster-shaped handles hanging from rooster-head hooks above the stove. My sister has a thing for roosters.

Janet did good for herself, I'll give her that. She married Brent the year after they graduated college. He does something in finance in New York City, and she manages a yarn boutique. Rich ladies come there to commission her and her staff to knit or crochet these really beautiful throw blankets for their designer living room couches. Janet was always good with her hands, and her marketing degree really helped her to grow the business. She started out just selling yarn. But now she also gives these how-to classes on Saturdays. She's even talking about having an online catalog. Like my mom says, Janet will always land on her feet and on the top of the mountain. My mom also says if you want to find a needle in a haystack, have Rena jump in because, for sure, she'll land right smack on top of it.

Handing me the tape, Janet asks, "Can I fix you guys something to eat on the plane?"

I squash a long piece into a messy ball and pat the sticky side up and down Stephanie's black leggings.

"No, that's okay. I packed some stuff for us. Brent's fine with me leaving the car here?" I didn't want the car sitting outside my empty house for so long. I had the house inside lights on timers. To maybe fool burglars into thinking someone's there.

"He said it was no problem." Janet takes the roll of tape from me and puts it back in the kitchen drawer. It's so neat in there with all the crap organized in separate plastic boxes for paper clips, pens and pencils, and sticky notes. There's even a container for a ruler and another one for a calculator.

"Are you excited about finally getting to leave?" she asks.

"Yeah. It's going to be tough, me and Steph getting set up in a new place and everything, but I'm so hoping it will all be worth it."

Janet hugs me and says, "I just know this doctor will be the one to figure things out."

I hug her back and say, "Keep praying for us, okay?"

"Of course. Always."

"Hey, did I tell you Gary finally made that appointment to have his stomach checked out?"

"Good, it's about time. Maybe it is genetic, who knows?"

"Right now, to tell you the truth, I'm hoping for anything. Just to get some kind of an answer, you know?"

"Absolutely understand." She hugs me again and says, "It'll work out fine, sis. I know it will. Stay strong."

I sniff and say, "I'm sure trying."

"Oh, I meant to tell you," she says. "Guess who I ran into at the grocery store last week?"

"Who?"

"Mrs. Hopkins. Remember her? You used to baby-sit for her son, Greg or Craig?"

"Craig," I say.

"Craig, that's right," she says, wiping the counter with one of the rooster dish towels. Of course, I can't see a crumb or spot anywhere on it. "She was in the check-out line, and we got to talking about when you used to watch him. All those ear infections he had. Remember?"

I did. He was this cute two-year-old with curly blond hair and really horrible ears. He'd even have pus and blood coming out of one or both of them. Poor little guy. Would scream all the time.

"Yeah, he really had it bad," I say.

Janet folds the dish towel exactly into thirds so the picture of the rooster shows on the front and hangs it over the oven door handle.

"So awful," she says. "Mrs. Hopkins said she felt terrible you couldn't sit for him anymore. She said she was really relieved when the infections stopped."

We walk back to the foyer.

"Well, thank God, most kids grow out of ear infec-tions."

Janet says, "She told me he's married now and she has two grandchildren. Lives somewhere in Florida, so she doesn't get to see them as much as she wants."

"Oh, too bad," I say.

There's a knock at the door.

"Must be the cab," Janet says. "Tell them to wait just a second, okay? I have something for Stephanie I think she'll love."

I let the cabdriver know. Janet goes into the pantry and comes back with a package wrapped in sparkly paper. She hands it to Stephanie.

Steph rips into it. She gives a little scream and runs over to Janet to hug her.

"Well, try it on, silly," says my sister.

"A real princess skirt," shouts Steph. It's a light blue tutu that's got silver stars all over it. She twirls around and around until she falls onto the floor, giggling.

"Stephanie, get up off the floor before you get all hairy again," I say.

"Wait," says Janet. "There's something else in there too."

"Oh, Aunt Janny, it's a wand. A magic wand. It's what I've always wanted."

Janet bends down to hug her. She says, "May all your wishes come true, mishmouth." It's a nickname Janet gave her when she first started talking because all her words were "mished" together. Stephanie giggles again and hugs Janet tight around the neck.

"Janet, you shouldn't keep giving her all these presents. It'll spoil her."

"Hey, I'm her only aunt. It's my job to spoil her. Besides, I feel like she's my daughter too."

I know this is true. They tried for years, but Janet just could not get pregnant. Something about her tubes being blocked or her uterus being shaped weird. I forget.

"Stephanie, we have to go now. I hope they let us take that wand on the plane. It's pretty pointy."

"I'm sure it'll be fine," says Janet.

"I want to say bye to Maxie," Stephanie whines.

"Good luck with that. I saw him run down to the basement," I say.

"Stephie, I promise I'll tell him you said goodbye when he comes up for his dinner. I'm sure he'll be up real soon to play with his cousins," says Janet, kissing Stephanie and giving her another hug.

My daughter seems to think this makes sense. But I know there's not a frigid virgin's chance in a whorehouse that Maxie will be coming upstairs any time soon to probably be scratched and hissed at by his "cousins." My bet is that it'll be at least a week of my sister taking plates of food down to him. In fact, I'd be shocked if she actually sees that damn cat the whole time Stephanie and me are in Arizona. But if that's what gets Steph going, the lie works for me too.

When we walk to the cab, Stephanie turns and waves her magic wand in Janet's direction and says, "Bye-bye, Aunt Janny."

"Bye, Princess Stephanie," shouts my sister.

Philadelphia International is crazy.

If traveling with a kid weren't hard enough, the jackass security guy yelling at everyone, "Take off your shoes, computers out of cases, everything from your pockets goes into a bin," over and over makes me want to fucking scream.

But the shit actually hit the fan before that, when I went to change our seats.

When Stephanie had to stay longer in the hospital, I needed to rebook the flight. The new seats we got were way in the back of the plane. We had less than an hour until we had to board, and there was this huge line to the customer service representatives, but there was no way in hell I was going to sit in those seats.

After twenty minutes, we finally reached the desk. I told the rep—Lynnie, according to her name tag—that our seats had to be changed.

She took my tickets and said, "Well, Mrs. Cole, let me see what we can do."

She clicked on her keyboard, frowned at me, and said, "Unfortunately, I won't be able to move you. This flight is at full capacity."

"Please see what you can do? My daughter, Stephanie, is very sick." I turned and pointed at Steph. She was sitting on the suitcase behind me, sucking the side of her pinkie. I bent down to hug her. "She was just released from the hospital." Stephanie looked up and Lynnie smiled at her.

"I'm so afraid the smell from the toilets will bring back her vomiting," I said. "Her doctor says she needs to be closer to the front of the plane and near a window."

"I understand, I really do, but I'm not seeing any options here," Lynnie said. She turned the screen around so I could see all the red blocks of taken seats. "Perhaps you could tell me what we could do to make your daughter more comfortable in your assigned seats?" She tugged on the ends of the blue-and-white scarf knotted around her neck.

"Nothing. There is nothing you can do. Like I said, those seats won't work. I will not have my daughter who is really, really sick and who just got out of the hospital after a very long stay, where she almost died, sit in the back of the fucking plane."

"Please, Mrs. Cole, lower your voice. I'm so sorry she's been ill, but—"

That's when I said, "Get me your supervisor."

Lynnie walked away and tapped the arm of a man who was loading luggage onto the moving carrier. I leaned down and whispered in Stephanie's ear that she needed to start crying. She began to whimper and asked, "Why, Mommy?"

"Just do it."

Lynnie and the guy bent their heads together. They looked at me, and then at Stephanie, who, after I gave her a tiny pinch on her leg, was now crying for real. Lynnie returned.

"My supervisor says that, while we normally don't do this, we will exchange your seats with two of our other passengers." She hit buttons, took the suitcases, and wrapped tags on the handles. She said a thank-you that sounded much more like a fuck-you and handed me our boarding passes with the new seats, 6A and 6B. Much, much better.

"Honey, it's okay now," I said, holding Stephanie's hand. I smoothed down her hair and used my sleeve to wipe off her cheeks. "Thank the nice lady for helping us."

Stephanie sniffed and whispered, "Thank you."

17
Claire

I don't need to hear what the doctor says. I can tell from my mother's face as she listens to the tinny voice on the other end of the line that my father is dead.

And it doesn't matter why. The fact that his heart was compromised from this and the strokes before, that his lungs started to drown in fluid, that then all the other organs miraculously keeping a human body running fell like dominoes, one after the other: kidneys, liver, large intestine. It doesn't matter. He is dead.

My mother crumples to the floor, a straw woman whose supporting framework has evaporated. I crouch next to her and try to gather her into my arms, but she's fluid and undulating, winding around herself and whimpering. The most I can do is try to anticipate her movements and place my arms and hands between her and whatever hard corners—the stairs, the couch leg, the door frame—are in her path. I reach for my cell phone and call Aunt Frannie, and she and Uncle Ted seem to appear the moment I disconnect, but time is slippery and funky. It could be fifteen minutes or an hour before they arrive. Aunt Frannie is finally able to coax my mother to a chair and have her sip from a glass of bourbon, the hardest, and only, liquor in the house.

Escaping to the bathroom, I sit and shake on the closed toilet seat. I turn on the water in the tub and the sink to stifle what comes out of my mouth, a keening sound that frightens me so much I clamp my hand over my lips to stop it. I force myself to breathe, in and out, in and out. Standing shakily, I rinse my face with cold water and reach into my pocket for my phone.

Cal's phone rings, and I lose count after fifteen. With a three-hour time difference, it's only eleven in Arizona, and I don't know why Cal isn't picking up. A slew of maybes I can't think about right now will have to wait.

The next few days rush by, a kaleidoscope of moments, some painted in vivid and garish oils: the obscene brightness of chartreuse grass in the field where we hold the farewell ceremony—my mother certain he would not have wanted a funeral. But most of the moments are hued in some variation of gray: the dimmed hospital room as we surround the bed to say goodbye to the mannequin who is as much my father as a toothpick is a tree. And another gray: the color of the ashes my mother tosses across that grassy field where she and my father spent afternoons the summer they first met.

Watching my mother spread my father's ashes, I remember a story my dad told me years ago when I was helping him during one of those many times he had to stay in bed resting.

He said Michigan used to have gorgeous Dutch elm trees. They would grow to over one hundred and twenty feet and would line the streets of the city, their canopies bending toward one another, creating lovely cathedral-like ceilings. He told me about a family living on a farm there. They had a bull they kept tied by a strong chain to one of those giant elms. The bull would walk around and around the tree, winding the chain during his trips, creating a huge groove into the trunk. Eventually, the family decided to move to Oregon, and they took their bull with them, but as the chain had become deeply embedded within the trunk, they had to leave it there, encircling the tree.

My dad explained that during the 1950s and 1960s, Dutch elm disease killed almost all the elms, except for this one tree. "You know why?" he asked, holding my hand between his two.

He told me the iron in the chain had somehow infused the tree with a mineral it needed to ward off the disease. See, he said, it survived even though it was grooved through, even though it had been damaged and was considered unsightly because of the chain. But that chain, that hardship, saved its life. "Get it?" he asked. I remember shaking my head because I didn't get it then. What I knew was that I was stuck taking care of my father while my mother had to work all the time and I was making dinners and reminding him to take his medicine while everyone else I knew was doing normal kid things. What did a stupid tree, living or dead, have to do with me?

Standing under skies overcast with dark clouds so heavy you can smell the rain in them, maybe I'm beginning to understand a little of what he was trying to tell me. That there are trials we have to face that may be undecipherable at the time as to why we're meant to go through them. I think he was letting me know that I would get stronger by what I was being asked to do back then. But this, his leaving us so soon, seemed an unduly harsh lesson, and I'm finding it impossible to fathom what future wisdom could be gained from it someday.

That night, after the ceremony, at Aunt Frannie's insistence, my mother sips a cup of chamomile tea and nibbles at half a banana. My aunt says she'll stay the night, but I tell her I think we'll be fine and that she should get some rest too. Crimping the foil wrapping on a pan of meat loaf provided by Mrs. Franklin from across the street, Aunt Frannie embraces me and says, "Call anytime, Claire. I mean it, any hour."

"I know." I blow my nose on a soggy handkerchief I vaguely remember being pressed into my hand by Edith Waverly, one of my mother's former clients. She drove eight hours to tell my mother how sorry she was, how she thought my dad was the loveliest man she'd ever met, and that whenever she'd seen my father and mother together in the shop or digging in the garden, she swore there was a giant golden bubble of light surrounding the two of them. I notice the hankie is embroidered with delicately sewn pansies and violets and smells vaguely of talcum powder.

I can't imagine how all these people find out about my father's death, but within hours, the phones ring so constantly we decide to mute my mother's cell and take the house phone off the hook. People—clients, neighbors, friends—arrive and, when we don't respond to the knocking, leave their offerings on our front porch: three green bean casseroles, two platters of brownies—one with nuts, one without, according to the index cards taped on top—and tins of cookies, at least half of which are labeled VEGAN. Bringing them inside, I keep a list of who gave what and jam what I can into the refrigerator and freezer. Neither of us has much of an appetite.

That night, after Aunt Frannie leaves, I sit on the floor outside my mother's bedroom. I'm trying to hear her. I need to hear her. I need to be heard. Crying or sobbing or screaming would be better than the hollow silence. Finally, I knock.

"Mom?" I'm not expecting an answer and begin to stand and walk away.

"Come in, Claire," she says, her voice raspy and soft, worn-out.

I enter, and we spend the next three days and nights in her bed, talking, remembering, crying, and trying to help each other through the inconceivable-ness of what's happened.

I don't want to leave my mother, but after five days, she convinces me to go. She's started to eat—not much, an egg or two and, occasionally, a piece of rye toast, but she's showered and is upright, shuffling slowly through the rooms and even, once, walking out into the garden with Aunt Frannie. My aunt promises she will stay with her at the house for as long as they both feel it's necessary. I'm able to book an early flight out of Philadelphia and text Cal to let him know my schedule. He'd called several times, but with everything going on, I missed the calls, and there was no answer when I returned the calls, so we've been communicating through voice mail and text. It's impossible to tell and, as I keep saying to myself, dangerous and stupid to do, but I can't help feeling his electronic messages seem curt and distant.

Sitting on the back patio with her now, with the sun just starting to rise, we're listening for the cab's horn. I ask her a question that's been in my head for the past few days: "Mom, do you want me to come back home to live?"

She doesn't respond immediately, and when she does, I think her answer surprises both of us.

"Let's see how I do. This is a whole new thing for me," she says, reaching forward to pull a dandelion from the clover surrounding our chairs. She sniffs, and I don't need to look over to know that she's crying when she says, "It will be good if I can learn to be alone, on my own."

"You're never . . . ," I start.

"I know." She takes my hand and stares at two butterflies twirling in a double helix above the hydrangeas. "It's a wonderful, terrible thing, isn't it? That this brought us back together, you and me."

"I want to help. You don't have to handle this all by yourself."

"Oh, honey," she says, squeezing my fingers. "I think I'm finally starting to know I'm not alone. Even with your dad gone . . . Of course, there's no one else who can be what he was for me, but your aunt, all those amazing people who called or came by, they'll be here. And you . . . We'll keep talking, all the time, right? We'll never lose this, never go backward. I'll make sure of that. And you'll visit again, very soon?"

"Of course," I say. "But—"

A honk from the front of the house announces the cab's arrival. She pulls me to my feet and clasps my forearms, green eyes focused on mine, a mirror image.

"What I don't want to do is repeat the messes of the past. I do not want you to feel responsible for me. That's not your job, and it never should have been." We walk to the waiting cab.

I toss my carry-on bag into the back seat and say, "I'll call when I get to Arizona."

"I'll come to Sedona soon. I can't wait to see that part of the country."

She takes me in her arms. I'm still not used to it, but I don't want to let go or be let go.

Under the garish overhead lights at Gate 7 in the Philadelphia airport, I'm squirming to get comfortable in the molded plastic chair, waiting to hear the announcement to board. Pulling out my phone, I push Cal's number again. There's still no answer, and I refuse to leave another voice mail. I alternate between anger and concern that he could be hurt and I would have no way of knowing. I had called Mindi after my dad died to let her know I needed to stay longer and thought about asking her to go to our place to check on Cal, but I was too embarrassed. What if he was there, and had been the whole time I'd been trying to reach him, watching old movies, eating stale popcorn and ignoring my calls?

Except, in my heart, I know the overriding emotion I'm feeling is actually fear. Surrounded by milling people going and coming amid a pervasive undercurrent of jet fuel fumes, when I can, momentarily, put aside my grief, I know I am terrified. Remembering the last conversation Cal and I had and adding that we've had zero nonvirtual contact since then, I feel like there's no guarantee he'll still be in the apartment where I left him. As I run through all the possible scenarios, it seems more and more likely he's finally had enough of my idiotic relationship rules of engagement or, rather, lack of engagement. That he couldn't continue with someone who was always keeping him at a distance, and so, he finally made his long-overdue escape.

The woman at the gate holds a microphone and notifies us we can get on the plane, and all I want is to be unconscious for the next five plus hours, to give my frazzled emotions a chance to recover a little bit before having to handle the next crisis.

I'd been relieved to score a window seat, figuring I'd lower the shade, cover my head with my hoodie, and block out everything and everyone. Except, there are two people, a girl and an adult I'm assuming is the mother, already in my row. The kid's in 6A, my window seat.

"Excuse me," I say to the woman. "I'm in 6A."

"Oh, sorry. Me and Stephanie got switched to these seats. My daughter, she's very sick, and she needs to be in this row. By the window."

I look around for a flight attendant, but they're all occupied, yelling at passengers to place their bags in the overhead compartments and sit down so the flight can take off on time.

Not having a bit of strength left to argue, I sit in the aisle seat, buckle up, and prepare to push myself into the oblivion of sleep.

My neighbor says, "Hi, I'm Rena," and thrusts a pudgy hand in my direction.

18
Rena

A woman holding a boarding pass stops at our row. She says Stephanie is in her seat. She's not too happy when I tell her the airline gave us these seats because Steph is sick. Looking around like she's going to make this big stink, she seems to decide it's too much of a hassle and sits down in the aisle seat.

I introduce myself, squeeze Steph's knee, and say, "And this is Stephanie, my daughter. We're taking a trip all the way to Arizona to see a new doctor, aren't we, sweetie?"

The woman nods, buckles her seat belt, and shuts her eyes.

She's so tall her knees are all scrunched up against the seat in front of her. Her lashes are long and fringy and I want to ask her what mascara she uses. And her hair is really shiny and lays exactly the way it should, just touching her shoulders. Maybe I could ask her about her shampoo too.

Stephanie squiggles around in her seat, so I give her a coloring book and crayons, and then I take the Xanax I brought with me. I'm asleep until I feel Steph shaking my shoulder, asking for some water.

My neighbor must hear her too, because she looks over at us with her eyes half-closed.

"The new doctor in Arizona is the best in the nation for treating stomach problems like what Steph has. Steph and me, we know she is going to fix her right up," I say. My neighbor opens her eyes the rest of the way. There's this piece-of-crap china figurine I got in a junk store a few years ago. One of those Japanese good-luck kitties holding up a paw. It has two fake emeralds stuck in the eye sockets—that's the color of her eyes.

"Pardon me?" she says.

"I said my daughter and me are going all the way to Arizona to see a specialist. A tummy doctor, right, Steph?" I pat Stephanie's stomach. She puts a finger in her mouth and starts to chew on the nail. I shake my head, and she moves her hand back to her lap.

"Oh," says the woman, "that's good."

"Do you live in Arizona . . . ?" I ask, leaving the air space for her to tell me her name.

"Claire . . . It's Claire. Yes, I live in Sedona."

"Oh, Sedona. I heard all about that place. The pictures of those red rocks are amazing. And isn't that where all those crazy vibes are?"

"Vibes?"

"You know, energy circles, shit like that."

"Yes, that's what people say." Claire moves around in her seat, turns away, and shuts her eyes again.

"I'm hoping this doctor is everything everyone says she is. We've tried so many. In and out of doctors' offices and emergency rooms and hospitals. But nobody can figure out what the hell is going on. It's been horrible. Like, not one doctor has a single clue what's wrong with her? You know what I mean?"

Claire turns back to face me, and I'm surprised to see she's crying. She reaches into her hoodie pocket, pulls out a crumpled-up hankie, and wipes at her eyes. Who even uses a hankie anymore?

"Hey, you okay?" I ask.

"I'm sorry." She sniffs. "My father just died."

"Oh, that sucks. Was he sick a long time?"

"Almost all of my life," she says. "Strokes."

"Strokes, they're the absolute worst. I was a nurse—well, a nursing student—and I can tell you those are the toughest on the families. Awful. I mean the person is just destroyed, piece by piece, right?"

She sniffs again, and her eyes fill with more tears. "Right," she says.

"Believe me, I know about this, how it takes all your hours and your energy. Actually, your whole life, when someone is that sick. With . . ." I point in Stephanie's direction. She's staring at Claire with her mouth wide open. I signal with my finger for her to turn around and mind her own beeswax. She mopes but does as she's told. "With Stephanie, it's been trauma after trauma, ever since she was born."

Claire nods and says something like, "I bet." But it's so soft, especially with the noise from the plane, it's hard to hear her.

"Hey," I say. "I got a question for you. Don't they have those mystical-type people in Sedona? You know, the ones who can tell you what's wrong? I mean, like physically? Like maybe they could find out what's going on with Stephanie? At this point, I'm willing to try anything."

Claire looks confused but then says, "You mean, like a psychic?"

"Yeah, maybe. Is that what they do?"

"Well, some do. They're called medical intuitives. They scan your body—well, actually, your energy—and supposedly can tell you what's going on inside."

"Supposedly?"

"I've only done it a couple of times, so I can't speak to whether it's always accurate or anything like that."

I practically jump out of my seat, I'm that excited.

"Wait, what the hell? You're a psychic?"

Claire doesn't answer for a long time. I'm about to ask again, but then she finally mumbles, "Yeah."

"Oh my God, this is awesome. Someone I know, my meditation teacher, Ricki, she's gone to a bunch of psychics. She keeps telling me to go, but with Steph, of course, I don't have a minute to myself. But maybe that's what I'll do once Steph and me are settled. Drive to Sedona. Is it close by to Phoenix? Do you have a card or something?"

"No, sorry," she says.

"Here." I grab my pen and a grocery store receipt from my purse and push them into her hand. "Write your name. Do you work in a store or out of your house or what? Write that down too, okay? Wow, I'm so excited you sat next to me." I turn to Stephanie and say, "Hear that, sweetie? Maybe you and me will drive up and see this nice lady so we can find out what's really going on with your tummy." She looks at me and then turns back to stare out the window.

The captain's voice comes over the intercom. "Ladies and gentlemen, we are about twenty minutes from Phoenix Sky Harbor. In a moment, crew members will be coming through the cabin and collecting any trash you may still have. Thank you for flying with us and enjoy your stay."

"Excuse me," I say, standing up and squeezing over Claire's knees. "Almost there, so I guess I better use the potty. Keep an eye on Steph for me, okay?"

19
Claire

Of all the seats in all the planes . . . I had to have the one next to her. To this woman named Rena. She's a frowsy, meaty blonde in desperate need of a root touch-up, with murky hazel eyes and ruddy skin. And a mouth that won't quit.

It's bad enough her kid's in my window seat, but then Rena, in the middle seat, will not stop talking. As soon as she sees the slit of one of my slightly opened eyes, she continues the conversation as if I hadn't been practically comatose next to her for the past four-plus hours. It seems she must tell me everything: her name, her daughter's name, her meditation coach's name, and her ongoing difficulties with the medical system.

Before she can start detailing for me the size and type of the shoes in her closet at home, I find myself giving her the Mystical Haven information. Apparently, she's always wanted to have a meeting with a psychic. Hopefully, someone who can tell her what's wrong with her child. It's very sad, I'm not saying it isn't, but she seems determined to include me in all of the anguish, and right now, I'm completely anguished out. I'm almost tempted to do the bait-and-switch thing, where you give the guy you meet at the bar your phone number, but it's actually the number for the zoo.

The captain announces that the flight attendants will be picking up our trash. I'm beat, I want to get to our apartment, and I want to find Cal, but mostly, right at this moment, I want to be as far away from the person sitting next to me as is possible to do when you're trapped in an aluminum box. Fortunately, Rena has to go the bathroom. Unfortunately, she asks me to watch her daughter, Stephanie, while she's gone.

"So, Stephanie, how old are you?" She's got the palest blue eyes I've ever seen. They're almost silver but dull and set deep in sockets surrounded by gray skin. Her blond hair hangs in droopy ringlets supported by two floppy red bows at the crown.

"Four," she whispers, twisting to stare fixedly out the window. I'm surprised because I would have guessed maybe three. She looks like she hasn't slept in a month.

"Is this your first plane ride?"

She nods stiffly, squeezing her palms into each other and intertwining her fingers until they're knotted together, her knuckles turning white.

"Uh-oh, better unwrap those or they may get stuck that way," I say, reaching over to gently lift one of her tiny pinkies. She jerks back as if I slapped her.

"I'm sorry. I just wanted to make sure you can play with your toys. It'll be hard to do with your fingers all scrunched up like that."

She giggles then, a sweet, pure sound. Her face pinks up a bit, and she finally looks at me.

"I brought Jeffrey with me and also some LEGOs."

"Jeffrey? Who's that?"

"He's my panda, silly." She giggles again.

"I bet he's a good friend. Do you and Jeffrey play together every day?"

It's like a switch flipped. Her face closes in, an origami, all folds and creases. She turns back to the window and mutters something.

Bending toward her, I say, "I'm sorry, Stephanie, I didn't hear what you said."

When she looks back at me, there's something in her face that's hard to decipher. Fear maybe, but definitely a sadness beyond what any child should carry.

She sighs and leans in my direction. I bend over

even more until we're close enough that she can cup her hand around my ear. She says, "Sometimes Jeffrey is very bad and he has to sleep in the cellar, on the floor." She pauses and looks up and around us and then says, "It's really cold and dark."

A whispered secret, her face a mask of resigned despair, like that of a person who's seen too much of life.

When my throat constricts and I feel like I'm going to cry again, I'm sure it's just a continuation of the emotional deluge I've been experiencing since my father's death. Suddenly, though, there's liquid in my mouth, and I have to keep swallowing to clear it. It tastes like the ocean, as if I've been sucked under by a wave and am taking in gulps of seawater. Like my salivary glands have been opened and I'm unable to activate the shutoff valve. I swallow and swallow, but the salty liquid keeps filling my mouth.

As we touch down, Rena rushes back, with the flight attendant close behind, hissing at her to take her seat.

When the plane stops rolling and the lights blink on, Rena grabs her bag from the overhead compartment and tosses Stephanie a stuffed panda that's sporting a ragged red-checked bow tie, and white ears and a belly that are mostly yellowed. I'm guessing it's Jeffrey. Stephanie closes her eyes and hugs him tightly to her.

I get my bag too and follow them down the aisle and

off the plane. In the terminal, Rena says she'll see me in Sedona and walks away, dragging Stephanie behind her by the arm. The little girl turns back and raises her hand in a limp wave.

I rush to the bathroom to spit into the sink. Much to the disgust of my fellow travelers, I'm sure, I stand there and spit and spit for at least ten minutes as the salty water continues to fill my mouth.

20
Rena

When Stephanie and me walk out of the terminal, I feel like I'm actually inside a fucking volcano. I heard it was hot here, but I thought that maybe since it was so early in the morning it wouldn't be too bad. Wrong. Sweat is dripping down my back, and Stephanie's face is all red. I take off her sweatshirt and tie it around her waist.

The cab drops us off at our new place, which is a shithole. There's no other word for it. It's a really small duplex on a square of gravel. No backyard. I look both ways down the street. All the buildings look exactly the same, just separated from one another by tall concrete block walls. There's not a tree or, really, anything alive over two feet high in sight. I'm not sure which one is supposed to be ours, so I knock on a door. No answer.

I move to the other door and knock again. Stephanie is poking the spikes of a cactus on the "lawn." She jumps back each time she gets stuck.

A fat woman with frizzy short black hair finally answers the door. She wipes her hands down the front of her apron, which is covered with flour, and says, "Yeah?"

"I'm Rena and, uh, I'm looking for Mrs. Lupito?"

"You found her."

I point to Stephanie. She moved away from the cactus and is dragging a broken toy truck across the dust and pebbles. "That's my daughter, and we're renting a place from you? You and me talked last month."

"Oh yeah, I remember now. You were supposed to be here like three weeks ago. I almost rented the place to someone else. You shoulda called me. Good thing you got here today. By the end of this week, it wouldn't be available no more." Her Spanish accent is pretty thick, so I have to listen real hard to understand what she's saying. Mrs. Lupito stares at Stephanie for a long time and then says, "She sick? She looks sickly."

"Yeah, really sick. That's why we're here. To see a stomach specialist at Sun Valley Memorial Hospital."

Mrs. Lupito grunts and closes the door. WTF? I'm about to knock again when she comes back out. She's got a key attached by a chain to a five-inch-tall plastic crucifix. She says to follow her and unlocks the door next to her place into the ugliest room I've ever seen.

There's a sofa with torn plaid fabric hanging off one arm and a huge purple beanbag in the corner. The scratched coffee table is covered with water spots and dust. I touch the beanbag with my toe. There's a hole (from a mouse?) near the bottom, and a pile of beans falls out onto the dingy shag rug. I didn't even know anyone had that type of carpet anymore.

It only gets worse from there. The bedroom is about the size of my closet at home. I can actually see the springs pushing up through the top of the mattress. There's hardly any space on the floor for Stephanie's sleeping bag.

The bathtub is filthy, all rust-stained and soap scummy.

"How far is the hospital from here?" I ask the landlady.

"Walking distance," she says as she moves toward the door. "Rent, first and last, due to me by end of today."

"Fine." I shut the door behind her.

21
Claire

Sun and shadow are warring over the buttes, light cresting above the ragged red edges, as I turn into our apartment complex. I assume Cal is still sleeping. My hand shakes so much the key drops to the front mat. Trying to open the door quietly, I'm rehearsing in my mind what I'll do, which already sounds ridiculous to me, like a bad soap-opera scene. Woman dresses in slinky robe, drops robe to the floor, and slides in next to her man, who is about to have a real eye-opening good-morning surprise.

Except the first problem is I don't own a robe of any kind, and the second, as I soon discover, is Cal is not in the bed. I walk back outside and stuff my hand in the mail slot hanging beside the front door. It's filled with at least a few days' worth of bills, magazines, and restaurant flyers. It appears as if Cal has not been home for a while.

All the words I wanted to say—how much I love him and need him—every single one becomes an extinguished firework, fizzling and hitting the ground as ash. I'm certain he's gone, as I had anticipated he would be. I check his closet and see his clothes hanging there, but I know at some point he'll come back for them and his CDs and his collection of ceramic owls, and then the apartment will lose all sense of its Cal-ness. How long could I honestly expect a good, sweet man like Cal to hang around waiting for someone like me?

My shirt feels too tight; everything feels too tight. I can't breathe.

Walking through each room, I hunt for a farewell letter, a sticky note, anything to tell me where he's gone, why he finally decided to walk away. Nothing—but I get it. What else could he possibly say after years of telling me how much he loved me, wanted to be with me, to marry me—shouting it into the great void of my heart and receiving not even an echo in return? It would be against all reason that he would stay, and now, beyond comprehension of why he remained for so long. I stand in the kitchen, marooned, and slip to the floor. I begin to sob, great belly-wrenching gulps that terrify me with their ferocity and my inability to control them.

Curling on my side, I gasp for air.

Eventually, I stand shakily, walk back into the deserted bedroom, and put on my running shoes. I need something familiar, an anchor to save me from this sensation of being unmoored.

The trail looks empty, as I would expect, given the early hour. I stretch and begin to lumber up the slight incline. Maybe it's from not running for the past week or so, but my legs feel leaden, my muscles stiff as an old bike tire. I trip over a fallen cactus. Vaguely, I can hear the whirl of helicopter blades and register that it's one of the morning tours. A group of chattering quails scurries in front of me, topknots bobbing.

My mind is struggling to find its lost stability, already grasping at alternatives for a new life, a life without Cal: I'll move to Pennsylvania and live with my mother; I'll go back to school and get a degree that could actually lead to a real job; I'll be an elephant trainer; I'll jump off the next lookout point. Images race through my brain, and in each one, there's a huge ragged hole, a place where Cal used to be. No matter how I try, I cannot imagine a life without him. Who will tell me the sound from outside is a dog and not a coyote? Where will I bring my tired mind when my thoughts become so tangled that only Cal can help me unravel them? When will I laugh again until I'm straining for air because of a joke so stupid it could only have this effect on the two of us? I know now, down to my core, that I want a future with him. I want to see what he does, what he becomes. I want to be there on his sixtieth birthday as he blows out a fire torch of candles on his cake. The tears start again, hot and blurring my vision.

All I want is Cal.

And there he is.

I'm so shocked, I stop midstride. He doesn't see me for a second since he's looking at his feet, a poor running technique I've been trying to break him of for years. Finally, he raises his gaze, and how his face lights up as he spots me only makes me cry harder. He sprints the distance between us, wraps his arms around me, and says into my hair, "Claire, I'm so sorry. It must have been horrible for you. I told you I should have gone. Why didn't you let me go with you?"

"Oh my God. You're here. You didn't leave," I push out between sobs.

"Leave?"

"You were angry. I know it. We didn't talk while I was gone, and your texts were, I don't know, distant. I went to the apartment just now and you weren't in bed and there was all this mail and there was no note and . . ."

He leans back to stare at me and starts to laugh. "You know me. Until this moment, and only because you reminded me, I probably wouldn't have checked the mail until it was falling out of the box. And why would I leave a note when I was only out for a run?" We walk back down the trail a bit, and he leads me to a stone bench to sit.

"Didn't you get my text that I was coming home this morning?" I gulp back sobs.

He reaches into his shorts pocket and says, "Damn. I'm really sorry, but I must have left my phone in the car. Again. But I did call you back. Didn't you get any of my messages?"

I nod and say, "I tried calling you too, but I guess, with the time difference, we never connected. And texts . . . They're so impersonal, you know?"

He wipes a palm over both my cheeks and kisses me. I feel my joints, connective tissue, even my organs, begin to soften and unknot.

"Yeah, I do." Cal looks at his running shoes, which are covered in red dust. He brushes one off with the sole of the other. "To be honest, you're right. I was mad when you left." He hesitates, and I can see the struggle as he decides what to say next. "I don't think it's a surprise to either of us that things have been tense between us for a while. I know you want me to do something with my life—the whole returning to school bit. And I started to think that maybe we were never going to get married, that maybe . . . you just don't love me as much as I love you. That I'm not the right person for you."

I turn his face toward mine so I can look directly into his eyes.

"Cal, I'm an idiot."

"Wait, let me finish. What I think made me so angry was not just that maybe you felt that way, but that I did."

"Huh?"

"That I wasn't the right person—for me. That I wasn't doing what I really wanted, what I needed to do. I mean, helping people decide which portable camping toilet to buy is fascinating work, but . . ." He nudges a small lizard with the toe of his shoe, and it scampers off into the low brush.

"The more I thought about it, the madder I got—at me. I've been taking it very easy, I know. Then . . . you left and didn't even want me to be with you during this terrible time. I felt like a loser on all fronts."

"Now can I say it? I'm an idiot," I repeat.

He starts to laugh, and I'm so relieved to hear the sound because maybe it means I haven't totally destroyed what I've trampled on for so long.

"I'm not sure how to explain it, but . . ." I tell him

about my mother, how we finally talked, truly talked, after all those years of being polarized and separate. How much it meant to me for her to tell me she was sorry about the burden I had to take on when I was a kid, how she truly loved me, and how we were able to grieve my father's death together.

He listens without commenting and then puts an arm around my shoulders and pulls me close. I can smell the sweat, which has an undertone of curry that tells me he probably went to Indian Paradise without me for dinner last night and that makes me start to tear up again, thinking of me not being with him for the curry chicken we both love. The possibility of us not together seems like the difference between falling off the cliff and almost falling off the cliff, like the tiniest of breezes or a small trip on a pebble could change everything. It feels that tenuous.

I'm crying again and babbling an avalanche of words that tumble and crash around one another.

"Maybe it was what happened between my mom and me, but . . . I started to get it, to really understand what it means. This love thing. I mean, I'm scared, like I don't want to get too excited about this change with her. I guess time will tell. But it felt so good to have that kind of love. And it reinforced for me how much I love you and how much I need you in my life. And I don't get to make decisions for you. Who am I to do that? You have to decide. Just you. Be what you want. The best damn supersalesman Mountain and Stream ever had or a plumber or research scientist or a logger or a monkey house cleaner. I mean, who am I to judge? I'm pretending to be a psychic because I couldn't get any other job and then was just too lazy to do anything else. Cal, be anything you want, but stay with me. Just stay with me."

"It's okay, Claire," he says, patting my back gently.

"No, it's not. I mean, what if it's the end of the world, and you're not with me? I want you with me. Who else would put up with me? I'm difficult, I know. And tough—I can be so tough. I'm sorry about that, I am, because you're not. You are the least tough person I know. Your heart is open and sweet, and all I've done is stomp all over it. I'm sorry. I really am. You're my friend, my best friend, and I don't want to be without you today or tomorrow or when the world ends. I can be better, I promise, I can try . . ."

Bundling me against him, he says, "Claire, you have to know by now . . . you couldn't keep me from loving you, no matter what you do or don't do."

I felt it then. Love. More than a little frightening, but so worth it.

22
Rena

STEPHANIE'S BATTLE BLOG

Posted on August 25 by Stephanie's Mommy

I know it's been a really long time since I posted.

You can tell by the pictures, me and Steph's place is definitely not the Taj Mahale. But its furnished. And it's near the doctor so that's all good.

Steph's stomach has been just Terrible. Last night she was in such huge pain so me and Steph spent alot of time on the brfloor. (see pic) It's really hard to watch your child in that much agony. All I could do was sit next to her and cry and cry. Our appointment is on Friday. Pls PRAY this doctor will know what to do and can help her feel better FAST.

But there maybe is some possible good news. My ex always had horrible stomach problems. I nagged and nagged at him and he finally went to a doctor. He said this doc tested him for something called fabric disease. I asked was this an allergy, like to wool or something? The doctor said it was GENETIC. Anybody know something about this? I want to make sure to tell Steph's dr at her appointment.

No good health food stores here. I did find a Momma Loves Baby class around the corner. Will check it out tomorrow. if she feels better. right now, she's as white as a ghost and can't keep nothing down.

Rena's Way to Well: Feed Your Kid Right

Don't believe everything the doctors tell you about your kid's diet. You are the MOMMY. You know best. They tell you organic doesn't matter. IT DOES!!! Don't put anything in your child that isn't clean and natral.

Yolandathegreat: I've been so worried about you since we didn't hear anything for a long time. How was the trip?

MartinaQ: Hey, glad you got there. When you get a chance, can you please send me that recipe for the quinoa pancakes?!

Kittieseverywhere: What doctor are you going to see? And where? Our son has terrible stomachaches since he was born and nothing anyone does seems to help. Would be so grateful if you could tell me who you be seeing. We will go anywhere to get Nathan help. Anywhere!!!

XY42: I work at a genetic clinic in CA and I think what you're talking about is Fabry Disease. It's an inherited disorder and pretty rare. Much more common in men than women. The body can't make an enzyme called alpha-galactosidase, which you need to break down fatty substances like oil and fatty acids. There are many symptoms, including pain and burning in hands and feet, small, dark red spots between the belly button and knees, cloudy vision and stomach pain. It's often misdiagnosed because the symptoms are pretty common and affect many parts of the body. The genetic defect for Fabry disease is located on the X chromosome. If the dad has the disease, there is a zero percent chance he'll pass it on to a son and a 100% chance he'll pass this altered gene to his daughter. Hope this helps and that your little girl feels better real soon.

KnitWit1: Rena, please call me. Where are you and what's with your phone? I haven't been able to reach you. You need to call me immediately. Love, Janet

Me and Steph were walking around the neighborhood one afternoon looking for the Laundromat and

saw a sign in the window of a kids' consignment clothing shop: MOMMY LOVES BABY: MUSIC, STORIES & FUN!
WEDNESDAYS, 10–11, ALL WELCOME!

There are only three other moms and their kids
sitting in a circle on a nasty-looking rug in the back
room of the consignment shop. The whole place smells
musty and kind of like BO. I'm guessing that's because
of all the donated clothes and crap. Lots of old toys and
kitchen stuff and coats (when the hell do they ever wear
those out here?) are piled up on open metal shelves.
Stephanie's being kind of shy, so I have to give her a
small push to get her through the doorway. Then she
hides behind my leg.

"Hi, everyone," I say. "I'm Rena, and this little
person attached to my hip is Stephanie. She's four.
Say hello, Steph." The women giggle, and Steph looks
around me.

"Aw, she's so cute. Come on, sweetie, sit here next to
me and Rex," says a fat woman with a fat kid. He looks
about five, but it's hard to tell because he's so huge.
The woman says her name is Connie.

I sit down next to Connie and Rex, and Stephanie sits beside me. The other two women tell me their
names and their kids' names. I help Steph take off her
sweatshirt.

"Too hot for this, right, sweetie?" I ask, folding and putting it on the floor next to us.

One of the women, Susan, says her daughter, Felicia, is three and a half. The kid looks a whole lot like one of those Pekingese dogs, with her pushed-in nose and all of her hair poking straight up.

"Is this your first time at Mommy Loves Baby?" Susan asks.

"We used to belong to a group back home. Me and Stephanie just got into town. We came to Arizona to see a special doctor here. She's a very sick little girl." I lick my palm and wipe at a smudge on Steph's forehead.

I see them all look at each other, so I say real quick, "It's not catchable. Stomach problems. She has a horrible time keeping food down. We've been in and out of so many hospitals."

Everyone seems relieved.

"So sorry to hear that. Where did you move here from?" asks Margaret, a Mexican-looking woman with a kid who could be about Stephanie's age. Margaret's daughter, Valerie, has big dark eyes and has been staring at Stephanie ever since we came in. I take off the rubber band from Stephanie's braid, finger-comb her hair, and rebraid it.

"Back east. We saw a ton of doctors there, but

they couldn't do shit. She just kept getting sicker and sicker. I did research and found the best doctor in the country for kids' tummy problems, and she's here in Phoenix."

"Well, welcome," says Connie. "I'm the coordinator for this group, but actually, we all take turns leading activities. Sometimes we have a lot of moms and kids, and sometimes it's a small group like today. Many people left the valley this week because it's been so dang hot. So, Rena, if there's anything you think our moms and kids might enjoy doing, please just let us know."

I nod and give Stephanie a hug.

"All right, then, everyone up," shouts Connie, her double chins jiggling. "Let's do a little exercise before we start on our musical instruments."

We stretch through a few yoga-type moves and do some jumping jacks. The dishes on the shelves bang against each other, especially because fatties Connie and Rex are really into the jumping.

"Stephanie, honey, you're a little out of breath," I say, taking her arm and gently pulling her down to sit next to me. "She has problems keeping up sometimes." Everyone stops jumping and sits down too.

The rest of the time we play recorders, beat on drums, and wave tambourines in the air to a CD of "Twinkle, Twinkle, Little Star" and the alphabet song.

For the first time in my life, I realize these songs have the exact same tune. So fucking weird.

When the hour's up, Connie asks, "Who brought treats this week?"

From a huge tote bag, Margaret pulls out a plastic container. She takes off the lid and everyone oohs and aahs over the cookies. They look like oatmeal raisin. She passes them to Connie.

"Are there nuts in those?" I ask.

"Of course not," says Margaret. "We're very careful about allergies here."

"That's good," I say. "How about white flour? Did you use white flour?"

Connie has three cookies in her hand. She's reaching in to get more, but then she stops to hear Margaret's answer.

"Yes, I used white flour. But I think it was un-bleached," Margaret says.

"Doesn't matter," I say. "Besides the gluten, all flour also contains pesticides. The USDA found like sixteen different kinds of pesticide residue in white flour."

Connie passes the cookie container to Susan, but Susan doesn't take any for herself or Felicia.

When the cookies get to me, Stephanie reaches in to take one, and I give her hand a little slap. I shake my head and pass the container back to Margaret.

"No, honey," I tell Steph. "We'll have our snacks when we get home."

"Sounds like you eat healthy," says Margaret. I know she really, really wants a cookie. She gives this big sigh, puts the lid back on, and shoves the container back into her bag.

"We try. It's not easy, though," I say. "I had to do a lot of research to find foods Stephanie can digest that are also super good for her. Like, for lunch, we're going to have gluten-free mac and cheese. Make sure you get the organic cheese. The other stuff is just pure crap."

"I wish I could cook healthier meals," says Connie, wrapping her cookies into a tissue. "But everyone at my house, including me, only loves all the bad stuff." She giggles.

"I know it's hard. I had to do it to save my daughter's life, but after reading a bunch, I know the way most people eat is killing them." I run my hands up and down Stephanie's back. "But sometimes, no matter what I make for Stephanie, it doesn't work, and then we have to hook up the feeding tube. Right, honey?"

"That's terrible," says Susan. She reaches over to touch Stephanie's knee. "Must be very hard for you, pumpkin." Stephanie looks at her and sticks her pinkie into her mouth. I pull it out and put it back in her lap.

"It's super hard on both of us, but she has to get her nutrition in some way, you know?"

Connie says, "I really admire what you're doing."

"Hey, I have an idea," I say. "Maybe at the next meeting, what if I bring a snack that's actually good for kids? I'll even share the recipe too."

Susan claps her hands, and Connie shouts, "Great."

Margaret still looks upset but says, "Sure."

When we get home from the class, I feed Stephanie lunch and tell her to go to her room and nap.

I call Janet, and she practically screams into the phone, "Where have you been? I've been trying to reach you for two weeks. I called Gary—who also, by the way, is pretty frantic—to see if he had heard from you. He hadn't, so I finally decided to go on your blog to reach you. What the heck, Rena? Why didn't you return any of my calls?"

"Wow, Janet, calm the hell down, will you? I'm sorry but I've been kind of busy here, in case you didn't know. Settling into a new place with a really sick kid? Also, I did talk to Gary."

"Apparently not in the last two weeks. He said he keeps calling. What's with your cell phone? Why didn't you answer your phone?"

"Pretty simple. I don't have that phone anymore. It was an old model, so I got a new one with a new number."

"And you didn't think to call me and let me know? We've been crazy here, worrying about you guys. Gary, he's spitting bullets, he's so furious. He keeps saying you may as well have kidnapped Stephanie since he has no idea where the two of you are. Plus, something about a doctor's appointment he had?"

"Like I said, I'm sorry, okay? This place was pretty disgusting and filthy, so that took a while. And, to be real honest, you and Gary are not first on my list. Steph's real bad, Janet. She couldn't even get out of bed today. I'm going to have to hook her up to the feeding tube tonight if she still can't keep anything down. I tried broth and applesauce, but nothing works." I start to cry.

Janet sighs and says, "You poor thing. I do know how hard it is for you and Steph. It's just that we're all worried and when we didn't hear from you . . ."

"I'm sorry. I really am. Sometimes I feel like I'm losing my mind," I sob and blow my nose on a paper towel.

"I know, I know, and I think you're doing a fantastic job. You're a great mommy, and it's horrible to go through this with your child. I'm just glad I finally get to talk to you, and now I have your new number, so we can at least keep in touch."

"Yeah," I say, sniffing. "That'll be good."

"Hang in there. I'm sure this new doctor will know what to do."

"I really hope so." I check my watch. There's a show I want to see. I'll only miss ten minutes of it if I can get Janet off the phone now. "Well, I got to—"

"Sure, but one more thing," says my sister. "I don't mean to add to your stress, but some guy from the hospital came by here two days ago looking for you."

"What guy?"

"Wait, I've got his card." I hear Janet pushing some papers around and then she says, "His name is Adam Marcus. The card says he's a patient outreach coordinator."

"What the hell is that?"

"I don't know, but he said he was from the Child Advocacy Center at St. Theresa's and that Dr. Rondolski asked him to get in touch with you."

Fucking Rondolski. "What did he want?"

"He didn't tell me much. Only that he was sent by the hospital to talk to you, and when he couldn't get you on the phone or reach you at your house, he looked in Stephanie's records and found me as your emergency contact. He wants to talk to you about her. Don't you know why?"

"Absolutely no clue. Some stupid hospital paperwork crap, I'm guessing." There's a cockroach running across the kitchen counter, and I splat him with the paper towel. "What'd you tell him?"

"That I didn't know where you were, which is the God's honest truth. He gave me his card and said as soon as I heard from you, I needed to tell you to call him."

"Good. That's good. I'm sure it's nothing," I tell Janet. "Give me his number, and I'll give him a call."

She tells me the number, which I pretend to write down.

"If he comes back, should I give him this new cell phone number?" she asks.

"Sure. How's everything there? How's business? Maxie okay?"

"Things are fine. I'm working with a web designer on the mail-order catalog, and Maxie actually came up and ate dinner in the kitchen last week. Big step and only a little hissing from all parties."

"Thanks again for taking care of him. I got to go now, but I'll call again soon. Steph and me see the doctor this week, and then I'll know more."

"Please, please keep me posted. And you should probably give Gary a call."

"Yeah, that's a good idea. When you get a chance, do me a favor and call him and give him this cell phone number, okay?"

"Sure. And will you please call me after you see the doctor?"

"Okay. Bye."

"Also, why don't you give me your address so at least I—"

I knock on the kitchen cabinet door and say, "Hey, Jan, that's my door. Can I call you back?"

"Okay, I'll talk to—"

I disconnect and yell for Stephanie.

"Get up and put your shoes on. We need to go to the mall so Mommy can buy a new phone."

23
Claire

I tell Cal everything. About my conversation with Aunt Frannie and my last time with my father. I think I must be all cried out, but when I talk about my dad, the tears come hot and rapid.

"Claire. I'm so sorry," he says. "He was such a good guy." I nod, my head wedged into his neck.

Then I tell him about Mom. How she apologized and even seemed to have become a little stronger through the experiences of the past week. And that a new and better relationship between us seemed possible.

We talk until the sun is almost at its peak, and then Cal and I leave the trail and go back to our apartment, undress each other quickly and without the need for a silky robe or any other provocative accoutrements, spend the afternoon in bed, becoming reacquainted. After our mutual confessions, it's as if we're—and maybe we are—different people, and as those different people, we need to discover things we don't yet know about each other or thought we knew but now realize we were wrong. Like, Cal looks into my eyes while we're making love, something I never knew because I always kept mine squeezed shut—until now. I feel myself unfolding and opening, to him, to myself, as the afternoon slides into early evening. We're starving but not yet inclined to untangle ourselves from the damp sheets. Fortunately, for some reason, Cal has a half-eaten chocolate bar on the table by his side of the bed, giving me an indication of what kinds of meals he did not make or eat while I was gone.

He props himself up on a pillow, breaks off a piece of the chocolate, and hands it to me, where I'm positioned sideways across the foot of the bed. I put it in my mouth and suck on it until it melts, and then I keep the liquid there a little longer to get the full effect.

After I swallow and yawn, I lean on my elbow and say, "Tell me that you haven't been living on chocolate bars in my absence."

"No, of course not. Lots of fast food, and last night I treated myself to dinner at Indian Paradise."

"Thought so. You smell a little curryish," I say, sniffing.

"I only did it because it reminded me of you. I know how much you love their chicken tikka masala." He grins, that lopsided goofy smile. "That was probably my only real meal. Besides that, it's been potato chips, and the occasional meat inside a bun that resembles but in no way is an actual hamburger."

"Ah, the all-American, heart-destroying, early-to-the-grave diet."

"Yes, but I ran every day, completely confusing my arteries, which didn't know whether to pump up or close down."

"Quite the conundrum."

"Truly," he says, grabbing my big toe and tickling my foot. I nudge him—very gently—in parts I plan to have additional use for later on, maybe tonight.

"Ow, watch the future generations, please," he says, laughing. "I'm glad you're back for so many reasons, not the least of which is to save me from my inevitable demise. And I did do other things in your absence. I didn't spend all my time eating Cheetos and watching game shows. Actually, I didn't spend any time watching game shows."

"Turner Classic Movies?"

"Of course. There was a great one about Alexander Hamilton and his affair. It was incredible and explained—"

"Later. Tell me later about Alexander Hamilton and more now about what else you did while pining away for me."

Leaning over to kiss me, he says, "I did pine, you know. Pined heartily." Switching positions and stretching out beside me, he continues, "That is, in between the times I was mad at you."

"I said I was an idiot."

"I know, but it actually was a great thing—me being angry with you but really at myself. Because . . ." He taps a drumroll on the mattress. "I did it. I registered for a class."

I sit up and stare at him. "No kidding? What class? Why? I thought you weren't interested. What changed?"

"Nope, not kidding. Aberrant Behavior and Its Effect on Society, to start. Because it was time. Because I actually never lost interest, but I realized I was taking the easy road, that I needed to finish what I started. And what changed? Before you get all guilty, thinking you forced me into it, yes, of course, you had some influence, but mostly because you pushed a little and made me start at least thinking in that direction. Then the idea wouldn't leave my brain. I figured out being a psychologist is something I've always wanted to do. Maybe working with troubled kids?" He adds this almost sheepishly.

I kiss him on both cheeks and say, "Lucky, lucky kids."

The next day, when I walk into Mystical Haven, Mindi jumps from behind the counter and wraps me in a bone-shattering hug.

"I'm so sorry about your dad. How horrible. But I'm so, so, so glad you're back. It hasn't been the same without you here. You would not believe how busy we've become. I'm not sure why. Maybe because Mars is finally out of retrograde. Or maybe because the weather has been beautiful. Whatever the reason, it's been crazy, and, well, I'm so, so, so happy to see you." She squishes me to her one more time and then leads me over to the counter and points to the appointment book, which is overflowing with names scribbled into time slots.

"Wow, you aren't kidding, Mindi. We're swamped."

"I know, it's crazy, right? Could you please, please, please take over some of these clients for me, or else I will go completely and totally insane."

Judging by the multiples of desperate *sos* and *pleases*

she's using, the intensity in her eyes and the slightly maniacal tilt to her smile, I can see she's only slightly exaggerating.

"Sure," I say and erase her name next to every other client and write in mine.

24
Rena

August in Phoenix is like having a front-row seat in hell. Me and Stephanie take a cab to the hospital. We probably could walk because it's only about a mile away, but I spent over an hour getting Steph into her new dress and curling her hair. Damn if she's going to walk in all sweaty.

Dr. Riley Norton's office is in the brand-new children's wing of the hospital. Stephanie's eyes grow big as pancakes when we walk in. There's this giant mobile— neon orange and blue fish, an octopus, a starfish, and a seahorse—hanging from the ceiling. The whole area has this under-the-sea vibe. Kids sit in little plastic chairs and play games on monitors stuck in the walls. You push buttons to "catch" the fish swimming on the screens. There's another area with a bunch of kids sitting on a rug watching cartoons. Stephanie starts to run there, but I grab at the back of her dress. She needs to sit next to me, right in front of the check-in desk. The clerk looks up when I say, "Stephanie, honey, you have to be very careful here. Lots of germs."

I mean, sure, everything is new and looks clean enough, but who the hell knows what kinds of diseases these kids might have? After all, they are in a damn hospital.

Finally, we're called in for our appointment. A skinny nurse takes Steph's height, has her stand on a scale, and then hooks her up to test her blood pressure (104/65), heart rate (90), and oxygen level (97 percent). She has me change Stephanie into a gown, and then we have to wait. The walls are covered with posters of kittens and puppies. There's a basket with books in it, but, of course, I don't let Steph touch any of them. She knows she just needs to sit there real quiet on the paper-covered exam table. I smooth the top of her hair. It's come all loose from the clip-in bow. I wonder if I have time to redo it, but then there's a knock on the door. In walks a teenager holding a computer tablet and a manila folder with Stephanie's name on it.

She puts her hand out, and I shake it. Then she bends down, looks at Stephanie, and says, "Hi, sweetie, you look so pretty today in your blue dress." Stephanie tries to hide her face in my shoulder, but I can see she's smiling.

"What brings you here today?" she asks me. That's when I realize this kid is not a candy striper (do hospitals even have them anymore?) but a real doctor, our real doctor, Dr. Riley Norton.

She's just like the new children's wing, all glowy and perfect. Her face looks like she just woke up from a full night's sleep, which I know can't hardly be possible, working in a hospital and all. Her coat is bright white, and she has these gold earrings in the shape of teeny elephants. They look like they have real diamonds for eyes, and they sparkle as she moves her head back and forth while she reviews Steph's information.

"Her blood pressure, heart rate, and oxygen levels look fine, but she's definitely on the small side for height and weight, isn't she? She's barely at the fifth percentile on the growth charts. Has she always been so small?"

"No, not really," I say. "She was seven pounds, six ounces when she was born, but she pretty soon started to have trouble gaining weight. That's the problem," I say, putting my arm around Stephanie's thin shoulders. "My baby can't eat right. I mean, she does eat, but most of it comes back up or goes back out, if you know what I mean. Like she can't keep nothing in her."

"Anything unusual with her birth? Any problems?"

"Nope. Long as hell, almost two days in labor, but she came out perfect," I answer.

"Hmmmm," says Dr. Norton, turning to Stephanie. "What do you like to eat, Stephanie?"

Steph mumbles something. I poke her in the side and say, "Speak up. No one can hear you."

"Do you like spinach?" the doctor asks.

Stephanie looks at her, eyes wide. "Noooooo," she says.

"Oh, okay, how about alligator tails?"

Stephanie giggles. "No, no," she says, slightly louder.

"Well, then . . . let's see, how about bicycle wheels?"

"What?" Stephanie laughs, her mouth wide open, and she practically shouts, "No way."

"Okay, okay, now we're getting somewhere. How about mac and cheese? Do you like mac and cheese?"

"Yum." She rubs her tummy round and round and says, "I do, a lot."

"Great," says Dr. Norton, looking at me. "So, Mom, how does Stephanie do when she eats mac and cheese? Is she able to keep that down?"

"Not always. Sometimes she can and sometimes not so much. I use only organic and non-GMO products. That way whatever I can get into her is the best. But some days nothing stays in. Then I have to feed her through the tube."

"A feeding tube? You have that equipment at home? And you do this procedure?" She looks concerned but also like she doesn't believe me.

"I have a nursing background," I try to assure her, but she doesn't seem to be all that convinced. "It's only been a few times, but when she doesn't have food for three or four days, what the hell else can I do?"

"I understand, Mrs. Cole. That's certainly frightening—not having your child eat—but it might be best for a doctor or a hospital to make the assessment to determine whether a feeding tube is necessary, and then . . ."

"Well, I guess that's why we're here, right? To find out what's going on?"

Dr. Norton looks at me. Then she makes some notes on the tablet and pushes the intercom button. "Sheryl, I have a patient who needs blood work. Stephanie Cole, in room nine. I'd like her also scheduled for a CT scan. The orders are in the computer." She turns back to us and gives Stephanie a hug.

I see my daughter stiffen up, but then she leans a little into the doctor's side.

Steph says, so softly I can barely hear the words, "I don't like that feeding tube."

Dr. Norton lifts one of her perfect eyebrows. She says to Stephanie, "Well, sweetie pie, that's why we have to figure out what's going on with your tummy and why you have trouble eating. Deal?" She puts up her hand for a high five. Stephanie gives it a tiny tap and grins.

"Mrs. Cole, we'll do a basic blood workup and CT, and then let's meet again to discuss the results. My office staff told me you've been trying to get her records transferred here, but we don't have anything yet."

"Damn that doctor," I say. "He promised me he was going to copy the file and send it over right away."

"Maybe you can contact the office again? It's important that I get a comprehensive sense of her medical history."

I help Stephanie jump off the table and say, "Thank you, Dr. Norton. I'll call the doctor as soon as we get home and see what's going on."

"That would be helpful. You'll be hearing from me. Bye, Stephanie," she says and waves.

Stephanie smiles and waves back.

"Oh, one more thing," I say. Dr. Norton stops with her hand on the doorknob.

"What's that?"

"My husband—actually, my ex-husband—has an awful stomach too, and his doctor is testing him for Fabry disease. I heard it's genetic, so maybe you should test Steph for that too?"

STEPHANIE'S BATTLE BLOG
Posted on August 28 by Stephanie's Mommy

Back from our first visit to the new doctor. The news isn't great.

She says Stephanie is a very, very sick little girl. In fact, she said she didn't know how my child made it this far, with all of the problems she has. She was really sweet. She wants to run a trillion tests and was even thinking about keeping Stephanie in the hospital overnight. But Steph looked so scared I begged the doctor to let me take her home.

I'm trying to get Steph to eat a little something, anything, but you all know how sometimes thats just impossible. I'm so afraid I may have to insert the feeding tube tonite.

Rena's Way to Well: Feed Your Kid Right

Doctors and other health professionals will tell you your child needs gluten. DO NOT believe this pack of shit. RIGHT NOW, STOP the pizza and cake and any other products with gluten. Your kid will thank you for it. There are even studies that this can improve or even PRAVENT autism!

Remember: right choices are not always the easiest ones. Be strong. Do whats right!

WhatIwant: Rena, this is so sad! I'm hoping, praying, sending you and your little girl love that this doctor will figure out what's wrong with you're precious one and that she can return to good health with the grace of the Lord.

KnitWit1: Please give my niece a great big hug and kiss from her auntie and keep us posted on your follow-up doctor's visit. Call me when you can and BTW, that guy from the hospital came by again. Did you ever connect with him? Keep in touch!!!

Onepotatotwo: You're a moron. Gluten free for kids is a horrible idea, unless the child has celiac disease. By going gluten free, you're actually robbing your child of the essential nutrients she needs to grow her brain and her body properly. Read up and don't post harmful and absolutely WRONG information. Because some other moron might actually believe what you say.

25

Claire

At first I was sure it was just luck.

I thought maybe since I'd been away from Mystical Haven for a week and then, after what could only be described as an emotional tsunami (Dad's death, my talks with Aunt Frannie and Mom, and my epiphany with Cal), maybe my brain was more clear and perceptive than it had been before.

That might have explained what happened with the first client I took for Mindi the day I returned to work.

Her name was Evelyn, and she was visiting from England and wanted her tarot cards read. She was dressed in a purple tweed suit with matching heels and bag, an unfortunate choice as it was still over ninety degrees outside. I felt overheated just looking at her. Her hair was tortured and swept into a snarled French twist, and the whole picture gave the impression she'd stopped by to see me on her way to high tea.

"I've been to oodles of psychics before, mostly in London, where we live half the year," she said, in her lilting accent.

"Oodles?" I asked.

"Oh yes, love, lots of them. I actually have one on retainer, you know? So I can call as often as I'd like to get her advice on things happening in my life. Very, very helpful. Last week, I was having a dreadful time with a decision I needed to make, so I rang Penelope and asked her what I should do, and lickety-split, she gave me the answer. She's a marvel, that one." Evelyn fiddled with a long string of pearls that hung nearly to her belly button and said, "But I've heard the ones in Sedona are simply beyond compare."

Not able to restrain my curiosity, I asked, "What kind of a decision did Penelope help you with?"

Evelyn's cheeks pinked up, and I almost apologized for my question, but then she scooted forward in her chair and explained, "I asked Penelope whether I should serve roast beef or lamb for Sunday brunch with my Women's Club subcommittee meeting. We were having a rather renowned philosopher speak on the relationship between education and happiness, and I wanted a meal that seemed both educated and happy. I was certain Penelope could read my cards and give me the exact right answer."

She leaned back with a contented sigh and said, "Lamb. Lamb was what the cards said. And, you know, she was right. Everyone there commented on how perfect the meal was."

Reaching behind me, I grabbed one of the many decks I had on the shelf, randomly selecting the Fairy Tarot deck. These cards have pictures of fairy kings, queens, and princesses, set against a backdrop of scenes of bucolic Glastonbury, England. Maybe it would remind her of home. I handed her the deck.

Or not.

"Oh," she exclaimed, shuffling the cards. "I've had these cards read for me many, many times, and I always connect with the fairies. I think it's because I have such positive energy and they recognize that. Also, they know I care about the earth, and so do they."

"That's, uh, great," I say, taking the deck from her. "It's important to feel attuned to the cards."

Because of disinterest and my inherent laziness, I long ago defaulted to a fundamental three-card read. It's very simple. You have the client select three cards. The first represents the past, the second one is for the present, and the third, obviously, is for the future.

"What can I help you with today, Evelyn?" I asked. Her eyes clouded, and the sides of her mouth drooped.

"How's my son? His name is Harry, and I want to know how he is."

Shuffling once more, I flared the cards into a fan and said, "Please pick a card."

She did, and I placed it facedown and said, "This represents the past." She selected the other two, for the present and future, and I was ready to start.

The first card I flipped was the Captive Man.

"See this man here?" I asked. "He's obviously trapped. Does your son have connections with something or someone who has bound him in some way?"

Evelyn's eyes moistened and she whispered, "Drugs."

"I'm sorry. That's terrible."

"It's got so bad that Alfred, that's my husband, and I haven't even seen our boy for almost three years. Three years. Can you imagine? Our own son." She sniffed, and I pushed across a box of tissues to her. She blew her nose with a loud honk.

I nodded. This was one of the other reasons I utilized only three-card spreads. Most clients wanted, needed, to talk about their issues, and the more cards, the more discussion, and pretty soon the hour was up and they'd be angry because we hadn't reviewed all the cards that had been placed on the table.

"Then he went away to university. At first we didn't think anything of it, but eventually, it was too obvious to ignore. The red eyes, the erratic behavior. He looked like a skeleton."

In between sobs, Evelyn apologized. "I'm sorry. I'm dreadfully sorry."

"It's fine," I said. "Let's see what the other cards say, okay?"

She squeezed two wads of tissues into her eye sockets and gave a tentative nod.

The next card, representing the present, showed a fairy with gray wings sitting on a large skull. At the top of the card was the word *Death*. Evelyn gasped.

"That means . . . Does that mean? . . . Is he dead? Is he going to die?" She screamed the last question, causing Mindi to peek behind my curtain. I mouthed to her, *It's fine*, and she shrugged and dropped the fabric.

"No, no," I quickly assured Evelyn. "Many times, what this card actually means is that it's time to walk away. Perhaps your son . . . Harry? Maybe he's ready to give up what's harmful in his life? To take steps and move from what's keeping him trapped."

As usual, I was just riffing. I knew from reading the

manual and from using the cards over and over, the standard meaning for each card. I was just hoping to find some fragment of truth in what I was saying relative to the card's interpretation and Evelyn's question. To maybe see that spark of recognition in the client's face meaning I'd hit or at least gotten close to the target I was fumbling for or, more important, what the client was hoping for.

Nothing. Evelyn was looking down at her palms, which were pressed together at her chest. She was muttering something I couldn't understand but assumed was some kind of a chant or prayer.

"Would you like me to go on?" I asked.

She didn't answer immediately but then looked up and said, "Yes, please do."

The third card, the one signifying what could happen in the future, was the King of Autumn.

I said, "What this card often symbolizes is the end of a very tough time, where you've had to face what seemed like insurmountable obstacles. But your hard work will end in victory, although it may not be in the way you expect."

Evelyn said nothing, and I suspected she was thinking this reading had been no help at all, that what I'd told her was pure bunk. She opened her mouth, I was certain, to say I couldn't be more wrong, and that the psychics in Sedona were highly overrated. But then she started to smile, a wide toothy grin.

She said, "You are brilliant. Straight on the mark."

Seeing my surprise, she explained, "Everything you've said—bull's-eye. Excellent. Truly excellent."

She lifted the first card and said, "Harry is being held prisoner by those awful drugs. I hate it. But it was his choice, and for a long while, my husband and I were pulled into the prison as well. He'd beg us for money, say it was for tuition, and then it would be gone. Obviously, for drugs. He even promised to go to hospital for treatment and asked for money to do that and then, of course, never showed on the day of admittance."

"That sounds very upsetting," I said, happy she was happy, that I'd hit most of the balloons in the shooting gallery. I glanced at the clock on the wall behind her and noted the session was up in three minutes.

"And this card, Death, I know exactly what it means now," she said, holding the card gingerly between her index finger and thumb. "This isn't about Harry's decision at all. It's about ours, Alfred's and mine. We've talked and talked about it, but now I know what we must do."

"What's that?" Two minutes left. I had an urgent need to use the bathroom before my next client.

"We must stop helping him hurt himself. As awful

as it will be . . . and it will be terrible . . . we must no longer give him any support—other than our love—that will allow him to purchase the drugs or engage in the type of life he's been living. We will not help him kill himself. He might remain captive but we must not."

I said, "I'm so glad this was helpful," and started to collect the rest of the cards, but she placed a hand over mine and then picked up the final card in her spread.

She said, "And now I know it will all turn out fine. Do you know why?"

"No, why?"

"Because of this card," she said, pointing to the King of Autumn. "Now I know if Alfred and I can make this very tough decision, we will be rewarded eventually. Harry will come to see the light. He will return to us, whole again, our son once more. A victorious ending."

She was beaming, delighted with the reading and her insight, and filled with the relief of her resolution.

I was about to wish her the best of luck, tell her to have safe travels, and that I hoped all would work out as she anticipated, but something stopped me.

It was like a series of snapshots flashing one after the other through my brain. I could see the ring, a gold band with a tiny red stone in the center. It was under a couch of some sort or perhaps a chair, it was difficult to tell, but whatever the piece of furniture was, it was covered in light blue fabric with birds on it. The ring was on a carpeted floor toward the back, next to a wooden piece I assumed was the leg of the couch or chair.

I shook my head, trying to dislodge the images, but they wouldn't leave. Evelyn stood, reached into her purse, and handed me a hundred-dollar bill.

I opened my mouth to tell her Mindi collected all payments at the front register, but what came out was "I know where the ring is."

"Pardon?"

"A ring? Are you missing a ring? A small gold ring with a red stone in it?"

Collapsing back into the chair, she said, "Yes. It's the ring Alfred bought for me when Harry was born. It's his birthstone, Harry's, a ruby. He was born on July the thirteenth." I noticed the bill was shaking in her hand.

"That ring is under a chair or a couch," I said. "I'm not sure which it is, but something that's covered with fabric that has birds on it."

"My Lord," she gasped. "That must be the love seat in the room we have here. It's upholstered in some kind of blue brocade, and yes, it does have birds on it. Doves, I think. I wondered where that ring had gone to. I had it two days ago when we checked into the lodge, but then I wanted to wear it this morning because, you see, I thought it would help me connect with my son. And it did, didn't it?" Her eyes sparkling, she looked at me and said, "He's coming through you, right at this moment."

I couldn't respond because my brain was still churning. Those visions of the ring and its location, the clarity of what I saw—it was all too bizarre. It had to be some kind of coincidence. But I couldn't deny what I'd felt, that it was important I tell Evelyn what I saw, that I knew what I saw belonged to her, and that I had the responsibility to share this information with her.

26
Rena

"Thanks a lot for watching her today, Mrs. Lupito. I'll be back in a couple of hours."

After living in Phoenix for almost two months, I really had to get out and do something. Come on, how much can you be with a four-year-old in a one-bedroom shithole without losing your mind? I know where the grocery store is now, but it has almost nothing as far as organic, non-GMO, gluten-free, or whole-grain stuff. I complained to the manager, and he gave me this look like I asked him for kangaroo tits or monkey balls. He said there was another store in Tempe that maybe had what I was looking for. I'm absolutely convinced the only food people eat out here is tortillas. They fill them with chicken or beans or cheese or pork, but it's still all tortillas, all the damn time. I checked the maps feature on my phone and found out the store the guy recommended was at least ten miles away, so I would have to take a cab. Maybe Mrs. Lupito would let me use her car, but I seriously doubt that. Last week she gave me a dirty look when I asked her for a plunger. Stephanie had clogged the toilet up even after I told her a thousand times to use no more than five sheets of toilet paper.

Besides, I need the money. Gary's punier-than-shit alimony and child-support checks get deposited in a bank that, luckily, has a branch not too far away from me. I never use checks or credit cards. As soon as his checks clear, I take cash out and pay everything that way—rent, groceries, whatever. But what he sends me barely covers what we need.

During our first weeks here, besides going to the Mommy Loves Baby classes, Stephanie and me went to a couple of local playgrounds. I was thinking maybe I could meet some other moms there. Except for a few smelly homeless people, the playgrounds were totally empty. And I think I know why. Stephanie actually got a burn on her ass, a real burn, from going down one of the slides. Forget about even touching the chains on the swings. I guess those are things kids around here only do, like, maybe November through March.

Mostly, we stay inside, but no matter how many

times I spray Lysol or wipe the walls with Clorox and water, it still smells like mold and dirty feet.

So I finally made the decision to get a job, something easy and part-time. Mrs. Lupito said she'd watch Stephanie while I looked.

Luckily, the second place I went to hired me. Bert's Pharmacy is a drugstore, and it's only two blocks from my place. There was a HELP WANTED sign in the window, but you could hardly see it since it was behind a bunch of stuff on a shelf there. Next to a pile of Beanie Babies (who even collects those anymore?), there was this dusty do-it-yourself blood pressure machine, a set of crutches, and for the back-to-school crowd, a plastic bucket holding markers, pens, and pencils leaning against a pile of spiral notebooks.

The inside of the place was just as bad. Half of the fluorescent ceiling lights were out, so it was pretty gloomy, and the aisles were really close together. Unless you kept your arms right by your sides, you would definitely knock things off the shelves. And good luck finding what you needed. The aspirin was next to the dog shampoo, and the Band-Aids were in aisle five in back of a display of picnic supplies. Maybe because people get scratched or bitten when they eat outside? Fuck if I know.

The job was for an assistant in the pharmacy. This

involved putting prescriptions in bags, stuffing those bags into deep drawers labeled with letters of the alphabet, getting those bags for customers, and then taking the money. Basically, idiot work. But I still had to spend almost thirty minutes convincing Joe Wolbit, the day supervisor, that I could probably manage to alphabetize paper bags and ring up sales on a register that did all the math for you. He put me on the ten-to-two shift, three days a week. And the best news was he agreed to pay me in cash.

Now I just had to figure out what the hell to do with Stephanie.

I thought about asking one of the women from the Mommy Loves Baby class, but they would probably expect me to trade off and sit for one of their kids. I wasn't up for that.

My only other option was right next door.

After agreeing with my new boss on a start date, I walk home and knock on Mrs. Lupito's door.

I can hear the TV blasting in the background. Some kind of annoying kids' program, maybe *SpongeBob*?

Mrs. Lupito yells, "Stephanie, must be your mama."

When Mrs. Lupito lets me in, Stephanie doesn't even look at me. Just stares at that damn cartoon.

"Hope she didn't give you any trouble," I say. I take the remote from the coffee table and turn off the noise.

"No, no. She was very good. Such a quiet little thing. No problem at all. So well behaved."

"Great. That's really great because I wanted to ask . . . Well, I did find a job . . . at Bert's, on the corner? I wondered whether you would maybe watch her on a regular basis, if that's at all possible? It would be ten to two, on Mondays, Wednesdays, and Saturdays. I could pay you, not much, maybe like forty dollars a week."

I can't tell if she's pissed off at being asked or upset at the amount I offered her. After staring at me for a while, she looks at Stephanie and asks, "Want to spend a little more time with me, *niña*?"

Stephanie jumps up and puts her arms around Mrs. Lupito's waist. They only make it halfway there. She shouts, "Yes, yes, yes."

I tell Mrs. Lupito I'll bring all the food for Stephanie's lunches and snacks since she has her special diet. We start on Monday.

"Don't be late picking her up, okay? I got my own stuff to do too, you know," Mrs. Lupito says to my back as we leave.

27
Claire

I hear Evelyn chirping at the register as she's paying for her reading, extolling my virtues and telling everyone about how "gobsmackingly accurate" my reading was, how it helped her make a decision she'd been struggling with for months, and how, "quite fantastically," I'd told her where to find her ring, a piece of jewelry "as dear to my heart as my own precious son."

To escape the adulation I'm still certain I don't deserve, I make a mug of tea and honey and go out the back door. Even standing under the sweltering midday sun, I can't stop shaking.

"There you are. Your next client is . . ."

I jump as if Mindi had attacked me with a hatchet and spill most of the tea on my sandals. The warm liquid seeps between my toes, and I can feel them getting sticky from the honey.

"Geez, Claire, I'm sorry," she says. "I didn't mean to scare you."

"It's fine," I say, bending down to take off the sandals.

"Hey, you do not look well. What's going on? Maybe you came back too soon? Of course, I didn't help by giving you such a big workload on your first day. Go home. I can handle it, really."

"No, it's fine. I'm fine. Probably just a little jet lag," I say, escaping her scrutiny by going back inside and into the bathroom. I tear off some paper towels and wet them to wash my feet. The leather sandals, spotted with tea stains, are likely a lost cause. Examining my face in the mirror, I have to agree with Mindi's assessment. I do look terrible. My cheeks are blotchy, and my eyes are red-rimmed. I rinse out my mouth with tepid sink water and splash some on my face.

Eventually, my heartbeat settles, and I tell myself it was obviously a fluke with Evelyn. I'm no more psychic today than I was yesterday or last week. I just got incredibly lucky that the cards happened to so closely match the situation with her drug-addicted son. I was in the middle of trying to also rationalize the visions I had of the ruby ring and had almost decided I must have seen such a ring recently, maybe in the airport gift shop, and that's why it popped into my mind when Mindi taps on the bathroom door. "Are you sure you're able to work?"

"Yes, I'm sure."

I leave the bathroom and she checks me out, apparently judges me fit for duty, and says, "Your next client's out front. She's very excited to meet with you, especially after the glowing recommendations from your previous client. As long as you're sure you can do this. You still look wobbly." Mindi reaches over and rubs my arm with her hand, which feels oven warm against my goose-bumped skin.

"No, really, I'm fine."

What I don't say to Mindi is that this has never happened to me before. Except for today with Evelyn, I've never had visions of any kind during a reading. Of course, I can't tell Mindi this because she has no idea that I've been bluffing my way through readings, tarot and otherwise, for the entire time I've been working for her. I feel like I somehow crashed into the topsy-turvy world of Wonderland without recalling having actually passed through the looking glass.

28
Rena

Sorry, but I haven't had a single second to write. Besides the new job, I'm not sleeping because I'm up with Stephanie all night.

Saw the doctor yesterday for Steph's test results. After we met with her in August, she had Stephanie and me get some more blood work done and even see a nurolagist.

But, get this! Dr. tells me NOTHING is wrong with her, except she's really underweight and small for her age. No shit. Tell me something I dont know. All those tests, the money to get here, the rent on the shithole we're living in, the time it took to even get in to see this doctor. And now she tells me Stephanie is fine?!?!

Then why is she, at this very minute, holding her stomach and screeming in pain?

I'm really, really not sure what to do. I called the doctors office this morning to beg her to PLEASE do more tests. Like a PET scan, but nobodies called me back.

SEND PRAYERS PLEASE!!!

Rena's Way to Well: Feed Your Kid Right

Do you know that you can diagnoze your child's health problems just by looking at her tongue?

Yup, that's right. Here are a couple of things to check for:

Bright Red=lack of Vitamin B12 or some other vitamin deficiency. To help, up the fruits and vegies and ONLY buy organic

White and looks like cottage cheese=yeast infection and thrush and too many of those idiot-perscribed antibiotics. Your kid's body does a great job healing itself without all those chemicals. They only kill the good bacteria along with the bad.

Kittieseverywhere: Oh, I'm so disappointed for you and for me. I thought/hoped this doctor could cure your baby and then I would make an appointment for my Nathan and go there too. So sad.

Naturalee: Hi, I was very glad to read your post about tongue diagnosing. I am a naturopath located in California and use this method all the time. A couple of natural remedies people can try are: cinnamon (creates an anticandidal environment), unsweetened cranberry juice (acidic environment), fermented vegetables like pickles, sauerkraut and Kimchi (strengthens the immune system), and coconut oil (swish 1–2 tablespoons in your mouth but don't swallow! because it contains bacteria and toxins). If anyone wants to contact me to get help with candida, write me at drleebhealthy@_____.

KnitWit1: Rena, I've been trying to reach you, but the number I have for you isn't in service? Please, please call me. I'm so concerned about Stephanie and you. Will you be coming home now? Love, Janet (P.S. Maxie's doing great. A couple of spats with his "cousins"—some biting and scratching—but everyone is getting along fine now!)

I close down the computer and pack up the rest of Stephanie's lunch (steamed broccoli and brown rice with organic cheese slices).

"Get a move on, will you?" I yell. She comes out of her room. She's holding one sneaker, and her hair is shooting up in five different directions. Yogurt from breakfast is still on her chin.

But I don't have time to deal with this shit right now. We go next door and knock. Mrs. Lupito opens up and gives me a look that's even nastier than usual. She reaches for the lunch sack and takes Stephanie inside.

The door slams in my face. No time to deal with that bitch either. I need to hustle or I'll be late to work—again.

29
Claire

Somehow I finish out the day with my three remaining appointments and, apart from one minor misinterpretation, these readings are also astonishingly on target.

Sharon L.: Tarot cards. She was crushed to hear her husband is sleeping with yet another one of his secretaries but not all that surprised because (as she told me after we finished) five days ago she did find purple lace panties wedged between two couch pillows.

Lyle O.: Psychometry reading. After he handed me his father's watch, I was able to tell him his dad "on the other side" did not want him to buy the house because it had undisclosed plumbing problems. Later, Lyle called the store and told Mindi that when he got home, the realtor was at his front door with news that the house he'd put a bid on had flunked inspection. Seemed there was a significant problem with pitting corrosion in the copper pipes.

Marilyn T.: Tarot cards. No specific question, just wanted a general reading. I told her, "These first two cards indicate you've suffered a loss and some emotional pain."

Marilyn didn't say anything. She sat in the chair, her face closed and her expression stony. I could tell she was one of those clients who liked to test psychics by giving nothing away.

As I was about to flip her last card, I had one of those freaky visions like I had with Evelyn, except this one was of a screen door open and blowing in the wind and something small, furry, and tan with white spots escaping through it, a blur running from the house and into the night. It looked like a puppy. I could hear someone crying from inside the house, a girl, probably young.

I glanced up from the cards and asked Marilyn, "Did you lose something? Like a pet? Maybe a dog?"

She glared at me but said nothing, so I continued, "This third card says you've been extremely angry. You and other people in your family are very sad and you need to open your heart to embrace forgiveness. Does that make any sense?"

Her face softens a smidge, as if someone airbrushed the edges of her hardened cheekbones.

She says, "I was so pissed. He's always doing stuff like this. My son, he's very irresponsible. I've told him and my daughter a million times, 'Close the door, close the damn door or Tanya will get out,' but do they listen? Then, surprise, guess what happens. He goes out to the garage to get a wrench to fix the leak in the kitchen sink, doesn't make sure the door is shut behind him, the wind blows the screen door wide open, Tanya gets out and is gone, who knows where. And now Butch and Laurie, they're all upset. Me too—Tanya was such a cutie."

"Tanya was your dog?"

"My dog? No, we don't have a dog. Tanya was a guinea pig. We'd let her run around free in the evening, which, except for guinea pig poop on the floor, was fine, if everyone could've remembered one simple rule. Keep the damn back door closed. I can't tell you how—"

I interrupted, "Marilyn, I'm curious, how big was Tanya?"

"How big? What do you mean?" She looked at me as if I'd asked her whether she had funds hidden in Swiss banks.

"I mean, about how much did Tanya weigh?"

"I don't know. The kids overfed her, that's for sure. Maybe three pounds, give or take. Pretty big for a guinea pig."

So it was a guinea pig and not a dog, but I still count the reading as accurate. After all, a puppy weighing about three pounds could look remarkably like a runaway guinea pig.

30
Rena

I walk through the door and pull my T-shirt down tight to show off the tops of my boobs.

"Hi, Joe." I wave as I walk past him.

He's so interested in my tits he doesn't even bother to look at the clock to see if I'm late. Works every time.

"New inventory's in. Can you unpack and price it? Then you can help Shirley in the pharmacy with some of last night's orders, okay?" he asks.

"Sure. Let me grab some coffee first."

It's an easy job and really boring, but I don't care. It gets me away from the house, and I can put Stephanie out of my mind for a little while. Most of the customers are nice enough, but I think the heat gets to their brains. They all seem kind of stupid.

I'm pricing boxes of foot cream when someone taps me on the shoulder.

"Joe told me to ask you about what kind of vitamins I should buy," he says.

Oh. My. God. He's fucking adorable. Dark brown wavy hair, a little long, but that's what I like. And almost-black eyes with these really thick lashes. He's probably an inch shorter than me, but so what? Those dimples make up for it.

"Hi," I say and motion for him to follow me to the vitamin aisle. I make sure to wiggle my butt a little as I walk.

I finally convinced Joe to get in some organic vitamins. With the other shit, you might as well be eating orange paper if you think you're getting any kind of vitamin C.

"My doctor wants me to take vitamin D. Man, there sure are a lot of choices," he says, looking at the shelf. Then he stares at my chest before finally getting to my eyes. I tuck my T-shirt back into my jeans so it pulls across my boobs to give him the full experience.

"Yeah, definitely." I see him noticing me checking out his thighs. The guy's buff, that's for damn sure.

"Why is the doctor concerned about your vitamin D?"

He moves closer to the shelf to look at the bottles. "I guess because I don't get out much. I work all day in a room with no windows."

"Where the hell do you work? A morgue?"

He laughs and says, "Sort of."

"Well, vitamin D is the sunshine vitamin. If you don't get enough of it, that's bad for your bones."

He nods.

"Also your testosterone levels, your sperm, and your ability to get and keep an erection."

He turns to me so fast he knocks a jumbo pack of tampons off a display. He bends down to pick them up, and when he notices what he's got, he turns even redder.

I start to laugh, and he does too.

He holds out the tampons to me and says, "I'm Louis."

"Rena." I tell him about the different types of vitamin D we carry. I can tell he's barely listening to anything I'm saying.

He decides on the organic ones from Blueberry Hill, a new vendor I told Joe to use.

"Vitamin D is one of the fat-soluble vitamins. You need to take this with your largest meal of the day, and that meal should contain fat."

"So, like, with a big steak dinner?" he asks, grinning.

"Yeah, that would be perfect." I move so close to him I can smell his aftershave. I do love a guy who wears aftershave. "It would probably be even better if you had someone to enjoy that dinner with."

Leaning in toward me to whisper in my ear, he says, "Well, I'm separated, and my wife is barely talking to me."

"Oh, that's too bad. Really too bad." I run my hand up his arm.

"Yeah, it would be a shame to waste a good steak dinner."

Joe walks around the corner, and I step away from Louis.

"Rena, can you help on the register?" Joe asks. Louis follows me.

By the time I ring up his vitamins, Louis and me have exchanged numbers and made plans for tomorrow night. We're gonna meet here in front of the drugstore at seven.

After my shift, as I walk back to Mrs. Lupito's, I check my phone. There's a voice mail from Dr. Norton.

"Mrs. Cole, this is Dr. Norton. I received your messages and your request for additional testing for your daughter. As we discussed during our meeting this week, I saw nothing of concern in either Stephanie's blood work or her CT. Except, as noted, she is significantly underweight and well below the height norm for her age group. This morning I got back her blood work for Fabry disease, and this was also negative, but just to be extra cautious, I've requested a genetic analysis as well. Sometimes we do get false negatives in females with this disease, so I think it's worth this extra step. It will, however, take another two to maybe three weeks to get the results. Perhaps, in the meantime, working with a nutritionist would be a good idea, and I'm happy to recommend one for you. However, my staff tells me you've called to request we now schedule a PET scan. I do not believe this is necessary. It's sometimes a difficult test for adults and even more so for children. As you probably know, it requires an IV needle for the contrast, an exposure to radiation, and many people, especially young children, find being in the tube traumatic. For these reasons, I'm advising against going forth with the PET scan you've requested. Please call me should you have any questions. And one last thing. We still haven't received Stephanie's medical records. Did you ever follow up on this? If not, please do so as soon as possible. It's important I have the full picture of her medical history so I can best treat her in the future. Thank you."

After listening to her go on and on in her oh-so-clinical voice, I want to scream. I throw the water bottle I'm holding at the mailbox on the corner. The blue box rattles. I wonder if it's a federal crime to hit a mailbox with a water bottle and then decide I don't give a flying fuck.

Who the hell does she think she is? Who made her the fucking queen of what tests my baby should or shouldn't have? Can't she see how sick Stephanie is? Don't I know what's right for my child? Jesus, I'm her mother.

I hit the numbers on the phone so hard to return the call I almost slap it out of my hand.

"This is Rena Cole. Is Dr. Norton there? Fine, yeah, I will definitely leave a message. You tell Dr. Norton she better have Stephanie scheduled for that PET scan immediately or believe me, I will be contacting the AMA." The dipshit of a nurse or receptionist or whoever answered starts to say something, but I disconnect.

I walk up the steps to Mrs. Lupito's. Before I can even knock on the door, she's there, holding out the bag that had Stephanie's food in it. I can feel it's still full, so I look inside. The containers weren't even opened. What the fuck.

"She don't like that stuff. She wanted a bologna sandwich and some chips. I also give her some carrot sticks and she's fine. No stomach problems at all," Mrs. Lupito says. You can tell she's all proud of herself.

Stephanie is behind her and peeks around at me.

"Let's go," I say to her.

Turning to Mrs. Lupito, I shout, "You were supposed to give her this special food. You had no right to not follow my orders. Are you going to be there at three in the morning when she's throwing up and shitting on the bed? Are you going to be the one to try to get her to take just a sip of water because the food you decided to give her made her so sick that nothing stays down or in? Tell me that, Mrs. Lupito. You've got some goddamn nerve." I grab Stephanie's arm and practically fly her over the steps.

Mrs. Lupito screams, "There's nothing at all wrong with that child. *Estas loco. Loco!* You, you're the one who's sick. Sick in the head. She's scared of you. You know that, right? You scare her."

She's still yelling when I yank Stephanie into our apartment. I slam the door and push her down onto the couch.

"Why'd you eat that crap she gave you? Don't you know by now it will make you even sicker?" I yell.

She squeezes herself into the corner of the couch and says, "But, Mommy, I feel fine. I do. I don't think—"

"That's the problem, you don't think. Ever. I'm

your mama. I'm the one who has to make these decisions. Not you. Not that fucking Mexican bitch next door. And not the fucking doctor either. It's me. I'm the one up with you all night when you're sick, taking you to all those doctors, making sure you get the tests you need. You think I do that for me? No, I do that for you. For you, Stephanie."

"Yes, Mommy," she whispers, biting her thumbnail.

"So don't blame me when you're sick tonight. No waking me up, crying that your tummy hurts or you shit your pants. Maybe go next door and see if your fat Mexican *mamacita* will help you."

First the doctor and now my bitch landlady. Definitely destroyed the buzz I had from meeting Louis.

And bologna? Christ, she might as well have fed her cyanide.

The main thing I need to do now is to try and get that poison out of my daughter.

I lie down on my stomach and reach for the supplies under the bed.

31
Claire

By the time I pull into our driveway, I'm so exhausted that extracting the key from the ignition feels like a major accomplishment and walking up the slight hill to our front door might as well be ascending Kilimanjaro.

Cal is sitting cross-legged on the couch, immersed in his books, notepaper strewn all over the coffee table, a laptop open to the right of him, and a bowl of pretzels to the left. A beer is sweating on the glass-topped end table, and the television is on mute, but I can see Humphrey Bogart mouthing to Ingrid Bergman, *Here's looking at you, kid.* It's a film Cal doesn't need to watch because he's seen it a million times and knows every line and nuance, so I guess it's more of a comfort to him to have it on in the background.

He looks at me and asks, "What's wrong?"

I push aside the pretzels to curl up next to him, snuggling close.

"You are not going to believe this day."

"Tell me."

"Apparently, I am a psychic."

Cal laughs and says, "I thought we'd already established a long time ago that you aren't."

"True. But now, I seem to be one, for real. I mean, I actually do have those skills—tarot, psychometry, mediumship, everything I learned when I was a kid and could do some of at that time but couldn't for a very long time and . . . it appears that now, I can."

"What? Wait . . . What are you telling me? That you actually can tell people their futures?"

I take a piece of pretzel and start breaking it into smaller and smaller bits, creating a pile of crumbs in my lap.

"Yes, that's exactly what I'm saying. Their futures, their pasts, their dead dads' warnings about plumbing." I brush the crumbs into a napkin, squeeze it into a wad, and toss it on the coffee table. "Also, I found a lost ring."

"C'mon. You're saying you saw all these things, like the whole sight-beyond-sight deal?" he asks, the question coming out in a slow and measured pace.

"Cal, stop that. You're acting as if I'm crazy."

"Well, you have to admit this is a little bit nuts. After all these years, suddenly, you have the gift?" He air-quotes *gift*.

"Listen, I'm as shocked as you are."

"This calls for a drink." Cal walks into the kitchen and comes back with two glasses of red, plops down on the couch, and says, "Okay, tell me everything."

And I do.

After I'm finished, he sits quietly for a while, sipping his wine and thumping his fingers against his thigh, a habit he employs when he's trying to work out something.

Finally, he stops thumping and turns to me. "Why do you think this is happening? Or, what I mean is why do you think this is happening now? Why, all of a sudden, do you think you're able to do these things?"

Walking to the kitchen to squeeze my empty glass in among the pile of dirty dishes in the sink, I realize I'm famished. Apparently, communing with the universe makes you ravenous. I grab two cookies from an open package in the cabinet.

"I have no idea." I get two more cookies and bring them back to Cal. "I thought at first it was an accident, you know, like before—when, on occasion, I would stumble onto the right thing. Like that time I guessed my client was a skydiver, and he was amazed because he'd just had a lesson. And that was because the door to the store was open and I'd heard one of the tourist sightseeing planes and that was the first thing that popped into my head—a guy jumping out of a plane."

I expect him to laugh, but he doesn't. Instead, he takes the cookies from me, disappears into the bedroom, and comes back with my running shoes.

"No way, I'm too tired to even move off this couch, much less—"

"Come on, we'll take it slow. I have a theory about what's happening."

"Fine, but can't you tell me this theory while we're relaxing in front of some mindless sitcom? That's about all I have the physical and mental strength for at this moment."

"Nope," he says, placing my shoes near my feet, hoping proximity will lead to the actual act of me slipping them on. "I need to think through it a little more, and running helps me do that."

It's more of a fast walk than a full-out run on Airport Loop Trail. Fortunately, it's nearly empty since it's a weekday night—most of the tourists won't be here until the weekend and the nontourists are either commuting home from work or getting dinner ready. We're able to travel leisurely up the slight elevation without worrying about obstructing hikers or runners who want to go faster, either up or down, than we do.

When we reach the summit, there are a few more people. One guy is sitting cross-legged and bare-chested in a yoga pose, eyes closed and arms outstretched to the west. The other three are tourists, maybe from Russia, based on what I can tell from their Slavic-sounding accents. They have their cameras on tripods poised to catch the sunset, which is still a half hour or so off. In the meantime, they take selfies: solo shots, then a pair of people, then all three of them, then a different pair. I try to do the math to see how many different combinations they could mesh but soon give up the mental gymnastics. My mind feels too bruised and numb to figure that out after everything it's gone through today.

There's a ledge slightly below the flat of the mesa where Cal and I always perch to watch the sunset. From there you can see the town of Sedona stretched out between the surrounding mountains. As the trail is set around and near the Sedona airport, it's also a great spot to watch the airplanes take off and land.

Lights begin to flicker on in the houses below, twinkling through the valley. I imagine a mother coming in with groceries and flipping the switch in her kitchen, or a dad playing with a German shepherd after turning on the table lamp in the den.

I sit between Cal's knees, lean back, and he wraps his arms around me.

"Tell me your theory, oh wise one," I say.

He points to a plane that's climbing, its silver nose piercing a sky that's gradually transitioned from a dusty blue to muted pinks and now is in a full bloom of fiery orange as if the sun is waging its last battle before giving up the day.

"Okay, here's what I'm thinking. Your father just died; you had an emotional breakthrough with your mom; you came home to me, thinking we're over, and we had this incredible open-hearted conversation—"

"And?"

"Stay with me here, Oz. When someone is . . . uh . . . closed off, not really able to let their emotions out—"

"Me?" I squirm in his arms and turn to face him. This is a bit dangerous because if I move the wrong way, I'll fall off the ledge and pull him with me.

Cal kisses me and says, "I'm not criticizing, but for the sake of my assessment of your current situation, can we agree that prior to this, you were pretty protective of your feelings?"

I turn back and watch as the sun glides under the horizon.

"Fine," I say, knowing that, of course, he's right.

"Good. So we can agree you've had a lot of emotional upheaval recently, and possibly, one of the outcomes might be that you've become more in touch with what's going on inside you emotionally . . ."

"Okay, probably true. Do go on."

"Sometimes what happens when a person decides to or has to open up, to become really aware of what they're feeling and face those emotions and, even more important, start to truly experience those emotions, even and especially the ones that are most painful— this can lead to unexpected outcomes."

"'Unexpected outcomes'?"

He stands and takes my hand to help me up. We crawl carefully back to the mesa top. Everyone else has left except for the guy doing yoga. He's wisely put on his shirt since once the sun set, the temperature must have dropped ten degrees. He bows to us, says "Namaste," rolls his mat, and starts the trek down. We wave goodbye.

"Tell me about these unexpected outcomes," I say.

Cal takes off his sweatshirt, wraps it around me, and begins to lead us down the trail. There's a little ambient light from the airport but not enough to help us easily navigate. It's a much slower trip down.

"What I think happened today was you were much more tuned into the emotional needs of others because you've become more open to your own emotions and were finally receptive enough to really hear your clients."

I grab the back of his T-shirt and pull him to a stop.

"What the hell are you saying?"

I can barely see his face in the dark.

"What I mean is that sometimes when people shut off parts of themselves because those parts are too painful, then it's hard for them to open up other parts of themselves. Emotions are difficult to compartmentalize. What I'm saying, I guess, is that once those gates are open, it's almost impossible to close them again."

We reach the trailhead and walk toward the car. What he's saying is very close to what Aunt Frannie said to me on the beach. My mind is churning, and I use whatever remaining brain cells I have to respond.

"You're saying because I'm more open emotionally now, essentially, I'm open to everything? That today wasn't an exhibition of my psychic talents? That all I did today was be an extra-good listener and that made my responses more on target than usual?"

"Yup, that's pretty much it."

I know in some respects he's not wrong. I have been more emotional lately. The other night, while we were watching a dog food commercial, I cried when the kid hugged his puppy. But Cal's explanation doesn't completely square with my experiences today. What about those things I could see and tell from the cards or from, I guess, the universe that were so specific, things I couldn't have gotten from a client by only close listening and guessing?

"Bullshit. I'm not buying it. Did you learn all this from just registering for your one psych class?" I ask, sliding into the front seat.

"Hey, no reason to get belligerent with me," he says as he turns the ignition. "And it was actually in an article in a women's magazine I was reading while I was waiting for the guy to cut my hair a couple of days ago."

Although I try not to, I laugh and say, "Very fine research, Professor."

"I thought so."

Serious again, I say, "Cal, it wasn't like that. I did see and hear and feel things I couldn't have known otherwise."

"Other than from the great beyond, you mean?" he asks, and cocks an eyebrow.

"Listen, you obviously think I'm still a fraud, so we're done talking," I say, jumping out of the car before he barely comes to a stop in our driveway. I slam the passenger door.

He runs after me, takes my arm, and turns me around to face him.

"Ozzie, can't you even consider that maybe you

weren't so much psychic today as you just had an over-abundance of stray emotions you projected onto others and . . . well, maybe you returned to work before you should have?"

He tries to hug me, but I yank my arm away.

"I'm telling you the visions, or whatever I had this afternoon, were one hundred percent the real deal. And I need to figure out how to handle this, with or without your help."

I'm angry with Cal, but I don't have time or energy to keep trying to convince him that what happened ac-tually did happen. The bigger immediate problem is what to do about it. All those images coming at me—it was overwhelming and frightening.

I go inside, and he follows me, many paces behind. As I bend down to untie my shoes, I know exactly what I need to do.

My mom answers on the third ring. In the back-ground, I can hear the scrape of a pestle on mortar, a sound that transports me immediately back to when I used to help in the shop grinding herbs for teas and medicines.

"Claire, I'm so glad you called. How are you, honey?"

"Good. Good. Everything's fine. Hey, remember you mentioned you were going to visit? When would be a good time for you to do that, do you think?" I can't imagine having the conversation I need to have with her over the phone. Definitely has to be face-to-face.

"What's wrong? You sound funny. Has anything happened?"

Obviously, I didn't do such a great job trying to sound like I was only asking a casual question about her potential travel plans. Cal was right about one thing. These stupid emotions keep creeping through when I least want them.

I cough and try to recover.

"Nope, everything's great. We talked about you seeing this part of the country and I just thought we should get going on that."

"Claire, I would love to. I know it's only been a day or so but I miss you already."

"So you'll come?"

"I think I can get Lisa—you know, that naturalist I met at the conference last year—to cover the shop while I'm gone. She can also water the gardens and watch over the house, Sammie, and everything."

"Great. Let me know your flight information."

32

Rena

It's not as hard as people think, putting in an NG feeding tube. Nursing students are taught how to do this really early on in their classes.

The nasogastric tube is a long, narrow tube that's soft and bendable. It goes through the nose and into the stomach. All you need is a feeding tube, a bag to attach to the tube, and an IV pole. Of course, I don't have an IV pole, but I can usually rig something up so the bag hangs high enough.

You get your patient to sit up with a pillow behind the head and shoulders. Coil the end of the tube around your index finger so it has a flexible curve—makes it go in a whole lot easier. Coat the end with lubricant, but don't use petroleum jelly. I forget why, but I remember some instructor telling us over and over not to use that. Instead, I have some kind of water-soluble shit that works just fine.

With the curve pointing down, insert the tube along the floor of the nostril until you can feel some resistance. That's how you know you're in the stomach.

Most patients will gag or choke a little, but you can usually fix that by changing the position of their head or neck. I can honestly say I've done a bunch of these and never had to call a supervisor or doctor to help me because I couldn't get it in right. I was successful 100 percent of the time.

Of course, Stephanie hardly ever gags or even coughs anymore, but she squirms a lot. It's not real comfortable getting this procedure.

She's curled up way in the back of the hall closet, behind the vacuum cleaner and a mop. I can hardly see her in the dark, but I can hear her sniffling.

"Stephanie, come out here. I don't know what the hell else that woman gave you but I need to take care of this. Get your butt out here now."

"No, no, Mama," she whines and scoots away from the tips of my fingers.

"Dammit, Stephanie, I don't have time for this bullshit."

"Mommy, I'm fine. Graciella gave me food at her house."

"Oh, so now you're on a first-name basis with her? You know what she gave you, Stephanie? She gave you poison. That's what it is. Like the powder we put in the basement to kill the mice that time. When we checked to see if it worked, do you remember what they looked like? Yeah, dead, with their feet in the air and all shriveled up, with that white foam coming out of their mouths. Pretty horrible, right? Well, that's exactly what bologna is, Stephanie. Poison. Come out right now!"

I'm afraid Mrs. Bitch Next Door will hear the screaming, so I tell Stephanie she can watch cartoons. This is something I hardly ever let her do, since I can't stand the noise and she sees so much of that crap with her new bestie. But the bribe works. She stops crying and starts to slowly come out of the closet. When she's close enough to me, I grab her hand and then carry her to the couch. Her arms and legs are kicking all over the place, but I am finally able to insert the tube.

STEPHANIE'S BATTLE BLOG
Posted on October 10 by Stephanie's Mommy

As you can see, my little pumpkin is hooked up to her feeding tube—again. (see pictures). I really thought this part of our battle was over at last. I was hoping and praying the doctor out here would know what to do. No such luck. She said it could still be Fabry disease and she's waiting for the genetic test to come back. I know it's bad to think this way but I'll be so pissed off at Gary if he gave something to Steph.

And now this doctor even refuses to do more tests. I left her a message and said either give Stephanie a PET scan or I will go to the AMA. And then the crazy neighbor who's been watching Steph gave her bolony today. BOLONY! No wonder Steph's stomach is such a mess now. She threw up everywhere when we got home. I had to put in the feeding tube. I didn't have a choice. Baby's got to get some nutrients in her some way.

One good thing did happen today, I met a really hot guy at work.

KnitWit: Oh, Rena, how horrible for you and Steph. What can I do? Do you want me to come out there and help? Please let me know and I'll be on the next plane. I hate to make things even worse, but both Gary and that guy from St. Theresa's Hospital came to see me this week, asking where they could find you. All I could say was Arizona—it was the honest response. PM me your address. Please.

Also, I tried calling you, but there was still no answer and no voice mail set up. Are you having phone problems again? Gary said he tried too but same deal. You need to contact him (and me!) right away and let us know how you and Steph are doing. PLEASE!!!

33
Claire

The following Tuesday morning, Cal and I make the drive to Phoenix to pick Mom up at the airport. I'm still upset with him for not believing me about my rediscovered psychic skills, but I make the decision to put my anger aside, at least for the week she's visiting.

It's mid-October, officially fall, and even after living in Arizona and in California for so many years, I'm still surprised and irritated that the temperatures are in the high eighties. I guess I'm an East Coast girl to my core, because I miss that first snap of cold in the air and the crunching of red leaves under my feet. At least Sedona is about ten degrees cooler than Phoenix, so it might not be such a big shock for her.

Cal leaves me at the curb and parks the car in the temporary lot while I go to baggage claim. I spot her immediately: a tall, slim woman with hair the color of orange sherbet. She's graceful even as she reaches over to sling a bulging suitcase from the spinning carousel, and when she turns, though I'm yards away, her green eyes that are identical to mine pierce through the distance as she spots me. She rushes over and squashes me in a giant hug.

"Hi, sweetie. You look so beautiful. Where's Cal?" Mom asks.

"He's parking the car. I'm really glad you're here." I turn away but not before she catches my eyes brimming with tears.

"Honey? Are you crying? What's wrong?"

"Nothing. I'm just happy to see you." I'm not about to start pouring out my secrets in the middle of baggage claim.

Even though the store was still busy, Mindi very generously gave me the week off to spend time with Mom. I think she figured the additional time away would be good for me.

But I was anticipating big-time retribution the week I returned in the form of an extra-heavy client load. Part of the reason for this is that in the week before my mother arrived, I became a very hot commodity. I knew there were clients booked for my week out who would reschedule for the following week because they only wanted to be seen by me. The phone in the store had been ringing constantly with people begging to get squeezed in whenever my schedule would allow. Mindi finally ended up taking on Helene, a local psychic who would fill in during my time away and see clients who weren't determined to sit only with me.

News of my astoundingly accurate readings had seemed to travel throughout Sedona within an hour, which only confirmed for me how desperate people are to believe in psychics.

Not only did my on-target readings continue with clients who came to me in the store, but I also started to be bombarded with information when I was out. During one trip to the grocery store, when I was trying to find an avocado that wasn't hard enough to be considered a lethal weapon, I felt a strange buzzing pressure behind my eyes. For a moment, there was a haze across my vision, almost like a thick fog in front of my face. I actually raised my hand to sweep it away, but there was nothing physically there. When it passed and I could see again, I noticed a woman one bin over picking through a pile of sweet potatoes. It was almost as if a magnet were pulling me toward her. I tried to ignore the sensation and quickly tossed two rock-hard avocados in my basket and turned the cart away from her and toward the dairy section for some cheddar cheese. Which would have been a good plan had a child at that moment not jumped in front of my cart, causing me to squeal to a stop. The sweet potato woman steered her cart parallel to mine.

"John Robert, why are you running through the store? Haven't we talked about this a million times?" She takes the boy's hand and secures it to the top of her cart, wrapping his fingers around the handle.

"I'm so sorry. Why is it they have so much energy at the exact same time of the day we have none?" she asked, chuckling.

"You need to have his appendix checked." I looked around after the sentence blurted out of my mouth, as if there were a ventriloquist nearby who actually said the words while I'd only mouthed them.

"What? What did you say?" the woman stuttered.

"I'm sorry, never mind. I guess I was just thinking out loud about other things. You know, like you said, tired and all that." I started to move my cart away, but she took hold of the side.

"No, I heard you. I heard what you said. You said I needed to have his appendix checked out. How do you know that? JR's had a bad tummyache for most of today. I kept him out of school, and he seemed better this afternoon, so I thought I'd do some shopping. It was a sharp pain in his belly and it came and went throughout the morning. Then, he said that he felt like he could throw up, but he took his nap and woke up better." She caressed the top of her son's head, smoothing down a cowlick that stood upright at his forehead. He was freckle-nosed and looked like the kind of kid who would stick a lizard down the shirt of the girl who sat in front of him in homeroom. He grinned up at me, and that was it. I had to tell her what I saw.

"This is going to sound bizarre. I don't even understand it myself . . . but I see things, like visions."

She pulled JR closer to her and backed her cart up several feet.

"I understand. I don't blame you, but I need to let you know what I saw because I'm worried about your son."

She swiveled her head back and forth, checking around her, as if wondering whether this was a spoof and she was actually being filmed for some reality show. When no one with a video camera leaped out from behind the display of lettuces, she leaned toward me and asked softly, "What did you see?"

Keeping my voice equally low, I whispered, "I saw a dark, black space, but then something red inside it exploded open, almost like a tomato being squashed."

Standing upright, she said in a normal voice, "A tomato. A squashed tomato."

"Yeah," I said, realizing how utterly ridiculous this must sound to a mother who simply wanted to buy some sweet potatoes.

"Why on earth would that make you think I need to have his appendix checked? Do you always stop people in the grocery store to tell them horrible things? I bet this is some kind of scam, right? You get people all upset and then tell them you can fix them with a witchy-witchy product they can only buy from you. You are a terrible person." Her voice was rising in volume with every insult, and people were starting to stare and congregate in a circle around us.

I was beginning to wonder where the pitchforks and rocks were when JR collapsed to the floor, clutching his belly and howling. He threw up and lay in a pile of vomit, and then it was all chaos. His mom screamed for someone to dial 911 while she was reaching for her phone and dialing 911. As the fire station was across the street from the grocery store, the EMTs arrived in under five minutes. They straightened JR out as much as possible, given that he was still coiled tightly in pain, gently palpated his stomach, noted his low-grade fever, and then said to his white-faced mom, "We need to get him to the hospital, pronto. Could be an appendix about to burst."

She gave me a look that was partially gratitude but primarily terror and rushed behind the paramedics as they raced the stretcher holding her screaming son to the waiting ambulance.

I deserted my cart in the produce aisle and walked out of the store before any of the rest of the customers staring at me, openmouthed, could decide to approach.

It happened several more times after that. Cal and I went to Taco Tuesday at Rosita's Mexican Grill. All I wanted was the taco platter they offered once a week and a margarita, but before I could dip the first chip into the salsa, I felt a prickling on the skin at the back of my neck. I tried to ignore it, tried to concentrate on what Cal was saying about Maslow's hierarchy of needs theory, but in increasingly louder interjections, a voice inside my head kept saying, *Tell him it wasn't his fault. He needs to know that. I was so sad, but there was nothing he could have done to help me. Tell him it didn't hurt.*

The man's voice wouldn't stop, like a tape on repeat, until I finally couldn't take it anymore.

I twisted around in the booth and tapped the guy behind me on the shoulder. He turned. A bulky guy in a worn denim shirt, sleeves cut off. He had a full beard and eyes so dark you almost couldn't see the pupils. He was not happy I had interrupted his burrito special and glared at me.

I gulped once and said, "Uh, did your father or some man close to you recently die?"

Cal asked, "Claire, what the hell? What are you doing?"

But the voice in my head refused to leave. It kept repeating things over and over. It was as if I had no choice but to keep trying.

"I'm sorry, I am, and I know this sounds nuts, but I keep hearing a voice telling me things and it's a man and he wants me to tell them to you."

The guy turned back to his meal snarling, "Sure, lady. You might consider adjusting those meds of yours." He snickered to his dining partner, a woman with a tattoo up her arm that read: RIDE WITH THE WIND, SLEEP WITH THE WOLVES.

"He says it wasn't your fault. It wasn't anybody's fault. He was just too sad. He didn't feel there was any other way out," I said to his broad back.

He stopped chewing, wiped his mouth on a paper napkin, took a long swallow of his beer, and turned back around to me.

"Who said?"

I tried to swallow around the grapefruit stuck in my throat.

Cal pleaded, "Claire, that's enough. Let the guy enjoy the rest of his meal."

"I'm not sure. I only know it's a man and it feels like a cousin but it could be a—"

"My brother. My older brother." His eyes softened, and his bottom lip started to tremble. "Suicide. Two months ago. But . . . but . . . how . . . ?"

"I'm so sorry. He wants me to tell you it didn't hurt."

"I don't understand. Did you know him?"

"No, I didn't. I know this is strange, but I'm a psychic, and sometimes I get messages."

He nodded once, stuck out a hand the size of a frying pan, and said, "I'm Hank."

"I'm Claire. What was your brother's name?"

"William, but we called him Whittle because he was always carving stuff."

"Hank, he's okay. Whittle's sorry for what he did, but he wanted me to tell you that you shouldn't feel bad about it. He feels finally at peace now."

"I wondered about it. We all did. We knew something wasn't right, but he never talked about it, you know? Pills. He took a bunch of pills one night, and that was it."

"I'm so, so sorry," I repeated.

"Well, thanks, thanks a whole lot for telling me," he said, turning back to his dinner. "That's good. That's real good. Hear that, Rhonda? Whittle's okay." She grunted and said something that sounded like "crazy nutcase."

Then, all of a sudden, the voice that had taken up residence in my head stopped. I realized during the time when all I could hear was Whittle, I couldn't hear anything else, not Cal, not the mariachi-band background music pumped into the restaurant, not the rattling of dishes from the kitchen. Now, everything came back, along with a pounding headache.

"Cal, let's see if they'll pack this to go. I need to get out of here." I knew Cal was as anxious to leave as I was.

It got so bad that all I could do was work and then come back home. We didn't go to movies or restaurants or even run, unless it was very early or very late, to make it unlikely we'd be near other people. I became terrified of being ambushed by information that I would then be compelled to share with a stranger at any random moment because apparently I now had a direct communication line to the universe. It was easier to keep isolated.

Word got out. People told people. I was seeing clients from eight in the morning until six at night, and judging by the feedback they gave me after each session, I was never wrong.

I was drained and frazzled to the point of collapse. Besides the physical exhaustion of being constantly attacked with images and words, it was like reading a newspaper from front to back and having every single story lodge into my brain. No, not only my brain, into my heart. I hurt. I hurt for the ones who were divorced and heartbroken, the ones who were suffering from pancreatic cancer or another terrible disease. For the dead mothers, the dead fathers, and especially for the dead children. Each reading left me more depleted. It was only when I was able to give a reading that was hopeful, to relay a comforting message from a loved one, or predict a sunnier future that I felt some bit of relief.

Besides spending time with my mom, I needed the week off to get rebalanced, to figure out what the hell was going on, and to clear my mind. I needed a spa treatment for my brain.

I knew my mother could help. If there was anything to know about the psychic world, she was the one to know it.

Through the years, when my mother would ask me about work, I'd always tell her it was fine. We never shared stories about specific clients, and she never pressed me for information about my techniques. My mother had a long-standing rule about this. She felt her relationship with her clients was very much like that of a doctor and patient, and required complete confidentiality. I was able in some ways to use her code of honor to protect my secret.

Cal and I'd made plenty of plans to entertain Mom during her visit, to show her around the area. I knew eventually I needed to talk to her about all the bizarre things going on with me. But if I was going to ask her for advice, I would first have to reveal that I didn't have the skills she'd thought I had all these years. Not a discussion I was looking forward to, but I was getting desperate.

34
Rena

I wake up to the screaming at three in the morning.

At first I think it's part of a nightmare I'm having. A pissed customer is chasing me around the drugstore. She's screaming she was poisoned by the vitamin C I sold her. Then her screams become really high-pitched and the woman turns into a bunch of charging monkeys who are all shrieking, "Mommy, Mommy, Mommmmmmmyyyyyy."

I jump out of bed. On the floor, Stephanie is rolling back and forth, grabbing her stomach.

I run over to Mrs. Lupito's and bang on the door for a full five minutes. I see a light go on in her living room. She finally opens the door a half inch and stares out at me.

"*Que?*"

"It's Stephanie. She's really sick. I need your car to get her to the hospital now," I shout.

"Call the nine-one-one," she spits out and begins to shut the door.

I kick it back open.

"Takes too long. You have to help us. Stephanie's bad."

She frowns but then says, "*Sí*, fine. I drive."

When she pulls her car down the driveway, I'm already there with Steph, wrapped in a blanket. I gently slide her into the back seat. Then I jump in front and shout at Mrs. Lupito, "Fast, dammit, get going."

On the way, I call the ER.

"This is Rena Cole. My daughter, Stephanie, is in extreme pain. Stomach. She's a patient of Dr. Norton's. Call Dr. Norton and tell her we're on our way."

I yell at Mrs. Lupito, "See? I told you. Her system can't take that crap you gave her."

Everything in the ER is a blur. People are shouting, and they grab Stephanie out of my arms and take her into a room surrounded by a curtain. I shove my way in, but a male nurse yanks me out and says, "Wait here."

"No fucking way," I yell, running past him. When I see Stephanie, there's a doctor doing CPR on her, and I scream, "No, no, no." I feel myself dropping.

"Rena? Mrs. Cole?" Someone is shaking my shoulder. I open my eyes. I'm in one of the ER cubicles.

"How is she? How's my daughter?" I try to sit up, but the nurse, whose name tag says DONALD, won't let me.

"You fainted, so we need you to rest here for a while."

"But how's my baby? I want to see her."

Donald puts a large, warm palm on my arm and says, "Stephanie's resting. I know Dr. Norton wants to talk to you. She's in with another patient right now, but she should only be a minute or two." He takes my pulse.

My forehead is pounding. I put my hand there and find a lump the size of a walnut.

"Yeah, you made quite the face-plant. I'll get you a compress for that."

I start to cry and say, "I'm so scared for my little girl."

Donald pulls a rolling stool next to the bed and says, "It's been real tough, hasn't it?"

"You have no idea. She's been sick for so long. I honestly don't know what to do anymore. She keeps getting rushed to the ER, and they always find too much sodium in her system, but they never know why." He hands me a tissue, and I blow my nose.

"I'm not a dad yet, but I can't imagine how hard it is to see your kid sick." He stands and pats me on the shoulder. "I can tell you're a good mom, though, and I bet they'll figure this thing out real soon."

I sniff and nod.

"Let me see if Dr. Norton's free, okay? Need anything?"

"A ginger ale maybe?"

"Sure thing."

He comes back with a plastic cup of ginger ale, and Dr. Norton is with him.

"Stephanie's hanging in there, but it was touch and go for a while. We weren't sure we could save her," says Dr. Norton.

I moan, "Oh, my baby. My poor, poor baby."

"What we don't know is what's going on with her. Especially perplexing," Dr. Norton says, flipping through a medical chart, "is her extremely high blood sodium level."

"Hypernatremia," I say.

Dr. Norton raises her eyebrows and says, "Yes,

that's what we're suspecting, but why would you mention this?"

"Because, uh, that's what she had before," I say, taking a sip of soda. "Didn't you read her medical records from the other hospital? That's what I was trying to tell you all this time. Something is definitely wrong with her, and that's why I said you need to do a PET scan to figure it out." I was shouting as loud as I could with my weak voice.

"Calm down, please, Mrs. Cole," Dr. Norton says, pushing back a piece of blond hair that came loose from her bun. "Unfortunately, we never got the records. I did tell you that in my voice mail, remember? If you can give me her doctor's number, I can certainly make a call."

"But when will you do the PET scan?"

She sighs and says to Donald, "Once the patient is stabilized, please see if we can schedule the PET scan while she's here. She'll need to stay at least one night anyway, so probably tomorrow morning would be best."

Dr. Norton turns back to me. "We're currently giving her IV fluids to slowly reduce the sodium levels. We can't do that too rapidly or we risk causing brain damage."

"Oh my God, brain damage." I roll away from her to face the wall.

"Please, try not to worry. We're doing everything we can. We'll know more in another couple of hours."

I nod and hear her start to walk away.

She stops and moves back to the bed. She puts her hand on my arm and turns me toward her.

"Mrs. Cole, do you have any idea how Stephanie could have gotten so much sodium into her system?"

"I have no clue," I say, turning away again. "But I'm sure the PET scan will tell us something useful."

"Dr. Norton, can I speak with you a moment?" Donald asks, following her out of the room. But I can't hear what he says to her, and their voices fade as they go down the hall.

STEPHANIE'S BATTLE BLOG
Posted on October 11 by Stephanie's Mommy

It's been a very, very long day or actually, night. It's eight in the morning now. Before I get some sleep, I wanted to update everyone.

Stephanie is not here with me. She had to stay in the hospital. She almost died last night. To much sodium in her system. AGAIN. They brought her back, but just bearly.

The doctor finally agreed to do the damn PET scan. They'll do it tomorrow before they release her.

When I wake up, I can hardly believe it's almost five o'clock in the afternoon. That Xanax I took really did the trick. I call the hospital.

"Hi, this is Rena Cole. I'm checking on my daughter, Stephanie."

"Yes, Mrs. Cole. This is Gretchen. I just got here, but I looked in on her and she seems much better. Even ate a little Jell-O. Such a sweet thing."

"Oh, that's really good. Did the doctor say when she could be discharged?"

"Let me check the chart. Says here, probably tomorrow morning if she remains stable through the night."

"Great, thanks."

After I hang up, I look in my closet to see if there's anything halfway decent to wear for my date with Louis tonight. My black slacks have a stain in front but nothing a long top won't hide. I get into the shower and am ready to go in an hour.

He's standing outside the drugstore, holding a white bag.

"What's that, more vitamins?" I ask, kissing him on the cheek.

"Nah, just a prescription I needed to pick up," he says. "I thought we'd have those steaks at a place around the corner. It's not a bad night for a walk, if that's okay with you."

I think people who live here must lose their ability to feel heat. It's in the nineties. The sweat is already dripping down my back, but I say, "Sure, let's walk."

Over drinks, I fill Louis in on Stephanie's history, all the doctors we've seen, the ER visits, the hundreds of tests.

"That's really tough. A sick kid's got to be the worst." He wipes some salad dressing from the corner of his mouth.

The restaurant we're at is a really popular tourist spot. Hanging from the ceiling all through the room are men's ties. Well, half ties. Louis says if a guy comes in wearing a tie, one of the staff will walk right up to him, cut it in half, and pin that half to the ceiling. I ask him if some people didn't get pissed. I mean, what if the tie's expensive? He says nope, everyone plays along. It makes the tourists feel like they're really in the wild, wild west.

I reach for the breadbasket. It's not actually bread but corn muffins with jalapeño peppers in them. "Yeah, it's been horrible with Steph so sick all the time," I say. "I'm wiped out, for sure."

"She's lucky to have a mom like you. I wish my kids were so lucky."

"Why? Isn't your wife a good mother?"

"My ex, Rachel? I mean, my almost ex. She's always screaming at them for something. That is, when she's not screaming at me. Which is all the time, especially lately."

He tells me how he met Rachel in high school. He said their dads had been in the National Guard together, and how happy their parents were when they started dating.

"It felt like they were tracking our every move," he says. "It was like they thought, of course we'd get married. Like everyone expected it, and we just went along."

"Why? Didn't you want to?"

He runs his hand through his hair and shrugs. "I guess so. I guess I did. We were just so young. Like I hardly dated anyone else except for Rachel. I kept thinking maybe I missed out on some stuff, you know?"

"Well, now you have a second chance, right?" I lean over the table and ask, "What exactly do you want now that you think you missed out on?"

Before he can answer, the waitress is standing there and takes our order. The steaks are fantastic. We split another bottle of wine.

"Ready for dessert? They have an amazing warm apple cobbler with vanilla ice cream," Louis says.

I stand up slowly and then bend over next to him so my tits are level with his eyes.

"I was thinking about a different type of sweet ending," I whisper into his ear. "Follow me to the ladies' room."

I check to make sure the one-stall bathroom is empty, and then I pull him in behind me. I give him a blow job that's so good he's still sweating and grinning as he hands the waitress his credit card ten minutes later.

All in all, a great first date. He takes me back to the drugstore, and I tell him I can walk home from there. He offers to go with me, but I tell him it's okay. No way do I want him to see that dump of a place.

"So, Rena. I had a really good time tonight."

"Yeah, me too."

"I need to go on a business trip for a week, but when I get back, maybe we can go away somewhere together. There's great hiking in Sedona. Maybe next weekend?"

"Sure, I'd love that."

I turn and walk away without kissing him good night. Let him keep replaying that last scene in the bathroom until we get together again.

35

Claire

During the first half of Mom's visit, Cal and I took her to all the usual Sedona and surrounding area tourist stops. We visited the Chapel of the Holy Cross, a church that sits two hundred feet above the road and looks like it was dropped out of the sky and then wedged between two jutting red rocks. I've been there dozens of times, even though I'm not Catholic. With the floor-to-ceiling windows offering gorgeous panoramic views, it's one of the most serene places you can go if you need to pray or just sit and think.

From there we went to Slide Rock in Oak Creek Canyon. It was still warm enough to sit on our butts in the shallow water and slide down over the slippery rocks in shorts and swim tops. The water was icy cold, though, and Mom bumped into a teenager and knocked him off his feet. Lots of cursing and apologizing followed.

We drove to Jerome, an old mining town that, after the ore ran out and the population dwindled, became practically a ghost town. Now, thanks to cute shops, great restaurants, and tons of motorcyclists, the town's had an impressive resurgence.

As we traveled, I talked to Mom about how she was coping. She'd tell me she was doing fine, but I'd find her staring at one of the rock outcroppings with tears running down her cheeks. We'd hug and she'd tell me she loved me and that things would get better. For both of us.

By Thursday of that week, we are all touristed out and decide to hang around, take an easy morning hike, and then go to Tlaquepaque, a shopping area outside of town. It has nice galleries and an even nicer outside courtyard, where you can get drinks and a decent lunch.

An amazing thing is that, during the week off, I wasn't having visions. Actually, I *was* having them, but for some reason, they weren't coming all the way through. It was like a radio station with a low but constant level of static. I'd hear something or see someone, but the sounds were muffled and it was like the vision or message was covered by strands of cotton. I couldn't make out what I was being shown or told, and pretty soon, I managed to relegate whatever was coming at me to the very back of my consciousness. It became like elevator music, ubiquitous and irritating, but able to be handled if ignored.

It's over the restaurant's signature crème brûlée that I decide to broach the topic.

"So, Mom, how's business?"

"Good, honey." She dives into the custard like the woman she is: one who only eats sugar on holidays, vacations, and birthdays. "Yummm, this is the most delicious dessert I've had this trip."

"That's saying something, since you've had dessert with practically every meal since we got here, including breakfast," says Cal, laughing.

"True. And I'm not apologizing for it. Although I will need to do a thorough cleanse when we get home, wash all this out of my system."

I start again. "Just curious, do you ever have times when your psychic abilities are more powerful than others? I mean, like, do they ebb and flow?"

"Ebb and flow?" she asks, licking clean the spoon before she drops it in the mini soufflé dish and then leans back with a satisfied sigh. A breeze lifts the branches of the tree shading us. It's the kind of weather that feels perfectly right, like you're submersed in a pool of your own body temperature.

"I mean, do they ever, um, disappear on you?" I take a sip of my iced tea, trying to look casual.

It doesn't work. It's almost impossible to try to hide something if you're sitting across from one of the nation's most renowned readers.

"What's going on, Claire? Is it your job? Tell me," my mother says, placing her hand on my cheek.

I glance at Cal, who says, "Go ahead, Ozzie, tell her."

Grasping the side of the table, I take a long inhale and say, "Mom, I've been faking it." It all gushes out of me: the years of pretending I knew what I was doing, and then the bizarre experiences of the past weeks, my 100 percent accuracy, the guy in the restaurant, the little boy in the grocery store, the multitude of customers begging for answers, the feeling of constant onslaught on my brain and emotions from every direction.

In the silence that follows, I can hear the cars on the main road that runs through town.

The waiter clears the dishes and brings our bill.

After he leaves, I continue. "I don't know how to deal with this," I say, looking down at my hands, which are clutched in my lap. "And I'm sorry, I really am, for lying to you all these years."

I finally look at her, prepared to meet her disappointment, but, amazingly, she's smiling.

"Oh, that," Mom says. "I knew."

"You knew? What do you mean, you knew?"

"It wasn't too hard to guess. After all, it doesn't take a psychic to figure out her daughter is making things up as she goes along."

"But ... . for how long? How long have you known?" I'm simultaneously shocked and relieved.

"Oh, I don't know," she says. "For a while now."

"Why didn't you say anything?" I ask.

Mom lifts her napkin to dab her lips.

"Your dad and I talked about it. I mean, you wouldn't have been the first psychic to do this. Let me ask you a question. Did you ever consciously deceive your clients or purposely cause them pain?"

I think this over and say, "No, it was more like I tried to tell them what they wanted to hear based on what the cards said."

"Like many, many other psychics would do, except they do not possess your skill level."

"My skill level?"

"Oh yes, you definitely had amazing talents. Regarding what you call 'faking it,' like I said, Dad and I knew, but we decided that when you were ready to tell us, you would."

"Did Aunt Frannie know too?"

"Yes, and it didn't change her opinion of you one bit. Besides, we were all certain that eventually, those skills would return to you."

"Return to me?" Then I ask the pivotal question, the real one: "How could skills I haven't had since I was a child suddenly come back?"

"A child? Oh, darling, you had your psychic abilities way beyond childhood. Don't you remember?" my mother asks with a look on her face that's troubling, although I can't decipher its meaning.

"Remember what?" I ask.

"Claire, what was the last vision you remember having—well, prior to these past couple ofweeks?"

It doesn't take long to recall, the way a football player in his old age can replay the memory of that final great game of his career.

"My birthday party. I was three. After that, I remember you trying to teach me, but I couldn't do it," I say, the guilt and frustration rushing in as if I were still in our front room failing to guess the right numbers or colors on the cards my mother held before me.

"You don't remember any other visions after your third birthday party?" Mom asks.

I don't, but then she reminds me and it all comes back.

36

Rena

"Up. Up. Let's do our exercises," shouts Susan. She's waving her hands in the air. Everyone at Mommy Loves Baby gets up to dance, except for Stephanie and me.

They all wiggle around to "The Wheels on the Bus." Susan stops the tape and asks, "Rena, don't you and Stephanie want to join us?"

I reach out and pull Stephanie closer to me. She squirms away.

"We can't. Well, Stephanie can't. She just got out of the hospital yesterday."

"I'm so sorry. Stomach again?"

"Worse than ever. I thought I was going to lose her."

One by one, the moms all come over to kiss or hug

me and Stephanie. They say things like "That's terrible. I'm so sorry. Feel better. Hang in there."

Susan says, "That's okay, we'll just cut our exercises a little short today. Leaves more time for games and reading." Everyone cheers.

At the end, I help Susan and Felicia pack up the games they brought. There's Candy Land, Ants in the Pants, Twister, and more. Everyone seemed to like them a lot. Even Stephanie smiled a little bit after she beat Rex, the fatty, at Candy Land.

"You sure do have a lot of games. I can never find all the damn pieces to any of the ones we have," I say.

"I have a system. Felicia has to put one away before she can bring out another game. Seems to work—most days anyway," she says, pointing at Felicia to get the wooden pieces of Blockhead back into the box. I hold the other end of a large plastic carryall, and Susan shoves in a game of Uno and a travel chess set. Of course, nobody knew how to play chess. I think Susan brought that just to show off.

"Sounds like a good method. Have to try that one."

When everything's packed up, we walk through the consignment shop to the front door. Susan stops to look at some clothes. She asks Felicia what she thinks about a yellow flowered summer dress.

"You've had quite the time of it, haven't you?" Susan asks me. She pulls out shorts and holds them up to Felicia's waist.

I look around for Stephanie. She's near the front door, and I mouth for her to come to me. She shuffles her feet but finally starts moving in my direction.

"Definitely. It was so scary. I mean, you'd think I'd be used to it. We've been in the ER so many times before, but this time . . ." I start to cry.

Susan puts her arms around me, pats me on the back, and says, "It's okay, it's okay. I can't even imagine what you're going through. How awful. If there's anything I can do . . ."

I pull back and sniff, "What I really need is a break. A break from all this stress. It's been so hard."

"I'm sure," says Susan. "On you . . . and Stephanie."

"For now, at least, she seems to be stable. We're waiting for some more test results, including the PET scan the doctor finally agreed to do. They said I should have those by Monday. I'm really, really nervous. I'm trying to figure out some way to occupy my mind over the weekend. Maybe get away or something."

"That would be great if you could. Where would you and Stephanie go? Might be nice to go north, maybe Sedona? Certainly cooler there." Susan hands ten dollars and the dress and shorts to the cashier.

"You know, I was thinking that exact same thing, but I don't know if it's a good idea to have Steph travel. Too many germs, you know?"

"Oh, you're probably right. I didn't think about that." She puts the two dollars and a quarter in change into a jar next to the register. It has a note on it: HELP FEED OUR HOMELESS.

"I was thinking about asking my neighbor who watches Stephanie when I work if she'd keep her for the weekend. But she's the one who gave her the damn bologna sandwich that put her in the hospital. So no way."

We walk out of the store. The sun bounces back off the white sidewalk and actually hurts my eyes. I can already feel the sweat dripping down my armpits.

"I can see why you'd be afraid to have her go there again," Susan says.

"The days I work, maybe it might be okay. Because it's not for very long and I can bring her Steph's food. I have no doubt at all that now she'll feed Stephanie only that food and nothing else. But I'm too scared to have my daughter with her for a whole weekend." I sigh and start to cry again. "Man, I need to get away, though. I'm so tired."

Susan looks at me and then bends down and puts an arm around Felicia's shoulders. "Hey, what do you think about a sleepover this weekend? Want Stephanie to stay with us for a couple of days?"

Felicia jumps up and down and shouts, "Yes, Mommy, please."

"I guess we have our answer, then, but . . . ," she says to me in a low voice, ". . . is it safe for Stephanie to be with us? I mean, if she's just out of the hospital and all?"

"Definitely. Her doctor gave her a full release," I answer. "I can get you a note, if you want it," I quickly add.

"No, no, that's not necessary. We'd love to have Steph stay with us."

"Oh my God, really? You are so sweet. I can't believe you'd do this. Really?"

"Of course, anything we can do to help. We moms need to stick together, right?"

"You bet. Listen, give me your address, and I'll be sure to pack up her food. Can I drop her off at, like, nine on Saturday morning? I want to get a real early start."

"That should be fine." She writes down her information on the consignment store receipt.

"Thanks again. Thanks so much," I say, walking with Susan and Felicia to their car.

"Stephanie, won't that . . . ," I start to tell my daughter but then realize she's not there beside me. I go back in the store. She's standing in front of some old ladies, trying on necklaces.

"Let's go," I say, taking her hand. She pulls it away from me.

"Stephanie, now," I say.

When I get home, I call Louis to let him know we're on for the Sedona trip.

I drag the suitcase out from under the bed. Most of Stephanie's clothes are still in there since we only have the one dresser.

Underneath her pajamas and underwear, I find the paper. Written on it is:

Claire
Mystical Haven
1 Canyon Village Way, Sedona

37
Claire

"Maybe we should move this party elsewhere," Cal says, pointing to the waiters who are beginning to reset tables for the dinner crowd.

When we get home, I set out a pitcher of ice water, cut some lemons, and pull together an appetizer platter with whatever we have around, which amounts to a slightly hardened block of cheese, some saltines, and a bunch of grapes. We're not hungry right now, but in case we want to nibble, it's there while my mother tells the story of my found and lost (and found) psychic abilities, which, until now, I was certain had ended at age three.

Mom and I sit on the couch, and Cal leans against some throw pillows on the floor.

She begins, "As a child, you weren't all that interested in reading tarot or learning the various other methods of the psychic arts. I was sure you had the gift and wanted to urge you to study, but your dad convinced me you should enjoy your childhood, and when and if you were ready, you would come to me to learn. That seemed right, so I backed off. Occasionally, you would sense something from a client and mention it to me after she left. You were nearly always right, but that was the extent of it at that time."

"What changed?" I ask.

"It started two weeks before your dad had his first stroke at the beach house."

I try to think back. What was going on in my life that summer in the weeks before we went to the beach? Nothing specific comes to mind. I was twelve, so I'm fairly certain whatever it was, it was age-appropriate and mundane. Learning to shave my legs? Mooning over some rising boy band? More than likely, I was running. Even in the off-season, I would train on my own, taking long runs and then stopping at the high school track to challenge my sprint times.

I shake my head and say, "I can't remember anything particular about that time."

"Maybe it's a good thing you don't remember. Sometimes our minds protect us by blocking out what's difficult to handle emotionally," says Mom.

"Why? What happened?" I ask.

She pours herself some water and adds a squeeze of lemon. She takes a sip and says, "At the time, we thought it was a seizure of some sort."

"What? I had a seizure?"

"That's what we thought. The first time it happened, I was in the front of the shop, about to open for the day, and I heard a crash from the kitchen. I ran in and found you on the floor on your back. You were wedged between the oven and that red step stool. You know the one we keep there to reach the pasta pot on the very top shelf?"

"Yes."

"I figured you needed something and then maybe fell off the stool. I tried to help you up, but you wouldn't move."

"What do you mean 'wouldn't move'?"

"Actually," she says, glancing at Cal, "it was more like you *couldn't* move."

"Was I having a seizure?"

"Like I said, that's what I first thought because you were so stiff. Your eyes were open, but you were definitely not focused on me or on anything at all. I was calling your name, but you didn't move. Except for your eyes, which kept darting back and forth. I was really scared. Your dad was at work, and I didn't know what to do. I ran to grab my phone to call 911. Then, all of a sudden, you sat up, shrieking, 'Daddy. Tell Daddy—tell him right now. He needs to know.'"

"Oh my God. You must have been terrified," I say, touching her knee.

She nods and continues, "I raced back and held you. You were shaking and kept crying and yelling that I had to tell your dad. When I could finally get you calmed down, I asked, 'Tell Dad what? What do I need to tell Dad?' And you said, 'What do you mean? What are you talking about?'"

"I didn't remember what happened after it was over?"

"Nope. It was as if the whole thing, which had lasted maybe ten minutes, had never occurred. You told me you were tired, went to your bedroom, and slept for pretty much the rest of the afternoon. When you woke up, I asked you again, tried to prompt you into remembering the episode, but you looked at me as if I were making the whole thing up. It was all very strange."

"What did it mean? What was I screaming about? And was it a seizure? Did you take me to the doctor?"

"Give her a chance to talk, Claire," Cal says, chuckling.

"Sorry, but this is more than a little bizarre."

My mom says, "Of course. It was for us too. The next time—"

"There was a next time?" I ask, my voice rising.

"Actually, two more times. Once the next day and one more the day after that. Of course, after the first one, when you got up from your nap, I did take you to the doctor's office. She checked you out, said nothing seemed wrong, but that we should keep an eye on you."

"Were they the same, the next ones? Same sort of a seizure type thing?"

"Pretty much," she says. "For the last one, Dad was there. He decided to come home early to mow the grass. You were in the garden picking tomatoes for dinner, and he said he heard you kind of yelp and thought maybe you'd been stung by a bee, so he rushed to find you. I was at the kitchen window and saw him running, so I raced over too. When I got there he was already crouched beside you calling your name. It was the same as the other times. You were flat on your back between the tomatoes and string beans, not moving, and when you sat up, you kept yelling those same words: 'Tell Dad. Daddy needs to know. He needs to know.'"

"What did Dad do?" Just thinking about my dad, I can imagine him there in the garden, next to me, with his deep, soothing voice, cajoling me to come back from wherever I'd gone.

"You were hysterical and crying. He kept holding you. This one lasted the longest of them all. I was about to call an ambulance when suddenly you stopped crying, looked straight at your father, and said, 'Please, Daddy, don't go,' and then collapsed again into his arms, sobbing."

Cal unfolds himself and stands to turn on the table lamps. I'm surprised to find the room filled with shadows.

"We probably should have taken you back to the doctor, but whatever these episodes were, they stopped completely after that final one. You had no memory of anything that had happened and seemed fine. Your dad and I figured it was like when you were a toddler and had night terrors. You'd be screaming and crying and you'd look completely awake, but you had no idea who we were and you wouldn't let us comfort you. We'd lay you on the rug and sit down next to you and you'd roll back and forth crying until you finally fell back to sleep. You eventually grew out of those, and we thought it was the same with this."

My stomach growls, and I reach for a piece of cheese and a cracker.

"I'm guessing I don't have a seizure disorder, because you never told me I did, and I've never had a seizure of any kind, as far as I know."

Mom says. "Nope, no seizure disorder."

"Then what does this have to do with my disappearing and reappearing psychic abilities?"

Mom stands and stretches. "Listen, I'm kind of stiff from all this sitting. What do you say we take a quick walk around the neighborhood? I love the way the desert smells at night."

38
Rena

I feel like a damn teenager getting ready for the prom.
In my high school, almost every girl planned to get her cherry popped after the junior prom. Girls made trips to department and specialty stores to find THE dress. Some even had appointments with hairdressers a few weeks before to get a "practice updo." There were even girls who went to salons to have their makeup professionally applied that day. Of course, I didn't do that, any of it. No money. But I was working at Walmart after school, and I had an employee discount. I got spiky false eyelashes and a new lipstick (Party Hearty Purple) and blush (Sprinkle Pinkle). Also a sexy black nightie with purple lace (to match my lipstick) and a built-in push-up bra. My friends and I had our "after" outfits ready too (leggings and a loose

top). The only thing left was to hope the guys remembered the condoms.

We went into the corners at the high school gym and giggled. We talked about whether it was going to hurt, how much blood there would be. We said how in love we were with our prom dates or how it was just time to get it the hell over with. For me, I was definitely in the second group. My date, Richie Baskin, was a nice enough guy. We were chemistry lab partners, and more than a few times he got my ass out of the fire by letting me copy his homework. But in love? No fucking way. He just happened to be attached to the part I needed to get the job done.

Packing to go away with Louis gives me that same kind of buzzy feeling. Like you're not sure what will happen, but you can't wait anyway. In the days before, I tried to watch what I ate. I know I've dropped a few pounds. Hard to tell without a scale. My face looks skinnier and maybe my ass too. I went back to the consignment store and found a cute pair of jeans that'll be good for hiking. They're only a little tight. I even colored my hair myself. It's not a perfect job, but at least now it's the same shade all over instead of black roots and blond ends. I didn't bother with a nightgown or anything like that. Why spend money on something I'll wear for less than six seconds?

Louis is going to pick me up at the drugstore in about two hours.

"Stephanie, stop screwing around in there, will you? I need to drop you off first, and I don't want to be late for work."

"Why can't you come home tonight like you usually do?" she whines. She's on her stomach under the coffee table and comes up with her ratty stuffed panda.

"I already told you a hundred times. My boss wants me to check out another pharmacy in the state, to see how they do things. It's part of my job, and I need to keep my job. Your medical stuff costs a crapload of money. Do you get it now?"

"Yes, Mommy," she says.

"Besides you get to stay with Susan and Felicia from class. That'll be fun, right?"

She skips off into the bedroom.

"Stephanie, where the hell are you going?" I yell. "I said we got to leave."

She comes back with her blankie and a book about ponies. I grab my suitcase and the trash bag holding her pj's, a change of clothes, and all her prepared meals and snacks. We get in the cab that's waiting outside.

Susan's house is a mansion.

The cabdriver says this part of town is considered to

be old Phoenix. The streets are lined with actual trees. Susan's house is two-story and brick with tall white pillars in front. I swear it looks like it's right out of *Gone with the Wind*. I almost expect servants to run out and carry in our luggage.

Felicia opens the red front door. She walks over to Stephanie and says, "Want to see my room?" They run back into the house.

Susan is waving at me. "Come on in, Rena."

"Hi, thanks again for doing this," I say and hand her the plastic bag.

We go into her kitchen through the hugest living room I've ever seen. Then I realize it's actually a living, dining, and TV room, all in one. A whole wall is covered with a big-screen TV. I'm thinking it must be like having your own private movie theater. In front of the TV is a sectional sofa, the kind where two of the chairs have cup holders and lean all the way back. A formal living area to the left looks like it came right from an Ethan Allen store. The dining area has a shiny dark wood table with twelve chairs around it. The chairs have some kind of needlework cushions. I get closer and can see the designs on the cushions are of horses chasing after a fox. The men on the horses are all wearing black top hats and carrying sticks, which I'm guessing they use to beat the horses.

"Do you have super-large parties here or what?"

Susan smiles at me and says, "Sometimes. My husband's in pharmaceuticals, and we often need to entertain his clients."

"I guess, I mean, I thought, since you were shopping at the consignment store, that—"

"Well, I believe in giving back to the community."

"Oh, sure, me too. I bought some jeans there yesterday."

I'm wondering why she goes to a Mommy Loves Baby class like ours. It's not in the best neighborhood. Then she says, "Felicia met Rex at the Children's Museum, and they became such great buddies that his mom and I try to get them together as much as possible. That's why we attend the meeting at the consignment store. Did you take Stephanie to that museum yet? I bet she'd love it."

"No, not yet. I work so much, it's hard to find time to do things like that."

"Hopefully, some afternoon you'll get to go. Maybe I can bring her next time I take Felicia? She adores all the exhibits. The kids can go through these play towns, where they can pretend they're running a post office or an ice cream store. It's loads of fun."

The kitchen is all stainless-steel fixtures and black granite countertops. It's like a glossy picture from a magazine. Susan takes the plastic containers out of the bag and says, "So, tell me what I need to know about Stephanie's food requirements."

I start to organize all the containers into different groups: breakfast (steel-cut oatmeal with organic coconut milk); lunch (tofu burger with a whole-grain bun and non-GMO baby carrots); dinner (bulgur salad with snow peas and free-range chicken pieces); and snacks (a container of blueberries and a package of organic string cheese). There are also bottles of spring water. Everything is marked for what meal it belongs to.

"I packed some extra in case you want Felicia to try anything."

"Thanks. We'll see. Felicia's kind of a picky eater."

"Oh, you need to stop that shit immediately. Once you let them decide what they will and won't eat, you can fucking forget about their health," I say, passing the containers to her that need to go in the fridge. She opens the doors of a double-wide refrigerator that's packed with so much food, I don't know where she'll put my stuff. But I notice a shelf at the bottom that's clear. This woman definitely has things under control.

Susan puts her nose up in the air and says in this snooty voice, "I appreciate the advice, and obviously, you know a great deal about nutrition and, of course, I know Stephanie's health is a priority for you." The unspoken words, I can tell, are *Stay the hell out of my life and if I decide to feed my kid horse crap, it's none of your damn business.* Can't say I didn't try.

"I guess I better get going." Susan walks me back through the foyer. There's this huge sparkling crystal-and-bronze chandelier. It gives off a glow from what feels like miles above our heads.

"Felicia, Stephanie's mommy is leaving," she yells from the bottom of the stairs. "You girls come down and say goodbye, okay?"

"Mommy, we're busy playing," Felicia shouts back.

"Stephanie, come down right now," I say. I hear her tell Felicia something, but soon she starts to walk slowly down the curving staircase.

I lean over to let her kiss me on the cheek. Turning us away from Susan, I squeeze Stephanie's arm and tell her, "You be good. Don't cause no trouble, understand?" I don't think Susan can hear me.

She nods once and runs back upstairs to Felicia's bedroom, which I'm sure is decorated in pink and has a bedspread covered with pictures of princesses. And there's probably a dollhouse taller than she is, filled with real wood furniture and lights that turn on and off.

I tell Susan I should be back by ten in the morning on Sunday. I'm out the door, heading to the cab, when I hear her running after me. "Rena, hang on—

you forgot to give me your phone number. You know, just in case."

"Oh yeah, sure," I say. "Except I plan on doing lots of hiking. I don't know if there'll be any reception out there."

"Really? We often go to Sedona, especially in the summer and have hiked many of the trails. We've never had any problem at all with getting a signal."

"Okay, good. That's good." I give her my number. She puts it into her phone, and I turn to walk to the cab.

"Wait, don't you want my number?" she asks.

I turn around. "Oh yeah, that's a good idea," I say. I type her number into my phone. "If you call and I don't answer right away, it's because I'm getting a massage or maybe sitting by the pool or something."

"I understand," she says, but there's definitely something in the way she says it. I know what she really means is, *I'm a much better mom than you are.*

39
Claire

We grab sweaters and head outside. Sedona is like the rest of Arizona, which people often forget is a desert. The days can be boiling hot, but the nights are cool in October, sometimes even cold. Our complex is in a cul-de-sac, so taking a walk amounts to three or so rounds of the circle.

My mother links her arm through mine, and Cal follows a few paces behind.

Mom sniffs the air. "What is that wonderful fragrance?"

"Probably the juniper trees, or maybe cypress. You should smell them after a storm. It's heavenly," I say.

We walk in silence for a while, and then she starts to speak.

"Your dad and I watched you closely in the days

after you had what turned out to be your last seizure, or whatever it was. Thankfully, nothing else happened. You were fine and very excited about going to the beach house."

"And?"

"And the first few days there were glorious. You remember, right? We sat on the beach and then that crazy miniature golf game in the pouring rain? All that thunder and lightning. I never saw lightning like that."

"Yes, I remember." The knot in my stomach ratchets into a tighter ball.

We've gone around the cul-de-sac twice when Mom stops and motions for me to sit next to her on the curb. Our place is only a couple of buildings away, and I can see the light from our living room. It looks warm and inviting, and I'm wishing I were there and not about to hear what she might say next.

"When your dad had the stroke that day, of course, we were all in shock. You probably remember this too—everyone was running around. To tell you the truth, I can't recall many of the details, but I can always pull up that horrible picture in my memory: your dad lying on the floor, his mouth . . ." She shudders, and I lean into her shoulder for comfort and warmth. "I know I went crazy. And I know I wasn't there for you that day, Claire."

Cal catches up to us and sits on the curb next to me.

My mom continues, "Aunt Frannie was the one who told me what happened with you after. She said you were inconsolable, which, of course, was completely understandable. No child should see her father in that condition. It was terrible for you, for everyone. But there was something else too."

"What?" I ask.

"You kept screaming. Finally, Aunt Frannie said she asked one of the EMTs to give you something to calm you down. Once the shot started to work, she said she could finally understand what you were yelling about."

"Which was?"

"You kept saying, 'It's my fault, it's my fault, I knew this was going to happen, I saw it happen.' Those phrases again and again, and nothing she said could convince you your dad's stroke was a medical problem and that you had nothing at all to do with it."

Sitting on the curb, now I begin to remember everything. Before this moment, my recollection of that disastrous afternoon ended with seeing my dad being slid into an ambulance. But now everything else that happened comes back, filling in missing pieces of memory I didn't even know weren't there.

That day, after my mother pushed me and my towel fell off, I grabbed it and tried to cover myself.

Somewhere, it registered in my brain that I should get dressed, but I didn't want to leave my father lying there. I thought if I stayed with him, right where I was, he wouldn't, couldn't leave me. My aunt ran to the bedroom and came back with my bathrobe, which she wrapped around me.

I also remember now everything I told my aunt later as she tried to assure me it would all be fine, that my dad was a strong man and would get well again. I sobbed and told her I was absolutely sure I had caused his stroke. Or, at the very least, I could have prevented it from happening. I told her those episodes I'd had the weeks before, the ones Mom and Dad had told me about—where I couldn't move—I could see now they were just like someone having a stroke. I told her these were obviously predictions of what was going to happen to Dad. The reason I kept pleading for my mother to "Let Dad know" was to warn him.

Surely, I should have done more to warn him. At twelve it was unlikely I could have put all this together—my seizure-like events and the signs of a stroke—before that day at the beach. But I told my aunt that night by my bedside that, obviously, on some level, I must have known this was coming, this first of his increasingly deadly strokes, and I was certain that my knowing it had caused it. I sobbed and told her I should have done more to stop it. No matter how many times my aunt tried to explain, using her nurse's terms, how a stroke worked, what factors might lead a person to have a stroke, I couldn't hear her. I *wouldn't* hear her. I'd caused the stroke and I hadn't stopped it. My guilt was suffocating.

I drop my head into my hands and begin to cry, sniffing into the sleeve of my sweatshirt. Cal puts his arm around me.

"After that, nothing I did could convince you to practice tarot or study any of the psychic arts. If you experienced any kind of pre-knowledge again, I never knew because you never said and you would always go somewhere else if I had a client in the shop. It was like you couldn't stand to be near any of it again."

She takes my hand.

"Claire," she says, "I'm sure you know this now, at least intellectually, but what happened to you physically did not cause his stroke, and there was nothing you could have done to prevent what happened."

"Maybe," I say, but her words only reach my ears and not my heart.

I mean, if I had paid attention to what was going on during those bizarre episodes, couldn't I have put it together, the similar stroke-like symptoms and my need to warn him? Couldn't I have nagged him until he made an appointment with a doctor, who would have run some tests or something and found a clot somewhere, ticking, ready to explode?

I readjust myself on the curb, listening to a mockingbird's call, which will continue all through the night. At least I know now the real reason I tried to distance myself as far away from the psychic arts as possible. But that still doesn't help with my current problem.

"Cal, why don't you tell Mom your theory about my recent visions?"

He hesitates, knowing this is a sensitive subject. "I only said that with all of the recent things that happened to Claire, with her dad's death, and the talk you and she had, maybe she was more open emotionally and that's why she started to have visions, or whatever they are, again. That, in some way, she became more receptive to her clients."

"Well, that makes sense, doesn't it? Once you allow yourself to be open to the universe, it's amazing what it will show and tell you," she says.

My mom bends over to pick up a brown leaf and twirls it between two fingers.

"Let me ask you a question," she says. "How are the visions since I've been here?"

"Honestly, not too bad."

She nods. "I suspected as much. The universe can

be very agreeable when treated right," she says, wiping her palms and brushing bits of leaf to the ground. "I think I've acted kind of like a bodyguard for you this week, like a shield protecting you from what's painful, while you try to figure things out."

"Thank you for that, but what's going to happen when you leave tomorrow?"

40
Rena

The drive to Sedona is amazing.

The landscape keeps changing as we head north. First, it's all cactus and scrubby bushes, and then puny evergreen trees. Finally, after we go around a curve, boom, incredible flat red mountains. Looks like something from another planet. Maybe Mars?

"Boy, it's really beautiful up here," I say.

"You miss New Jersey, Rena? From what I've heard, it's kind of a crappy state." Louis rolls down his window to let in air that smells great, really clean and fresh.

"There's some truth to that," I say, laughing. "Nope, don't miss it, not at all."

He pushes his aviator sunglasses back onto his head and wipes his palm across his forehead. His hands are so . . . manly. They're strong-looking and big, much bigger than what I'd expect on a guy so small. Well, you know what they say about big hands.

"But I know it's hard for Gary, my ex, not to see Steph," I add.

He slips the glasses back down over his eyes. He shifts gears on the Mustang to pass a truck as we climb a hill. In this car, with this guy, I feel cool, like one of those girls in my high school, the ones with the straight, shiny hair whose mothers always sent them to school with cash for whatever they wanted to buy at lunch (not the stale bread with one slice of wrinkled dry salami and brown mustard I got).

"I can sure understand that. Justin and Emily, they're the best part of my marriage to Rachel. It's hard to even think about not seeing them every day. But I feel like I'm fucking suffocating."

I reach over and touch his shoulder. "It's so hard, isn't it? Being a good parent at the same time you're trying to be the person you were meant to be." I read that in *TV Guide* a couple days ago.

"Yeah." He looks over at me. I'm wondering if he thinks the new makeup I'm trying—smoky eyes and pouty lips—is sexy. "That's a really good way to put it. I feel like everything totally changed in the last two years, and not for good. Rachel's constantly bitching at me to make more money, fix stuff around the house, spend more time with the kids. More, more, more. Like I'm not already working eighty hours a week to pay the mortgage on the big house she had to have, the one like her damn cousin's. We never have fun anymore, never do things like this . . . get away for the weekend, see something new, do something different. It's all work, chores, bills, and stupid-ass TV at night."

"I know exactly what you mean. It was the same with me and my ex. I didn't know what to do. But for Steph's sake, I had to make a move. If you and their mom don't love each other anymore, then it's probably better for everyone if you split up."

"You know, you're really easy to talk to," he says.

"Hey, look," I say, pointing to a billboard for a casino in a town called Casa Verde.

"Let's go there. Is Casa Verde very far away?" I ask.

"Not too far," he says, grinning. "A casino, huh? You a gambler, Rena?"

"Fuck yeah, but really small-time. Mostly slots. You?"

"Tell you the truth, I only went once, and that was just for a beer. I didn't even gamble. Rachel's real religious, and she thought it was a sin. I always wanted to go back."

"Then what the hell are we waiting for?" I ask. He takes the next exit.

The casino is a blast. It's on an Indian reservation stuck out in the middle of the desert, with nothing else around it.

We lose at craps but make it up on roulette. Louis lays out the money for the bets, and I tell him I'll pay him back—in trade. He definitely likes that idea. He tries to get me to begin the payment plan immediately, behind the quarter slot machines. I tell him he'll just have to wait. Mostly, we get stupid drunk and have to double up on black coffee at the restaurant there before we can even think about getting back on the road.

"I can't believe how much fun this was," says Louis, blowing over his steaming cup.

"I just knew you were a gambler at heart." I'm sitting as close to him as possible on the booth seat.

"Rena, you're amazing, you know that?" he says. He leans over to kiss me. "I can't remember the last time Rachel and I did anything on the spur of the moment like this."

"Oh, just wait until you see the next fun thing I have planned," I say, squeezing his crotch under the table. "And I'm really, really curious about the other things Rachel thinks are sins."

———

When Louis and me finally get to Sedona, it's early in the afternoon. We stop at the visitor's center for some trail maps and take a couple of short hikes. Then we go for ice cream on the main road in town. As far as I can tell, most of the shops here are jewelry, western clothing, or junky souvenir stores. There are some art places with huge paintings of Indians doing all kinds of weird dance moves. Not exactly my taste.

Desert Dessert and Café is a small place with an old-fashioned counter. There are a few booths covered in red vinyl. It even has a tall jar filled with straws on the counter and a jukebox that takes quarters on each table. Very fifties-looking.

Louis and me sit on the counter stools, and I can see his face in the big mirror across from us. He's such a cutie pie.

"Good hiking," he says.

"Yeah, the best." I don't tell him this much walking in one afternoon is more than I've done in all of the past year. Or mention that my bad knee is fucking killing me. I reach into my back pocket and get the two Advil I put there before we started up the first trail. I swallow them with a drink from my water bottle.

"You okay?"

"Sure," I say. "Vitamin C. I need to make sure I

THE PERFECT FRAUD • 317

don't get sick. For Stephanie's sake. With her condition, we can't afford any germs."

He gets a sundae, hot fudge on the side. I have a root beer float with chocolate-chip ice cream.

When we finish, he takes out his billfold, which I can tell is leather. It looks soft and expensive. Then he peels off a hundred to give the clerk, and I notice there are a lot more hundreds behind that one. He must be really good at his job.

Turns out I'm not wrong. At dinner I ask Louis about his work.

"Well, I used to be an accountant, but I decided to change professions."

"Oh yeah? What do you do now?"

He holds two fingers up, letting the waitress know to bring more beer, and then bends toward me and says, "If I told you, I'd have to kill you."

I giggle and ask, "What is it? Something undercover? A spy? Assassin?"

He sits back. "Nah, nothing that exciting. I'm working for a company now where my accounting skills are put to really good use. Mostly, I make investments."

"Investments?"

"Yeah, big-time. I help people with lots of money make lots more of it," he says.

"Well, congrats to you," I say, tipping my beer glass against his. It's my third drink after the margarita we had before dinner. I'm starting to feel loopy.

"I guess. There's one problem, though. They want to move me to California."

"That's a problem? I never been, but I hear California is like the dream place to live."

"Except it will be so far away from Justin and Emily."

"Who?"

"My kids, Justin and Emily. I don't know how often I'd get to see them."

"You're right. That would be tough. When would you have to go?"

"Not for a while."

"Oh, good. Would you live near the ocean?"

I'm sure it's the booze. But I can't help where my mind is going. Louis and me in California. We're living in one of those adorable pink bungalows a block from the ocean. No, maybe right on the ocean. Our place is all white—white walls and couches, with blankets in sea colors spread over them and framed pictures of flowers on the walls. We light candles every night and snuggle under one of the blankets in front of a stone fireplace. Just the two of us.

"Rena? Rena?"

"What? Sorry, you say something?"

"I asked if you want to call Stephanie after dinner, maybe check on her?"

"That's a great idea. Wait, what time is it? No, better not. She's probably asleep by now, and any time I can let my baby get some rest, I don't mess with that."

"You're a great mom, you know that?" he says, helping me from the chair and leading me to the car.

It's an un-fucking-believable room. Louis told me he got it using credit card points because of all the travel he has to do. He said sometimes he even has to go to South America because his company has clients there.

The bed is a king, and it's across from a huge picture window. There's a full moon, and if you listen real good, you can even hear the creek below. I don't want this weekend to ever end.

I turn out the lights and he moves toward me. He pulls my shirt over my head and unzips my jeans. I think how right I was not to buy a nightgown. I push him back onto the bed, which is like layers and layers of the softest feathers in the world. I keep bringing him to the point of explosion and then making him back off. Finally, I know he can't take it anymore, and I pull him inside me. When it's over and we're lying there in the light from the moon, all I can think about is that house by the ocean, decorated all in white, with just Louis and me and the fireplace and the candles.

I hardly remember I'm not on the pill and that I didn't think to ask Louis whether he brought any condoms.

41
Claire

The next morning, we all wake up early to enjoy breakfast together before Cal needs to take my mother to the airport.

"Sleep okay?" Mom asks, squeezing lemon into her tea.

"Not really," I say, yawning so wide, my eyes tear up. "Truthfully, I'm a little scared to go back to work today."

"I guess I can understand that," she says.

"All those images, the issues, and the secrets, they go straight through me. I feel like a human sieve."

"Maybe you won't even have the same experiences. You've been gone a week. Maybe it's all, I don't know, out of your system," Cal says, retrieving a slightly burnt bagel from the toaster oven.

I flip around to glare at him. "It's not like I had the stomach flu or temporary insanity, Cal. I'm pretty sure it hasn't gone away."

He holds up his hands in defense and says, "Fine, fine. Well, maybe you can filter these things a little. You know, protect yourself." He's slathering the bagel with butter and jelly, a combination that always horrifies me. He leans against the counter and takes huge bites. "Is that even possible?" he asks through a filled mouth, directing his question to my mom.

"I wish," I say. I reach to break off a yellow leaf from the potted philodendron on the table, the only type of houseplant with a minuscule chance of living under my care.

"It's a hard thing to do, trying to filter what comes through," my mother replies.

"But it's possible?" asks Cal.

She takes a deep breath, turns toward me, and says, "There is something you could try."

"Like what?" I ask, not surprised to hear desperation in my voice.

"You could try refusing to participate," she says.

"Refusing to participate? What, like unsubscribing, or removing her name from a list?" Cal asks, laughing.

"Kind of like that," says Mom. "That's what I did when I was pregnant with Claire."

"When you were pregnant? Why?" asks Cal.

"Maybe it was all the baby hormones, but my readings became increasingly more powerful during that time."

"Powerful? How do you mean?" I ask.

"The visions were much more vivid. I'm not sure how to explain this, but it was like they were painted in thick oils, where before the pregnancy, I would see things in light watercolors. Does that make sense?"

"I guess I can understand that," I say, remembering how physically and emotionally shaken the visions had left me.

"It got more and more difficult. Each reading would leave me exhausted, but I figured it was because I was pregnant. I was early into my second trimester, and you had just started to move." She smiles at the memory. "One day, a woman came into the shop for a reading. She said she was worried about her daughter, Georgia, who was in the ninth grade and not doing at all well. She was flunking almost all her classes, and the mom suspected she was hanging with the wrong crowd. I set out her cards, which did confirm a bad influence around Georgia, but then, all of a sudden, I had this vision. It was so painful."

"Painful? What do you mean, painful?" Cal asks.

"Like pain. Real pain running from one side of

my head to the other. It felt like my skull was about to break in half. A second after that, I saw her daughter. She was engulfed in these flames. I could see her sitting in a classroom, dressed in a pale blue sweater, jeans, and high-top sneakers—every detail was crystal clear—and she was surrounded by this yellow-and-orange fire." My mom's face drains of color.

"Oh, Mom, that's terrible," I say, standing to get her a glass of water.

"Not only was the vision horrible, but bizarrely, in addition to the pain in my head, I also started to have other weird physical reactions."

"What do you mean?" Cal asks. I put the water down near her hand, which I notice is shaking.

"My skin actually felt like it was burning," she says, gulping the water and then setting the glass down carefully. "I touched my arm and it was cool, but I still felt like it was pressed against a hot toaster. I couldn't breathe. It felt like my throat was closing. My eyes were watering so much I could barely see the client, who, of course, had no idea what was going on."

"What did you say to her?" I ask.

"I hardly remember now. I think I told her I was having a very bad allergy attack and I would have to cut the session short. I wouldn't take her money. As she was leaving, I felt I had to tell her that, yes, her daughter was surrounded by a negative influence, but also that Georgia should be very careful around fire. The woman started to ask for more information, and I'm sure I seemed rude, but I basically shut the door in her face, locked it, and ran into a cold shower."

"Did that help?" I ask.

"That, and letting some time pass. I finally calmed down, but you . . ." She taps my arm with her finger. "You did not. You were rolling around in my stomach as if the whole experience had seriously agitated you. I tried everything—chamomile tea, a warm bath, meditation—but nothing seemed to help. Finally, your dad came home, and after I told him what happened, he began talking softly to me and to you while massaging my shoulders. It was as if you finally felt safe, because you stopped racing back and forth."

"That sounds like Dad. He had a way of always making things right."

"I went to sleep and was prepared to start seeing clients again. But the next morning on the news, there was a report that a local girl had died in a house fire that apparently started because of faulty wiring in the family's basement."

"Oh no. Was it Georgia?" Cal asks.

"When the reporter announced her name, I fell apart. That poor girl and her family. Then, I know it was selfish, but I thought, *I just can't put myself—and my baby—through something like that again.* I couldn't chance it. What if, during my sessions with clients, I saw more horrible visions? What if something I experienced during these sessions crossed through the placenta to Claire and somehow harmed her?" Mom touches my hand and says, "That's when I decided to close up the shop until you were safely delivered."

"Were you better then?" Cal asks, starting to clear the table. I knew it was getting close to the time he and my mom needed to leave, but I couldn't let her go yet.

"Yes and no. I wasn't seeing clients, but every time I went out of the house, even just to take the dog for a walk, if I was near a person, I would pick up a vision of some sort and have that terrible pain in my head. I needed to figure out a better way to protect both of us."

"Sounds like what happened to you, Claire," says Cal.

"What did you do?" I ask. "Decide not to have any more visions and they went away?" I'm thinking, hoping, maybe it was just that simple.

"No, but that was a part of it. I figured if I could identify what was happening in my body and mind when a vision started, then perhaps I could stop it before it took hold."

"How? Did it work? What did you do?" asks Cal.

"It was a lot of trial and error at first, and it wasn't

easy. I had to figure out the triggers I would get when a vision would start. Then, once I did that, I developed methods of dealing with the visions. Like, I would repeat statements to myself."

"Statements?" I ask.

"You know, like mini mantras. I'd say things like 'No thank you,' or 'I prefer not to help,' or 'Please find somebody else to visit.'"

"That worked?" I asked, not fully convinced.

"Most of the time. I also trained my mind to substitute a blank slate of color to fill my head. Essentially, block out the vision. Usually, I chose a deep blue, or sometimes burgundy. It took weeks and weeks of practice, and until I got the hang of it, visions kept slipping through. Like one time the mailman came to our door with a package I had to sign for. I saw a crack running down one of his arms, and I couldn't help myself. I felt I had to tell him he should be very careful, that something might happen to his left arm."

"Did he listen to you?" asks Cal, placing the butter back in the refrigerator.

"He pretty much blew me off. I don't think he believed in the whole psychic thing. But on Monday he delivered our mail with his left arm in a cast and sling. He told me he'd broken it in a beach volleyball game. He kept asking me over and over how I'd known."

"What did you say?" I ask.

"I said it was just a lucky guess. He told me I shouldn't be fooling around with witchcraft and left. After that, he never said another word to me when he brought our mail."

I laugh. "Yeah, I'm guessing you spooked him. But you were able to stop the visions, right?"

I pass Cal the sugar bowl and pointedly ignore his hand motions signaling they have to get going.

Mom looks down into her lap for some time before she says, "Pretty much, but emotionally, it wasn't easy for me. I knew that, at least during the pregnancy, I was not going to take any chances. Still, I felt incredibly guilty."

"Guilty, why?" asks Cal, tapping his foot and then leaping up to grab the sponge and sweep it across the table. Subtle, he's not.

"Like, when I was still having breakthrough visions, I noticed the guy from the electric company who read our meter monthly had what looked like a red outline of a heart sort of shimmering on his uniform jacket. I saw a jagged tear running through the heart. He probably had heart disease or maybe was about to have a heart attack or something, but I knew if I told him, like with the mailman, he would think I was evil or, at least, crazy. I also knew receiving and passing on even one vision would likely open my mind up to more and more visions coming in. I couldn't take the chance of anything happening to Claire."

"But why did you feel guilty?" I ask, standing, giving in to Cal's edginess to leave.

"I knew I was sent the visions for a reason, that not everyone was chosen to do this, to have this talent. On some level, I felt I had a responsibility to share what I saw."

Getting up from the table, she says, "So, honey, I guess you have a decision to make. Now that you know it may be possible to block your visions, you need to figure out whether that's actually what you want to do."

42

Rena

I wake up at the sound of the hotel door opening and closing. Louis hands me a steaming cup.

"Hey, thanks," I say, taking a sip of what has to be the best damn caffe latte I ever had.

"It's beautiful out. Want to take one more hike before we start back?"

"Sure. But there's something else I want to do too, if it's okay."

"What's that?"

"A psychic."

He opens the curtains with a whoosh. The glare of the sun makes me squint.

"You're shitting me, right?"

With the sheet wrapped around me, I walk to the bathroom. I feel stupid because, come on, the guy's already seen more of me than anyone else has in a really long time. But what looks (or feels) good under the covers in the dark can lose a whole lot of appeal in the daylight.

"No, why? You don't believe in them?" I ask. I leave the door a little open so I can hear his answer. It sounds like he says, "That will make us late getting in," so I say, "It shouldn't make us too late. It's fine if I can't, but I'm guessing it won't take more than an hour."

Louis stands outside the bathroom door. I like that he's a gentleman. Another thing that definitely kills the romance the next day is watching someone take a piss.

"I'm not worried about the time. What I said was 'They all work for Satan.'"

I flush and come out. He's sitting on the edge of the bed, looking at his fingernails.

"Maybe that's exactly why I want to go," I say, standing in front of him. I bend down so my face is nose to nose with his and whisper, "Maybe I work for the devil, and the way he communicates with me is through a psychic."

He pulls me onto the bed, laughing.

"Funny, very funny, and maybe a little bit true," he says, nibbling my earlobe. Him and me have a repeat performance of last night's show, complete with intermission and an amazing second act.

After a short hike, Louis drops me off at Mystical Haven. He says he saw a sports bar nearby where he can watch the World Series.

"Hi, I'm Rena," I tell the woman at the counter. She's wearing this scarf that's wrapped around her hair and piled at least a half foot above her forehead. I can't help staring at it. I keep thinking maybe there's a bird stuck in there somewhere.

"Namaste, and welcome to Mystical Haven," she says and gives a small bow.

"Yeah, hi. I met a woman named Claire a while ago, and she said if I was ever in Sedona to make sure to come see her for a reading. See, here's her information," I say, showing the woman the piece of paper.

"Claire's wonderful, isn't she?"

I nod. "Is she here? Can she take me now, do you think?"

"She's been extremely busy, especially recently, but let me check."

She walks through a curtain that, I'm guessing, leads to where all the psychics do their shit. I wander around the store. It's filled with Buddhas of all sizes. Most are sitting, cross-legged, with their hands in their laps. There's a big one, probably three feet tall, that has one palm facing out. I feel like I should return the high five. A lot of them are inside a flower of some kind. The ones I like best are the fatties who have these huge smiles and their arms are spread wide open, like everything in the world is fucking great. Kind of like how I feel right now. I walk back to the cash register, where there's a display of necklaces made of leather strips. They have small silver pendants shaped like symbols attached. I'm trying to figure out what the different symbols mean when the woman comes back.

"Claire said she can see you now."

Since I've never been to a psychic before, I don't know what to expect. I guess I thought there would be these big stuffed pillows on the floor and some fabric draped from the ceiling. Like a harem I once saw in an old black-and-white movie.

But it's just a small space with a table and two chairs and some books on the wall shelves. The only thing giving it a psychic vibe at all is the incense stick burning. It's stuck into a hole at the edge of a carved wooden base. An ash about two inches long drops into the base as I sit down.

Claire's the same as I remember, with light red hair and those green eyes.

"Hi. Remember me? Rena? I was with my little girl, Stephanie, on the flight from Philadelphia to Phoenix. Let's see, it was back a bit, maybe like—"

"Yes, Rena," she interrupts. "I remember you."

"Oh, good. Well, I wanted to come see you. You know, for a reading. I'm in town with my boyfriend. We've been hiking. And to the casino. It's sure beautiful up here." I know I need to stop talking, but I can't. When a person stares at you without blinking, it's hard not to feel kind of nervous.

She shakes her head, like those horses at the farm my mom took my sister and me to. Like she's got flies on her and is trying to get them to stop landing. And she's so pale. She's got a redhead's skin, but it's even whiter than I remember.

"Hey, you feeling okay? You look sort of—"

"No, I'm fine. Let's start," Claire says. She reaches for a deck of cards from behind her, shuffles them, and sets out three on the table in front of me.

I find Louis in the bar. He's leaning over a beer glass, looking depressed.

"They're losing," he mutters. "Why don't they replace the pitcher, for Christ's sake. Such a royal fuckup." Not his first beer, I'm thinking.

"Aw, that's too bad. But, look, I got you something." I pull the necklace out of my pocket.

Louis waits for the commercial before he turns to me and says, "Hey, you didn't have to do that." He fingers the leather string and the silver amulet and then hangs it around his neck.

"It's the evil eye, supposed to ward off bad things," I say, kissing him on the cheek and signaling for a beer.

"Well, I could use that right about now," he says.

"Bad game?"

"Yeah, that and I just got a call from my boss. They want me to move to California sooner than I thought."

It feels like somebody reached into my chest and grabbed my heart and squeezed really hard.

"Why? When?" I can't help it, I can feel the tears starting.

"One of the investments I handle just crapped out big-time. And I'm not sure exactly when, but real soon."

"One of your investments? You need money?"

"Yeah, that would help, but sources have pretty much dried up here in Arizona."

"Well, maybe you could invest for me." I'm trying to come up with anything to keep him from leaving. Shit, we just got together.

He looks up from his glass.

"You've got cash to invest, Rena?"

"Not yet, but I will."

He looks disappointed, takes a big gulp of his beer and starts to watch the ball game again, so I say, "I'm expecting a lot of money pretty soon. Stephanie's birth was really complicated, really hard, and they think that may be one of the reasons her stomach's so messed up. The lawyer says we'll get at least two million dollars from the hospital. Of course, I'll need to split that with Gary, but still . . ."

On the drive back, I tell Louis about the reading.

"It was amazing. She said I'm going to travel. Somewhere near water, probably the ocean."

"How does she know that? I think they just make shit up," he says, turning on his headlights.

"How the hell do I know? She put these three cards out on the table and then told me what each one meant."

"Yeah, the same things she told every sucker before and after you. It's a bunch of crap, Rena, like I said."

"No," I say, rubbing his arm and then moving down to push my palm against his inner thigh. "What you said was that it was the work of the devil."

"And it is. I say stay the fuck away from those people. They take your money and tell you whatever the hell you want to hear."

"Well, that part's right anyway. She told me there was a new man in my life. Someone who can make all my dreams come true."

He turns to me, smiling.

"Okay, so maybe she's not that far off." He pushes a

button. The roof of the car slides back, and I can see all the stars. I wrap my sweatshirt around me and lean my head against the leather seat. "So tell me more about this settlement you're expecting," he says.

"The what?"

"The hospital settlement you mentioned in the bar? I'm guessing it's for malpractice? Like you get money for pain and suffering, some shit like that?"

"Uh, yeah, something like that. It's been tied up in court for a while now."

"But it'll be, what did you say? About two million?" he asks.

"Yeah, maybe even a little more. Our lawyer's a real shark."

He smiles, squeezes my knee, and says, "I can definitely help you invest that. So maybe when you get home, give your lawyer a call and see what's happening?"

"Okay, sure. I'll do that. And guess what else? The psychic said she's coming to Phoenix to do a group reading real soon. She said she'd let me know when so I can sign up."

My phone buzzes. It's Susan again. It's, like, the tenth fucking call since this morning. We'll be there in another hour, so I don't call back.

43
Claire

After teary goodbyes and *talk soons*, Cal leaves with my mom for the airport, and I have fifteen minutes before I need to go to work. I make myself another cup of tea and sit down at the kitchen table to think.

Do I honestly believe I have a responsibility to relay psychic messages? A responsibility to whom? To the person? To the universe? Sometimes the messages can be so random that it feels like tossing darts at a board where the center circle keeps moving. Psychic reading isn't an exact science or, as many would argue, a science at all. Maybe Cal's right and my emotions just took over, maybe I had a run of fantastic luck and made some really, really good guesses.

I am not my mother. She's the real thing. The images, feelings, and interpretations I'm now receiving? Can I honestly support these as a credible foundation for giving information that people, my clients, will take seriously and possibly act upon?

The answer comes to me quickly. A resounding *NO*.

I am not willing to take on the burden of delivering such possibly bogus messages.

Washing my cup and spoon at the sink, I reflect back on Mom's vision-prevention methods and think— and hope—I can make them work for me.

It's time to go to the store and test this. I grab my purse and head out the door.

Success!

My first client of the day is Sophia. She's on a waiting list to adopt. After years of tests, treatments, and the heartbreak of infertility, she wants to know if and when it will happen. As I lay out her cards, a vision begins to sneak into my brain, and quickly, I shut my eyes and say loudly, but silently, to myself, "No, thank you. I prefer not to help." The image begins to fade, eventually turns to smoke and disappears. I tell Sophia about her cards, that the Page of Cups and the Page of Swords both have a connection to babies and that the Sun is the card of joy. Her face lights up, and she thanks me profusely, having drawn her own conclusions that a baby could be waiting on her doorstep when she returns home. I didn't lie. I did give her the common interpretation of those cards, but since I thwarted the vision that threatened to break through, I didn't have anything to add. For all I know, her cat could be having a litter of kittens and this will be the prognosticated future joyful experience, because—well, everyone likes kittens. Seems like I'm back to doing things the way I used to.

What a relief. I can feel my mental and emotional stability returning, that the ground has become solid and I am finally, once again, in control of my thoughts.

Mindi peeks inside my curtain and says, "I had a call from your eleven o'clock. Tooth abscess and needs to cancel."

I'm about to say, "Great, I could use the time to . . . ," when she continues, "but there's a woman who just walked in who would like to sit with you—right now, if you can. Rena, I think she said her name was. Says she knows you."

"Rena?"

"That's what she said."

Of course, I know her, the woman who talked nonstop on the plane and who left me to look after her kid while she went to the bathroom. My body starts to buzz, like there's a low-level current doing flips up and down my spine.

"Claire?" I'm surprised to look up and find Mindi

still standing there. "Can you see her? Um, maybe not. You're looking kind of sick. You all right?"

"Sure, yes. I'm fine. Give me a minute? And then . . . bring her back."

After Mindi leaves, I put my arms on the table and lay my head on top of them. I'm not sure what's happening except that whatever control I thought I had just minutes ago has been obliterated. Unsuccessfully, I try to modulate my breathing. It's as if my body has forgotten the pattern of in-and-out breaths and instead they come and go in a random and syncopated rhythm. I whisper over and over, "No, thank you. Please find someone else. I don't want to see or report any messages. Please, not me," while simultaneously trying to paint different colors inside my brain. I first pull in a bold red but find it only increases the tension in the clenched muscles along my back and up my neck. I try a deep purple and think I have it locked in when all I can see inside my head is purple, but it begins to dissolve until eventually it looks like weak grape juice circling a drain and then disappears. I'm about to try a tie-dyed version, thinking maybe the psychedelic pattern and colors will allow me to fixate and hold on to its inherent complexity, when Mindi returns, pulls back the drape, and says, "Claire, here's Rena." My hands are shaking so much I need to sit on them to make them stop.

She's pretty much as I remember her, except she's lost a little bit of weight, her hair looks better, and she's wearing lots more makeup. Her eyes are rimmed so heavily in black she resembles a rabid raccoon, and her lipstick is an intense fuchsia, some of which has smeared across her left incisor.

"Hi. Remember me? Rena? I was with my little girl, Stephanie, on the flight from Philadelphia to Phoenix. Let's see, it was back a bit, maybe like—"

Taking a gulp around the saliva accumulating in my mouth, I manage to choke out, "Yes, I remember you."

"So, how does this shit work?"

I shuffle the deck I used for Sophia. Normally, I'd have Rena shuffle but I'm doing anything I can to speed things along.

"Here. Cut the deck, please."

"Okay," she says.

I lay out her three cards.

The Six of Cups–reversed.

The Nine of Wands–reversed.

The Six of Swords.

My hands are sweating, and I rub my palms against my thighs before I speak.

I touch the Six of Cups card. In an upright position, this card indicates the client does or is about to spend a lot of time with a child. But in a reversed, or upside-down position, this card can mean a child is in trouble and in need of support. Suddenly, it's like a TV set has been turned on behind my eyes. The picture is fuzzy, but I can still make it out.

Squeezing the sides of my head with my hands, I attempt to block the vision: Rena's child on that plane. Those haunted eyes with the bags underneath them. How fragile she was, how skittish. Like a rabbit in a trap.

"How's . . . how's your daughter? What was her name again?" I sputter.

Rena pauses and then answers. "Stephanie. Her name is Stephanie, and she's good. Why? Is there something about her in that card?" She looks closely at the Six of Cups, seems to consider the pictures (a garden, a sweet-faced person handing a bouquet of flowers to a child), and then sighs and says, "Actually, not great. She was in the hospital again last week. I'm not sure what else to do." She hangs her head and sniffs.

"Yes, I can see that because, uh, this card, when it's reversed, means a child may be in trouble."

Another vision flashes, and there's pulsating behind my eyeballs: Rena standing above Stephanie. All I can see is Rena's back as she leans over the little girl. Rena's got something in her hands, but I can't make out what it is. Then it all fades away.

I grasp again for a color to blanket my brain. At the same time, I'm frantically mumbling, "No, thank you. Go away, please. Get someone else." I think my voice is only in my head until Rena says, "What? I didn't hear what you said."

"Oh, sorry. Nothing. I was just considering your second card, the Nine of Wands." I point to it and say, "This card usually means you've gone through some kind of battle and won. You're worn-out but resilient."

"Right. That makes sense. All this hospital and doctor crap has been nothing but one big fight."

"I'm sure that's true," I say. "But, see, this card is also reversed." I don't know how to phrase my next question to her as the Nine of Wands, when upside down, can indicate the client might have psychological issues. Another image strikes behind my eyes, sharp as a lancet. I see Rena's face, but it's not actually hers. It's more of a mask, a dark cover with holes cut out for eyes and a nose, but not for the mouth. What is she not telling me? What is she hiding?

"Yeah, so?" she asks.

"So, Rena . . . How are *you* doing with all the medical issues?" I say, placing emphasis on the word *you*.

Rena gives out a long exhalation that ends with "Shit." She says, "I'm so tired, I can't hardly stand it. You never get a break. This weekend, here in Sedona, with my boyfriend . . . it's the first time I've been away in years. You need to be separated from your kid once in a while, for your own sanity, you know?" She fingers the card and asks, "Why? Is that what this card says?"

"In a way," I say, choosing my words. I can practically feel the nerve endings pinballing back and forth in my head. My only hope is that all the frenetic neuron activity, combined with my failed attempts to shove the images away, has seriously scuttled my abilities to even get close to reading these cards accurately. I'm basically hoping everything I've seen, on the table and inside my brain, is completely wrong.

All I can think about is finishing the reading and getting Rena away from me and out of the store as quickly as possible.

The best response I can manage is "Yes, this card shows you're under considerable stress in your current situation."

"No shit," she says, flicking off a long ash of the incense stick burning in the holder. Instead of dropping into the base below, the ash blows across my table. I brush it away with my palm and continue.

"Finally, this card, the Six of Swords—"

"Well, at least that one's facing the right direction," Rena says, chuckling.

"Yes. This card usually means a move away from something, maybe a trip by or to water?"

She gasps and puts her hand over her open mouth. "Oh my God, that's fucking fantastic. I was talking to Louis—he's my boyfriend—about moving to California. He's getting a big-time promotion there. We want to get a place by the ocean."

I'm about to tell her that another interpretation of the Six of Swords is that there will be a transition as a result of a decision made, and to get clarity, she might need to let something go. At that moment a picture of Stephanie blazes through my brain and I can't tell whether it's a vision or a true recollection. It's her hugging that stuffed toy and waving goodbye to me (perhaps at the airport?). I know then that it's not a thing Rena might be off-loading. It's her daughter.

My mouth begins to fill with saliva. Except it's not normal saliva. It's salty and briny-tasting. I swallow, but it keeps coming back, and then I remember: it's the exact same reaction I had after I sat next to Rena and Stephanie on the flight from Philly to Phoenix.

It won't stop. Every time I swallow, my mouth fills again. In between gulps, I tell Rena there's nothing more I can see from the cards and that our time's up.

She looks at her watch and says, "But it's only been

forty minutes. I thought this was supposed to last an hour."

I swallow again and stand to lead her to the front. "I'll ask Mindi to give you a ten percent discount on any purchase you make today."

"Fine, I guess," she mutters, as she walks to the cash register and starts to look at some of the leather necklaces hanging there.

Racing to the bathroom, I throw up in the sink, big rushes of salty water. I keep the faucet running so, hopefully, I can't be heard. After three more times of vomiting liquid, the extra saliva finally starts to dissipate. I turn off the faucet and run back, just in time to see Rena opening the door to leave.

"Wait, Rena. I wanted to get your email or phone number or whatever. I'll be doing a group reading in Phoenix very soon and thought you might want to attend." Taking a piece of paper and a pen from the counter, I hand them to her. She stares at me for a beat but then writes down her contact information.

44

Rena

Susan is royally pissed.

She's standing in the doorway with her hand on her hip. Stephanie and the trash bag with her things are next to her. I ask Louis to wait in the car.

I get within three feet of her and she spits out, "I cannot believe you are this late. I thought you said you'd be here to pick up Stephanie this morning, and here it is . . ." She looks at her watch. ". . . past nine o'clock. On a school night. I couldn't get Felicia to sleep because Stephanie is still here, and frankly, your little girl is exhausted from staying up and waiting for you."

Stephanie is standing close to Susan, holding a piece of her robe in her hand.

"Okay, okay, I'm sorry. I didn't realize it was so late.

We hit a bunch of traffic. And a terrible accident on the way down." I'm almost out of lies, and still, Susan's face is like a damn igloo.

She looks down at Stephanie and says, "Honey, why don't you go up and see whether Felicia is all ready for bed, okay? Maybe you and she can read a book together under the covers?"

My daughter runs up the stairs. Susan still hasn't asked me to come into the house.

"What I can't understand is why you didn't return any of my calls," she says through her teeth. "What if something had been wrong with your daughter?"

"Why—was there something going on with Stephanie?"

I guess this isn't exactly the right thing to say, because Susan gets very red in the face and snaps at me, "She's your child, Rena. Seriously, I'm shocked you didn't at least want to check on her, even once, during the time you were gone. Especially since she was just in the hospital."

I'm about fed up with this holier-than-thou shit.

"You know what? Maybe you should mind your own fucking business," I shout. I see a porch light go on at the neighbor's house to the right, which is pretty surprising since the houses here are so far apart. How can they possibly hear what's going on? I guess nosiness is common in this part of town. I look back at Louis's car. I'm glad to see his windows are still closed up.

I can tell Susan is trying really hard to control herself. She's taking deep breaths and opening and shutting her fingers.

"You're right. It is none of my business, Rena. I'll tell you this, though, Stephanie seems troubled. She cried in her sleep both nights. And then this morning, when I was packing up her things to go home, she started crying again and telling me she didn't want to leave. She said she wanted to stay with us."

"I'm sure she did. It's like a goddamn palace here," I say. "She doesn't have all kinds of cool toys at home like I'm sure your precious Felicia does." Louis honks, rolls down the window, shouts at me we have to get going, and then rolls the window back up.

Susan sighs like she's so annoyed with me she can't stand having my face in front of her for even another second.

"It's not that. It's not the toys or our house. It's . . . it's how she jumped the first few times I tried to touch her. Eventually, she let me hug her, but I could still feel her shaking. And the food thing. She was begging to try Felicia's waffles. Finally, I gave her some. Just a little. And she was fine. No stomach upset. Not even nausea. I kept asking her, and she kept saying no, that the waffles were so yummy and could she have them again at lunch?" She stares at me and then says, "I can't help feeling something is not right."

I poke my head around her and yell, "Stephanie, let's go. Right now." She shuffles slowly out of Felicia's room and looks down at me from the second-floor railing.

"I said, right now."

She makes her way down the steps, stopping on each for a few seconds, until she finally reaches Susan. Susan puts a hand on Stephanie's shoulder, and my daughter leans into her, hiding her face in the fluffy, white robe.

Susan says, "It's okay. Your mommy's here for you now." She bends down to hug her. Handing me the trash bag, Susan says, "I take the care of children very seriously, Rena. I want you to know that." She shuts the door. Bitch.

I grab Stephanie by the hand and walk her to the car.

After I buckle her into the back seat, I say, "Louis, this is my daughter, Stephanie."

He turns around in his seat and says, "Hi, Stephanie. Did you have a good time at your sleepover?"

She doesn't say anything, just stares out the window.

"Stephanie, sweetie, please answer Louis's question."

"That's okay. My kids were really shy at that age too."

Stephanie sticks her thumb in her mouth, something she hasn't done since she was a year old.

I tell Louis he can drop us off at the drugstore. He offers to take us to my place but I really don't want him to see where I live and I can tell he wants to get home. When we get to the drugstore, Louis lifts my suitcase from the trunk.

I kneel down next to Stephanie and give her a big hug.

"Mommy missed you so much. I hated being away from you. Did you have fun playing with Felicia? She has a lot of neat toys, doesn't she?" I reach up and gently remove her thumb from her mouth, but she immediately pops it back in.

"Poor little thing. She looks pooped," Louis says.

"Yeah, it's way past nighty night, isn't it, Stephie? We should get you ready for bed. I'll read you your favorite story, the one with the unicorns, okay?"

Stephanie just stands there, sucking her thumb, with this dumb look on her face.

"Tell Louis bye, okay?"

She whispers, "Bye."

I give him a big kiss on the lips and say, "Thanks for an awesome time."

Once he gets in the car and drives away, I take Stephanie's hand and pull her down the block, rolling the suitcase behind us.

When we get to our place, there's a note taped to the door.

See me right away.
There's a message for you.
Graciella Lupito

Jesus Christ. Whatever that bitch has to tell me will just have to wait until tomorrow. Tonight, I have other things to deal with.

"Stephanie, into the house. Now."

45
Claire

As the door closes behind Rena, my knees are so rubbery I grab one of the merchandise shelves for support. I'm shaking, and all the Buddhas begin to jiggle and dance across the surface.

Mindi comes to me and says, "Claire, what is it? Did she say something to upset you?" She takes me by the hand, as if I'm a lost child in a department store, and gently pushes me onto the stool by the register.

Walking to the front door and flipping the sign to CLOSED. PLEASE COME BACK TOMORROW, she asks, "What's with that client anyway? I picked up a weird energy from her when she was buying one of the necklaces."

"A weird energy?" Now I have chills and everything

around me feels muffled and slow. It's as if I'm hearing Mindi's voice through layers of ice cream.

"Claire?" Suddenly, everything clears, and I jump because she's yelling my name.

"What? Why are you yelling? Stop yelling. It's making my head hurt," I say, rubbing my temples, which are throbbing rhythmically.

"Listen, I'm driving you home, and then I'll come back and take your final two clients of the day. You need to rest. In fact, maybe you need to take another week off." I wave my hands at her and start to tell her no, but she says, "Not a request. You are taking more time off."

I'm huddled in the corner of the couch with the lights off when Cal opens the door, carrying his textbooks.

"How was class?" I ask.

He slams his hand on the side of the wall and lunges for the umbrella in the bucket by the door.

"Geez, Claire, nice way to give a guy a heart attack. And why are you sitting in the dark?"

"It's been a strange day. Sorry I scared you," I say.

"What happened?" he asks. Walking through the room, he turns on the light on the side table and the standing pole lamp, which splay pools of yellow on the rug. Throwing the couch pillows to the floor, he sits next to me.

I say, "I didn't tell you something before because, frankly, I didn't even remember it again until today."

"What's wrong? Something at work?"

"Hang on. I need to explain what happened before, because I think there's a connection to today, but I have no idea what to make of it."

"Sounds confusing . . . and intriguing."

"On the flight back to Phoenix after Dad died, there was a woman who sat in my row with her daughter. There was something off about both of them, but I didn't know what it was. Besides, I was a mess then with my own stuff, not exactly thinking straight."

Cal nods but remains silent, and I can imagine him as the psychologist he'll one day be. Patient and gentle. Someone easy to talk to.

"Her kid, Stephanie, seemed so . . . I don't know . . . lost. It's hard to explain, but I could sense even through my own misery that she was in pain."

"How old and what kind of pain?"

Stephanie's face comes back to me then. That pinched look, like she was on high alert, watchful and nervous.

"I don't know. She was so little. I think she told me four, but she was definitely a small four. It was like she was burdened somehow, like she had more stress on her than any kid should. The mom told me her little girl was sick and that they were going to Phoenix to see a new doctor." I shook my head. "But it's what happened after the plane landed that freaked me out." I swing my legs over his lap.

Cal rubs his hand up and down my calf. "What was that?"

I tell him about the salty water that kept filling my mouth and that I had to run to the ladies' room to keep spitting it out until it finally stopped.

"What? That's crazy," says Cal, and I make a mental note to remind him not to use that particular word with future patients.

"Today, this same woman, Rena, comes to the store for a reading. I gave her my information on the plane, and one of my clients happened to cancel so I had time to see her."

"How was the reading?"

"Very strange. On the plane, she wanted to know all about medical intuitives, a psychic who could evaluate Stephanie's condition, but you know what? She didn't even bring Stephanie with her today and never asked me one question about her illness in the reading. I was the one to bring it up."

Unwinding himself, Cal walks to the kitchen and returns with two cold beers, caps off.

I take a long swallow. It's refreshing, and I can feel the tension in parts of my body start to loosen.

Sitting back down, Cal takes a swig and asks, "So, what's the problem? This weird woman comes to see you but doesn't ask you about her child?"

I vividly remember Rena's cards and can still feel the absoluteness of the conclusions I made in the reading.

It's too awful to say, but I do anyway. "Cal, I think Rena is hurting Stephanie."

"What? That's a pretty strong accusation."

"I realize that, but the cards—"

"You're saying the cards told you this?" He raises his eyebrows.

"But—" I start.

"Oz, I know you've recently had some amazing readings, in and out of the store, but now you're getting into dangerous territory here."

"But, the cards were so . . . definitive. Except it wasn't just that. I had visions too, bizarre but very clear visions."

"Of what?" Cal asks, taking another sip of beer.

The image of Rena standing above and over her tiny daughter flashes back and again, the sense of malevolence strikes me violently. My head feels like I pounded it against concrete, and there's a cramp in my stomach that causes me to double over in pain. The same salty liquid fills my mouth, and I have to keep swallowing.

"Claire? Ozzie? What's the matter? What's wrong?"

"I don't know," I moan, as sweat drips down the sides of my face. Cal leaps up and returns with a wet kitchen towel, which he presses to my forehead.

The liquid dissipates, and slowly, the pains in my head and stomach go away.

When I can finally speak, I say, "I don't know what that was, but I think somebody or something is definitely trying to get my attention."

Cal's a good listener, but I know it's my mother I need to talk to.

I leave a voice mail, and she calls me back within minutes.

"Sorry I missed you. What's up, honey?" she asks.

I tell her about the cards and Rena, how they indicated Rena was mentally unbalanced and seemed to predict her child is being or will be harmed in some way. I describe how my visions coincided with and supported the cards, and the horror they foretold. I tell her about the final card, the one forecasting a trip, maybe to the ocean, and how thrilled Rena was because she might be moving to California with her new boyfriend.

"At that moment my mouth filled with what tasted like ocean water. I had to keep spitting it out. It was the strangest thing. Mom, has anything like that ever happened to you?"

It's quiet on the line, but I can hear her fiddling with the delicate wind chime that hangs in the kitchen window. It's made of brass, and the chimes are shaped like butterflies. My dad got it at a flea market for her a long time ago.

"Occasionally I can sense what's happening when someone is ill or might become ill. Like, I'll have trouble breathing, which might mean the client should watch out for pneumonia. But no, nothing that sounds like what you experienced," she says.

"What do I do?"

"Do?"

"You know . . . with this information. How do I handle it? Should I call the police? And what would I say?"

Cal has obviously been listening to the conversation, or at least my side of it, because he shouts from the kitchen, "Call the police? And tell them what? That the spirit world wants you to play detective because some probably way overprotective mommy is legitimately concerned about her sick kid?"

"Mom, can I call you back?" I ask.

Racing into the kitchen, I yell at Cal, "What the hell do I need to do to convince you that the visions I'm having are real?"

Cal whirls around from the stove, where it looks like he's concocting some sort of an omelet. There's a frying pan heating, and eggshells and grated cheese are strewn across the counter. Butter has started to blacken in the pan, and he flips off the burner.

"Can you really blame me? All these years you've told me you had zero psychic abilities, that you were just trying to make a buck. So forgive me if I'm a little confused here."

"But now they're back. I do have these abilities now, so—"

"Fine, maybe I could accept that your long-lost skills have returned. But you want to bring the police into this? To accuse someone of possible child abuse? Can't you see the potential horrible ramifications of this? Lives ruined?"

"I can't just ignore what I saw and felt today."

He wipes his fingers on a dish towel, bridges the distance between us, and takes my hands in his.

"Why not? You've told me many times the cards can be interpreted in different ways. What if your interpretation is off this time?"

I rip my hands away. "And what if I'm exactly on

target? Do you really think that, if something horrible is happening to a child, I can stand back and do nothing about it? Then, Cal, you don't know me very well. And, frankly, now I'm wondering how well I really know you."

I turn from him, march into the bedroom, and slam the door. I'm furious. I can't believe Cal is still doubting my abilities, but more important, that he can't see I have to help this child. But in my heart, I know my anger is fueled by something else—recurring self-doubt. What if everything that happened today and in the last couple of weeks is just an impressive streak of bull's-eye good guesses? Do I really want to call the authorities based on guesses?

I crawl, wounded, to bed. After an hour, I finally fall asleep but toss all night, replaying the battle.

46

Rena

Someone's pounding on the door. I bury my head under one and then two pillows. Stephanie moans in her sleep but doesn't wake up.

But it won't stop. I stumble to the front door, swing it open, and shout, "What?"

Mrs. Lupito doesn't even blink. She hands me a business card and says, "Here, this is for you. Some guy came to my house yesterday and said for me to give it to you right away." She smiles with just the corners of her mouth and says, "It's from a Detective Larson."

"Fine. You delivered the damn message. Good for you." I start to close the door, but she slaps a hand on it.

"Listen, I don't want no trouble here. I never had problems with my renters before, and you better not be bringing any to me now. Understand?"

I slam the door in her face and throw the card on the chair. I head back to the bedroom to catch a couple more hours of sleep. But as soon as I lie down, my cell phone starts to buzz. I really want to ignore it. Then I think that maybe it's Louis.

But, no. Not his number. It's from the hospital. Dr. Norton's administrative assistant, who says her name is Campbell.

"Rena, Dr. Norton asked that I call you. We received the test results back from Stephanie's PET scan, and she was wondering if you could come in this morning to meet with her."

"This morning?" I yawn.

"Yes. She has an opening at eleven. Would that work for you?"

"Yeah, sure." I hang up and call the pharmacy to let them know I can't work today.

Stephanie and me are only ten minutes late for the appointment, but Dr. Norton looks like she's been waiting for us for about a week. She's got this aggravated frown on her face. I'm really glad to see the scrunched lines between her eyebrows and send up a silent wish that they'd stay there forever.

"Mrs. Cole, come in. Please take a seat." Her desk is huge, all light wood. Besides her computer, there are piles of papers neatly stacked in a slotted metal organizer on one side. On the other side is some kind of ugly-ass carved wood statue. I'm trying to figure out what the hell it's supposed to be. It just looks like round circles glued to other round circles with a pointy thing coming out of one side. I decide it's some kind of modern art shit that has no meaning whatsoever but probably costs more than I could make at the drugstore in three years.

Stephanie walks in before me and waves at Dr. Norton.

"Hi there, pretty girl. How are you feeling today?"

I put my hand on Stephanie's waist and have her sit next to me in the leather chairs facing the desk.

"She's fine," I say.

Dr. Norton hits some keys on her computer and then turns the screen so it faces me and Steph.

"Here are the results of Stephanie's recent PET scan," she says, pointing to some blobs on the screen. "These are shots from your daughter's upper and lower gastro-intestinal tract. I know it's confusing to interpret, but the good news is there is absolutely nothing wrong in either of these areas."

"How about that genetic test for Fabry disease?" I ask.

"It's going to take another couple of weeks, at least, for those results." She turns the screen back toward her and says, "It's great news that the PET scan showed nothing. Of course, the bad news is we still don't know what caused the dangerous increase in her sodium levels."

"Maybe you need to do a bone marrow test?" I suggest.

Dr. Norton stares at me and then turns to Stephanie and says, "Honey, see the little table in the corner that's just your size? Why don't you go over there? I know there are some coloring books and crayons in the drawer I bet you'll love."

Stephanie slips down from her chair, stops, looks at me sideways, and then walks slowly to the table.

Dr. Norton waits until she's settled and then says in a low voice, "Mrs. Cole, do you have any idea how painful a bone marrow test is? There are no test results, nor any clinical rationale for performing a bone marrow aspiration relative to the symptoms with which Stephanie is presenting. Why would you want to put your daughter through that?"

"Because something is very wrong with her, and I want you to do everything . . . do you hear me? . . . fucking everything . . . to figure it out," I shout.

"Please keep your voice down. I don't want to upset Stephanie."

"Believe me, she's upset plenty already. In pain all

the time. We're both upset, to tell you the truth," I say, only slightly quieter.

"I'm sure that's true," Dr. Norton replies. "But, frankly, I think it's time to look seriously at other possibilities for Stephanie's ongoing problems."

"Such as?"

She hesitates but then leans forward, like we're a couple of gal pals out for drinks.

"I think it would be a good idea for you to meet with the hospital psychologist, Amelia Bately. She's wonderful. I know you'd like her. Perhaps she can help."

"Help? Help with what? How the hell would me seeing a stupid psychologist help with the pain that kept my daughter awake screaming bloody murder for over three hours last night?"

I leap up from the chair, knocking over her hoity-toity, *look at me, I'm so rich I can buy something that looks like dog shit but everyone else thinks is so fancy* wood statue. It crashes to the floor, and the arm or leg, or whatever the hell it is, breaks off and rolls under the desk. I grab Stephanie's arm and yank her to stand up. I pull the red crayon from her fist and toss it onto the table.

"You know what? Maybe you should concentrate on spending more time finding a cure for my daughter's illness and less on a good mother who is only trying to do the right thing."

I hear her calling my name as I race Stephanie down the hallway.

When we get back to the duplex, my heart is still thumping so hard, I can hear it in my ears. *How dare she? Who the hell does that bitch think she is?*

Flipping open my laptop, I log into my blog. I want to tell my readers what's going on. I know they'll be as furious as I am.

There's a message from my sister.

KnitWit1: Rena, that guy from the hospital came back again today and I told him (again) that the only information I had was that you were in Arizona trying to get help for Stephanie from a famous doctor there. He asked me what kind of illness Stephanie had and I told him she's had stomach problems all her life. I wanted to let you know because I'm pretty sure he's going to try to find you there. What's happening? Why does he want to see you? He asked me if I knew the doctor's name (which, of course, I don't). I think about you guys all the time. PLEASE tell me how you both are and what, if anything, I should tell this guy if he stops by again? Also, Gary's called at least twice a week to see if I've heard from you and if I know where you're living now. Call him . . . and me! Your loving sister, Janet

47

Claire

Cal's gone when I wake up. I tell myself that's a good thing because I can't stand the thought of picking up the fight where we left it last night. Physically I feel better, though, and I've pretty much decided I'll go back to the store today.

I fix tea to drink on the back porch. Just as I'm sitting down, I hear my phone ring from inside the house. Thinking it's probably my mom after I failed to call her back last night as promised, I run in and finally find it twisted in the bedsheet.

But it's not her. It's Cal. I push decline.

He immediately calls back, and I answer this time, spitting out, "What?"

"Don't hang up, okay?"

"Fine, but make it quick. I need to go to work and give some more fake readings."

"Claire, please—"

"Please what? Cal, I don't know what else we have to say to each other right now. I'm trying to get my head around not only my rediscovered psychic skills but also the possibility that a child is in real danger, so—"

"You're right," he says.

Caught off guard, I ask, "What do you mean?"

"Oz, I didn't sleep at all last night. I went out and walked around and around and here's the conclusion I reached: I do know you, and I know you've never lied to me, but more important, I've never known you to lie to yourself."

"So?" I'm not sure where he's heading with this.

"So if you tell me you've got your psychic mojo back, then I believe you."

I start to tear up.

"Cal, really? Because it's important to me to know I can trust you with all this. It's been so crazy, and I've been feeling like I'm completely alone with it."

"I know, and I feel awful about that. I really do. I mean, I'll be honest, it's hard for me to comprehend because, well, it's kind of out there. But last night I remembered what your mom told us about her experiences, and I think I finally began to understand what you've been going through."

"I can't tell you how much that means to me," I say over the lump in my throat.

"I love you, Claire, and I never want you to think I don't support you."

"Thank you," I choke out. "Thank you so much."

"But, besides apologizing for my stupidity, I called for another reason."

"Which is?"

"This morning on the way to school, I was thinking about your client, Rena, and remember that made-for-TV movie we watched? I think it was last January? Or maybe December? I can't remember exactly, except I know we still had the Christmas—"

"Cal, did you really call to ask me about some stupid movie?"

"I did. This is important. Because the movie was about a mother hurting her son. Don't you remember? She was this seemingly perfect mother, went to every PTA meeting, made brownies from scratch? And nobody had a clue she was doing horrible things to her kid."

Then I do remember: Cal and I curled on the sofa under an afghan, a bowl of popcorn between us, watching this terrible movie (besides the truly disturbing subject matter, it had awful writing and dreadful acting) and wondering how a mother . . .

"For attention, right? She was hurting him and always bringing him to doctors and emergency rooms for his symptoms, just so she could get the attention," I say, feeling nauseated thinking about it.

"That's right. She was getting off on all the praise from the doctors and nurses for being this great mother of a really sick kid, when she was the one causing all the symptoms."

"What was it called? What she had? Something to do with donuts?"

"Munchausen by proxy syndrome," Cal says. "Donuts?"

"Sorry, what popped into my mind just then was Munchkins. Do you really think Rena has this Munchausen thing?"

"Yes, I think it's possible."

I take the phone outside, sip the lukewarm tea, and think about Rena with Stephanie on the plane.

"I know it doesn't square with the reading or my visions, but I've got to tell you, Rena appeared, at least on the plane, to be genuinely concerned about Stephanie. Traveling across the country to see the best doctor and all that."

"It's what they do, these moms. They are really over-the-top with what they show the world. On the surface, they look like the perfect parent. But it's all an act, just for the attention."

"Lots of people need extra attention, and they don't hurt their kids to get it."

"These are not normal people."

"You're saying they try to get the doctor to pay attention to them through their kid?"

"Yeah, and get this. The mother will create more and more symptoms. The doctor keeps buying into the apparent illness and loses sight of the fact that many of the symptoms or test results just don't make any clinical sense. Meanwhile, the kid's being tortured, first by the mom, and then through all the testing."

"Wait, what do you mean 'creates more and more symptoms'?"

"Some moms will lie to doctors about their kids' symptoms, but some will actually cause the symptoms."

I shiver even though the temperature has to be creeping toward ninety already.

"Cal, do you think Rena is actually causing Stephanie's stomach problems?"

Pieces are starting to come together, creating a frightening picture.

Rena on the plane, seemingly a loving mother, willing to travel far away from home in order to finally discover why her daughter is so critically ill. Like someone who should receive the mother-of-the-year award. Then, Stephanie, a fragile specimen of a child, beyond shy. I see her clutching that stuffed toy (a panda? Jeffrey?) and suddenly recall what she said to me.

"Cal," I say, "Stephanie told me sometimes her stuffed panda was bad and had to sleep on the floor, somewhere where it was dark and cold."

There's silence, and then Cal says, "I'm betting Stephanie was there with that panda during those times."

"Oh God. Poor little girl."

Right then, that bizarre salty liquid returns to my mouth in such a rush that I race into the bathroom and barely make it to the toilet, where the saliva or whatever it is keeps replenishing. I vomit several times. From a distance, I can hear Cal's voice, tinny through the phone I threw onto the bathroom floor. "Ozzie? Are you okay? What's going on? Something you ate?"

48

Rena

After I close the laptop, I'm about to turn the TV on for Stephanie, figuring I'll take a nap. But then someone starts banging on my door, which seems to be the routine for today. Goddammit.

I'm afraid it's Mrs. Lupito again, so I put my finger on my lips to shush Stephanie.

After a minute or so, the knocking stops. Then I hear the person at Mrs. Lupito's door.

"Hello, Mrs. Lupito. Detective Larson. Sorry to bother you again, but I was next door, and Mrs. Cole still doesn't seem to be home. Do you happen to know when she'll return?"

Shit. What the hell does this asshole want anyway?

"Hey, listen, I'm her landlady but I don't check on everything she does, you know. She came back late last night. I give her your card first thing this morning, just like you say to," Mrs. Lupito says. "But that one, she's sneaky. I don't think she call you back."

"Why do you say that?"

"Don't know. Just a feeling."

"What do you know about Rena Cole, Mrs. Lupito?"

"I know she a real loony bird. She makes a big deal about feeding her daughter all this healthy food, but she don't seem to care much about what that little girl is doing most times. She's weird, that's all I can say. And something is very wrong with her and Stephanie, that much I know."

"Stephanie. Her daughter?"

"Yeah, her little girl. I watch after Stephanie when Rena works. Sweet child, but it looks like she afraid all the time when her mama comes to pick her up."

"Where does Mrs. Cole work?"

"At Bert's Pharmacy, on the corner."

"Thanks. Here's another card. Could you please tell Mrs. Cole I need to speak to her right away?"

"Yeah, sure."

"Thank you, Mrs. Lupito."

"*No hay problema*. And you should know something else too."

"What's that?"

"Sometimes I hear that child crying. She scream in the middle of the night."

"Why? Why is she screaming?"

"How would I know?"

Stupid bitch. Why can't she mind her own fucking business and just make her tamales all day? I hear the detective walk down the steps and Mrs. Lupito's door closing.

My phone buzzes with a text message.

Hi, Rena. This is Claire from Mystical Haven. Thank you for coming to see me. As promised, I will be in your area and would like to invite you to a group reading. It's tomorrow, at the West Park Inn on Central Avenue in Phoenix, at 2:00. Please let me know if you can attend. Looking forward to seeing you again.

I'd have to take Stephanie with me. Obviously, my next-door babysitter arrangement is totally over. I think about it for a second and then text: COOL, I'll be there. Rena.

49
Claire

I flush the toilet, put the lid down, and sit on it, shaking. I reach for my phone.

"Rena's hurting her child," I sputter. "The salt water in my mouth that comes from nowhere? It's a sign I'm supposed to pay attention to. I'm sure of it."

"But you don't even know this woman—"

"You're the one who suspects Munchausen by proxy. Now you're still thinking Rena's just some overprotective supermommy?"

"No . . . I don't know, but . . . ."

The rational part of my brain is saying, *Don't be ridiculous. Rena is a mom who's trying to do right by her child. You've just started having visions that, for some reason, are turning out to be valid.* But then the emotional side, which I've come to think of as directly linked to my psychic side, presents the counterpoints: *Remember the child's face, how gray and scared she looked. Something's not right here, and you know it. And it's up to you to do something about it.* Much as I hate to become enmeshed in this nightmare and would like to crawl back under the covers and forget about this mother and her kid, for the first time since I had to take care of my father when he was sick, I feel I have to take responsibility for another person. I don't want to, but I have to. I can only hope I'm prepared for the job.

"Listen," I say, gripping the phone with a sweaty hand. "Not only am I sure Stephanie is in serious danger, I think it's up to me to do something about it."

"You what? Claire, come on. What are you thinking you can do about it?"

"Call the police."

"And tell them what? That you've had visions about a mom hurting her child?"

I go to the bedroom and struggle into my jeans and a T-shirt, moving the phone from hand to hand as I do. "I really don't know what I'll tell the police. I only know I have to do something to help this little girl." Cal begins to say something else, but I hang up.

"Phoenix Police, Second Precinct, Officer Mallory. Can I help you?"

All of a sudden, everything Cal has been trying to tell me floods my mind, and I can't think of anything to say that doesn't make me sound like a raving lunatic.

I decide to start with the basics.

"Hi, my name is Claire, and I live in Sedona. I'm a psychic here, and I think one of my clients may be trying to hurt her little girl."

Office Mallory coughs once and then says, "What makes you think your client wants to hurt her child?"

I tell him about the cards and their possible meanings and then about the visions I had during the reading and finally about the salt water.

"Then, my boyfriend, Cal, who's studying to be a psychologist, mentioned this condition, Munchausen by proxy, where the mother will do anything she can, including hurting her own child, to get attention, especially from doctors."

"Uh-huh, I see, and what was your name again?"

"Claire. Claire Fontaine."

I have no idea why I decide to do this—give him my mother's maiden name. I don't know, maybe it's the tone of the officer's voice, which is more than a little snarky, but I don't want to tell him my real last name.

"And your phone number?" I provide him with my cell phone number.

"Tell you what, if I hear of anything going on that sounds like what you believe might happen because of your crystal ball, I'll let you know, okay?" I hear snickering in the background before he hangs up.

The door swings open, and, seeing my face, Cal asks, "Not the response you were hoping for?"

"What are you doing here? I thought you had class."

"I decided to bag it. What did the police say?"

"Pretty much exactly what you predicted. Hope you're satisfied," I snap.

"Now what?" he asks.

"Sometimes the direct option is the best one," I say. "I'm going to Phoenix."

"Right now?"

"No, but early tomorrow morning. I invited Rena to meet with me tomorrow afternoon. I told her I was doing a group reading."

"You're doing a group reading?"

"That's what she'll think. Before she left yesterday, I was so upset that I got her cell phone number. I wasn't sure what to do with it yesterday, but now I am."

"You are?" he asks.

"No, not exactly. But the first step that feels right is to get to Phoenix. If the police aren't going to help, then I've got to do something myself."

I go to the bathroom and start pulling out toiletries to pack.

Cal follows me, grabs an overnight bag from the closet, and says, "Okay, Nancy Drew, I'm going with you. There's no way I'm letting you go alone to meet this potentially crazy person."

50
Rena

After I don't hear from him for most of the day, I finally end up calling Louis. He says he wants to come over to my place so I can cook him dinner. No way that's gonna happen. I tell him I'll get a sitter for Stephanie so we can go out.

I'm in the shower when someone knocks on the front door. Stephanie opens it before I can tell her not to.

"Daddy," she screams. "Look, Mommy! Daddy's here."

I tighten the towel around me and try to put a smile on my face. "I can see that. Hi, Gary."

When I come out of the bedroom dressed, Stephanie is sitting on his lap on the couch. He kisses her cheek and says, "Steph, honey, can you go to the bedroom with Jeffrey for a few minutes so Daddy can talk with Mommy?"

"Yes, Daddy. Then can you color with me?"

"Sure, honey." He pats her back, and she skips away.

"I . . . I didn't know your company sent you to Phoenix," I say.

The smile he gave Steph is completely gone from his face.

"They don't."

"I was going to call you tonight," I say, trying to brush the knots out of my hair.

"I'm not buying that," he says, standing up. I can see his jaw clenching and unclenching. His voice is so low it sounds like he's growling at me. "I've been trying to reach you for weeks, and nobody, not Janet, not even your own mother, knew where you were. Then I get a call from this guy, Adam something, from St. Theresa's, who said he's also been trying to talk to you about Stephanie. What in hell's name is going on here, Rena?" His neck is getting red, which I know from our time together means he's really pissed.

"Hey, listen, I've been busy with doctor's appointments and everything. Did you know she was in the hospital last—"

"Cut the crap," he shouts, but then makes himself whisper. "It's not right I can't see my daughter. I had to figure out on my own where you were. I contacted the insurance company, and since the policy's under my name, they were able to tell me the hospital you've been going to. Through some finagling, I found out the address of this . . . place." The disgust at where we're living shows all over his face.

I go to the kitchen and grab a paper towel to wipe at my eyes. He follows me.

"I'm sorry, I really am. I didn't mean for you not to see her. It's that everything happened so fast, and I got wrapped up in caring for her and not sleeping and then . . . fuck, the time just goes by."

"Yeah, well, I also called the Phoenix police, I was so concerned," Gary says.

"Police? Jesus, Gary. You know what I'm doing out here. Why the hell would you call the police?"

I fill a glass with ice and tap water. I add the slice of lemon I know he likes.

"The water here is crap. Tastes a lot like pipe," I say, handing him the glass. He takes it like he's doing me a fucking favor. He walks back to the couch and sits, trying to avoid the torn cushion.

"Because I was frantic, that's why. It was a while until I could make a trip out here," he says, taking one of the mildewy couch pillows in two fingers and throwing it onto the floor. Dust flies up where it drops.

"How long are you staying?"

"I guess that depends. How is she? How's my little girl? I have to tell you, she looks pretty bad."

I give him the summary of what's happened since we got to Phoenix, including my request for a bone marrow test and Dr. Norton's flat-out no. I leave out the part where she suggested I see a shrink.

"Well, maybe she's right, Rena. Maybe another test isn't the answer."

"And what do you think the answer is, Gary? Tell me, please, because then I can stop working on this fucking problem like I've been doing the past four years, twenty-four hours a day, every single day. And, by the way, I'm still waiting on the test results about that horrible disease you probably gave her." I'm yelling, and Stephanie pokes her head out. I signal for her to go back into the bedroom. She does, but not before she blows a kiss to Gary. He blows one back.

"Calm down, will you? You'll upset her. That's one of the reasons I've been trying so hard to reach you. I wanted to let you know my test results were negative for Fabry. And I only meant that maybe we should look at other resources. Like maybe other doctors. Or . . . ?"

I look at the wall clock, turn to Gary and say, "You know, you're right, and that's really great news on the

Fabry thing. We should definitely talk more about this. But I can't right now. Stephanie's little friend is coming here to spend the night, and I promised the mom I would feed them both dinner. Want to come by early tomorrow, maybe for breakfast? We can all catch up then and talk about plans and next steps and everything."

"Fine," he says, getting up and calling for Stephanie, who runs from the bedroom and takes a leap into his arms. Gary tickles her, gives her another kiss on the cheek, and sets her down. He promises her he'll be back the next day, and then they can color. Before he's out the door, he turns to me and says, "I'm spending all day with her tomorrow. Understand? I'm her father, and that's what I'm going to do. And you and me . . ." He points a finger in my face. "We'll have a long talk. I want to know everything. Every test that was run and each and every result. Why the guy from St. Theresa's wants to talk to you. Everything, Rena."

"Of course," I say, closing the door behind him.

51
Claire

We're on the road by eleven the next morning. I packed lunch, so the only stop we make is midway to switch drivers. Pulling into a rest stop off the highway, I hand the keys to Cal. He's been sleeping most of the way, and now it's my turn to catch up on what I missed last night.

We trade places. I unwrap the turkey-and-cheese sandwiches and pass one to Cal, who holds it in one hand, takes a bite, and turns the key with the other. He pulls onto the highway.

"You know what confuses me?" I ask, folding the foil on my lap into something resembling a duck.

"What's that?"

"Why these women aren't caught. The things they

do to their kids are so awful and sometimes, right there in the hospital. Why don't nurses or doctors notice?"

"I don't know. These women are pretty slick."

"But why don't the kids say something?"

He wipes his mouth on his napkin, hands it to me, and gestures to the bottle of water on my lap. I twist off the plastic cap and pass it to him.

After a gulp, he answers, "From what I can tell, like any abuser—emotional or physical—these moms are masters of manipulation. They can pretty much get their child to believe anything, even maybe that what they're doing to them is good for them."

As we get closer to Phoenix, I can see the ring of smog pollution hovering above the valley, like some alien spacecraft.

"I guess I can understand how a mother could manipulate a little kid, like someone Stephanie's age, but what about the older ones? Don't they say anything? Don't they tell the doctor or teacher or their grandmother or someone what's happening?" I ask, redoing the buttons on my shirt, which I just now realize are fastened all wrong.

"Ozzie, there's a bunch of mind messing going on here. It's the kid's mother. It's probably impossible for kids to believe their own mothers could hurt them.

And the rest of the world? They can't believe someone apparently so caring could be doing such horrendous things."

"So, does it happen mostly with younger kids?"

"Yeah, I think so."

I have a terrible thought then, one I'm afraid even mentioning will make true. But I have to ask.

"Cal, what happens when the mother no longer gets the attention she needs from making up or causing these illnesses?"

He's quiet for a long while before answering.

"She may up the ante by making the kid sicker and sicker until she can get back the attention from the medical staff. Or . . ."

"Or?"

He looks at me and says, "She decides the child is no longer worthwhile for her to have around."

We turn into the hotel parking lot. I realize I didn't get the nap I'd anticipated, but I highly doubt I'd be able to sleep now anyway.

There are signs all over the lobby touting new renovations. Based on the room we enter, it appears like putting up signs was as far as the renovations went. It's a sad space with worn bedcovers and two identical prints of a forest scene positioned over two queen-sized beds.

The bathroom looks like it does have a new shower-head, but that doesn't make up for the broken tiles on the floor and the rust around the base of the toilet.

I text Rena to let her know I'm in room 312 and ask her to confirm she'll be here at 2:00 for the group reading.

"When she gets here, maybe excuse yourself and go downstairs," I say to Cal.

"Sure, and leave you with a potential killer. I don't think so."

Realizing he has a point, I suggest, "Fine, then you can be another person at the reading. After all, it's supposed to be a group. You can be a group of two."

"You know this is nuts, right? What are you going to do after she gets here? Say she actually admits to hurting her daughter, then what? I tackle her to the ground and you wrap her in duct tape?"

"Hey, you didn't have to come with me."

"Like I'd leave you here alone."

I go to the bathroom and while I'm in there, my phone rings.

"Can you get that, please?" I yell.

"Hello, Claire's phone," he says in a chipper voice. He comes to the bathroom door and announces, "It's for you."

I finish up and reach for the phone.

"Hello?"

"Is this Claire Fontaine?"

I start to tell him he has the wrong number when I remember the alias I hastily threw out to the officer I called this morning. "Uh, yes, this is Claire Fontaine." Cal raises his eyebrows.

"Miss Fontaine, this is Detective Larson with the Phoenix Police Department. I had a message from one of my officers that you called this morning."

I mouth to Cal, *It's the police*, before responding, "Yes, I did call before, but, frankly, Officer Mallory didn't appear to take my concerns very seriously." Cal's head is dropped, and he's shaking it from side to side.

"Would you mind telling me those concerns? It would be helpful to hear the issues directly from you."

I repeat basically what I said to Officer Mallory, trying very hard not to sound crazy. I tell him about our Munchausen by proxy suspicions. He's familiar with the syndrome.

"Then my boyfriend and I decided to drive down to Phoenix, which is where we are now."

"You're in Phoenix? Why is that, Miss Fontaine?"

It's only then I realize how what I decided to do might sound to someone who does not do what I do for a living.

"When Rena came to see me in the store, I was

concerned, so I got her phone number by telling her I wanted to invite her to a group reading in Phoenix. Cal and I are in a room at the West Park Inn on Central waiting for her now."

I can hear the detective chewing on something I think may be gum, but then he swallows and asks, "What were you thinking of accomplishing by inviting her to this group reading?"

Fumbling for an answer, I again realize I don't exactly have a clear idea of what I was trying to do getting her to come see me again, except maybe this: "Uh, I wanted to double-check my first reading conclusions to confirm the information I gathered was correct."

"The first reading that told you she might harm her child?"

"I know it probably sounds ridiculous to someone who doesn't believe in psychics, but—"

"You're right about that, Miss Fontaine. As far as I'm concerned, it's up there with Bigfoot and the Loch Ness Monster. A lot of malarkey."

"Then why are you calling me?" I say, trying, but not succeeding, to keep the anger from my voice.

"Because it may all be bullshit, but there's a kid involved who might be in trouble, and I happen to have received three calls about this Rena person in the past two days."

"Calls?"

"I shouldn't necessarily be sharing this information, but now that you're somewhat involved, I can tell you. One call was from the kid's doctor here, and another was from Rena's ex-husband."

"They both had the same concerns?"

"Not exactly. The ex-husband wanted to see his kid, and his ex-wife has not responded to him or shared with him her address since she moved to Phoenix over two months ago."

"And the doctor?"

"Said she did every test she could think of and even one she didn't think was at all necessary, but the mom demanded it. Said she couldn't find anything wrong with the child and that she refused to administer another test the mom wanted her to do. Doc said she had concerns about the mom—nothing she could pinpoint, but said something just didn't feel right. She told me the last thing she suggested to Rena was that she see the hospital psychologist."

"How'd she take that?" I ask, checking my watch. Rena should have been here six minutes ago.

"Not good. Apparently, she ran out of there, dragging the kid with her. That's when the doctor called us."

"You said there was a third call. Who was that from?"

"A social worker or advocate or someone like that from the hospital in New Jersey where Rena last had Stephanie seen. Apparently, he's been trying to track her down. Turns out a doctor there is also worried about the kid." He takes another bite of whatever he had in his mouth before but this time his speech is gar-bled around it. "When's she supposed to get there?"

I look at my watch again. "Seven minutes ago."

"I'm betting she won't show."

"What do you want me to do?" I ask.

More chewing and then a swallow.

"Okay, here's what I think. Why don't you text her again and tell her nobody else showed for the group reading, but if she gives you her address, you'll be happy to go to her house for a private session. You guys do that kind of stuff, right?"

"Sure, I guess. I mean, I don't personally, but I know some psychics who make house calls."

"Good. Text her and then give her five minutes to respond."

"Then what?"

"I'm heading over to her place now. Her husband gave me the address. He called me again this morn-ing and said he was supposed to pick Stephanie up, but there was nobody there, so he's upset. If she knows you're coming, and if she's interested in what you're selling, maybe she'll let you in, and we'll be right there too."

"So I text her and if she responds?"

"Tell her you'll be right over."

"And if she doesn't?"

"Go to her place anyway. Like I said, I don't believe any of this psychic crap, but since she seems to be a real escape artist, I guess I can use all the help I can get to trap her, even the crazy kind."

He gives me the address, and I send the text. Rena doesn't respond, even after ten minutes, so Cal and I get in the car.

52

Rena

"Stephanie, listen. Lock the door behind me and do not open it for anyone, got it?"

"Yes, Mommy," she squeaks from under a blanket on the couch. Since the TV is on the cartoons channel, I'm sure she'll be right there when I get back. "I mean it. You don't move, not even a little. Understand?"

"Yes, Mommy."

"And if you get tired, just go to sleep."

She hugs Jeffrey closer to her and whispers, "Okay." I walk out the door.

After I finally got Gary to leave, I rushed around like a crazy woman, getting dressed and pulling together some dinner for Stephanie. Louis and I decided to meet at the same restaurant as before, which was great because I could walk there from my place.

After we sit down, he says, "You look terrific." I'm glad I took time to put some curl in my hair.

"Did you find a sitter for Stephanie?" he asks.

"Yeah, it worked out fine. Her dad came into town today, so he's watching her."

"Oh, that's great. I bet they're really happy to see each other," he says. He reaches for one of those yummy corn muffins.

"Yeah, they are."

"So, did you get a chance to call your lawyer about that settlement money?"

"Huh?"

"The money you're supposed to get from the hospital that I could invest for you?"

"Oh, that. No, with Gary stopping by and everything, I didn't have any time. But I promise I'll call real soon."

"Sounds good. Hey, how was the doctor's appointment?" he asks. "Did you get the results of the PET scan from last week?"

"She said the PET scan didn't show anything, but she wants to do one more test, a bone marrow aspiration. Just to be sure she's not missing anything."

"Wow, isn't that painful? I don't know anything about it, other than what I've seen on TV on the doctors' shows, but it always looks like it hurts like a son-of-a-bitch."

"No, it's not too bad. I think they use a local anesthetic or something. Anyway, the doctor and I are committed to finding out what's going on, once and for all. I'm really glad she suggested it."

"I bet. Sounds like a great doctor."

"Nothing but the best for my kid."

He orders a bottle of wine and clams casino for an appetizer. I always wanted to try them.

For dessert we have the delicious apple cobbler Louis told me about last time but happily did not have.

"Well, looks like I have to leave for California sooner than I thought," he says.

I put down my fork.

"Really? When?" I feel like I could scream.

"Right away. Tonight, in fact."

"Tonight? Why? Why does your company need you to go right now?"

I gulp back tears and make myself concentrate real hard on the ice cream melting on the hot cobbler. I couldn't eat another bite if I tried.

"It's a business problem, like I told you before. I need to generate some capital really fast."

"But why can't you do that here? I mean, maybe I can help with my settlement and all?"

He stirs cream into his coffee and then says, "Yeah, I wish I could stay, but they think it's better if I work out of the California area for a while. But maybe . . . ?"

"What?" I ask, my heart flip-flopping.

"We could keep in touch, and when you get your money, like I said, I'll be glad to help you with investments and everything."

I can't stand this. I can't fucking stand the idea of Louis leaving, moving away. He's the first good thing to happen to me in years.

"How about if I go with you?" I say real quick, before I can lose my nerve.

He doesn't answer right away, and I hold my breath.

Finally, he says, "Yeah, you know, I think that's a great idea. It could be a blast, you and me together out there. And I could really use help finding a place and everything."

I am so, so relieved. "Oh my God, are you kidding me? I would love to." I jump out of my seat and hug him. "I can be ready to go right away. Just say the word."

Louis looks at me for a long time, so long I'm sure I blew it, that he thinks I'm being way too ballsy. But then he says, "Really? That would be awesome. But don't you have a ton of medical things to do with Stephanie?"

We walk out into the hot night.

"Let me check. I bet Gary can help. I might even be able to arrange things so I can go with you tonight."

It's time, I think, *to go*. I definitely need a break, away from the doctors, the social workers, the police, the nosy neighbors.

"Hey, if you can, that would be fantastic," he says, hugging me. "But do me a favor, will you?"

"Sure, anything."

"Maybe, when you get home, send an email to the attorney and ask him about the timing on that settlement? I could really use a quick win when we get to California."

"Absolutely."

I practically run back to my place. I'm so happy I can hardly keep it all inside. That perfect little bungalow, right on the ocean. I can almost feel the heat from the fireplace Louis and me are sitting in front of. Just the two of us, cuddling under the softest blanket in the world.

53
Claire

We find the address, get out of the car, and are greeted by a tall guy with a mustache who flashes a badge and introduces himself as Detective Larson. He's holding a package of red licorice in one hand and a spiral notepad and pencil in the other.

Next to him is a smaller guy, slightly balding, with a paunch.

"This is Rena's ex-husband, Gary." We shake hands. "This is the psychic I told you about," says Larson.

Surprisingly, Gary doesn't react to this information in either a positive or negative way. He seems numb.

"I already knocked on Rena's door, but no answer. I was about to try the landlady. I should warn you, she's pretty feisty," says the detective.

We follow him up the walk, where he pounds on the

door of the place next to Rena's and finally, a woman answers. She's wearing a threadbare pink housecoat that's ripped at the pockets and has her hair in rollers, covered by a faded blue kerchief.

"What, you again?"

"Yes, Mrs. Lupito," replies Detective Larson, stuffing a piece of red licorice into his mouth. If I had to guess, I think he may be a smoker trying to quit. "Sorry to bother you, but I really need to speak with your neighbor, Rena. I tried her door, but there's still no answer. Do you know if she's in?"

"How do I know what that crazy girl does? Maybe she has men in all day, different ones, how do I know? You was one of them yesterday," she cries, pointing at Gary.

"I'm her ex-husband. I was visiting my daughter."

"Oh, you Stephanie's papa? She's a sweet thing. So well-behaved, but I got to tell you, your wife, your ex-wife, she's a loony bird. Always saying Stephanie can't eat this, can't eat that, and you know what, I give her real food when her mama's at work and she's fine. Nothing wrong at all. Somebody sick, but not the girl," she says, giving us a knowing look.

"Do you happen to know where Rena and Stephanie are, Mrs. Lupito?" the detective asks.

"Not a clue. Been cooking all day. I got to get up

early tomorrow. My grandkids are coming by." She almost smiles.

The detective takes this in and offers her a piece of licorice. She shakes her head and says, "I don't like that stuff." Staring at him and then looking at the rest of us, she asks, "You know what else was strange?"

"What's that?" Larson asks, flipping open his notepad.

"Stephanie, she was real sick a week or so ago. I could hear her screaming, even before her mother knocked on my door in the middle of the night and said I had to drive them to the emergency room right away."

"And did you?" Larson takes a bite of licorice and makes a note.

"I did, but here's what was weird. First off, Rena just sort of throws Stephanie into the back seat, like she don't care how she lands. Then she gets herself in the front seat. She don't check on her kid the whole way there. I never see her look in the back seat at all. And guess what? When we get to the hospital, she says to me, 'Drive around.' So I say, 'What? You don't want to go straight to the ER?' And you know what she does then? She gets out her compact and powders her nose, fixes her hair, puts on lipstick, and then she tells me to pull up to the ER. Like I said, she's *muy loco*."

The detective looks at Gary and us, nods, and says

to Mrs. Lupito, "Yes, you're right, that does sound strange. Here's the problem, Mrs. Lupito: we're also concerned about Rena and Stephanie. I think we need to check her place to see if they're okay. Can you help us with that, please? You have a key, right?"

For a second, she hesitates, but then she tells us to wait a second, goes back inside, and returns with a ring of keys.

She leads us to Rena's, where the detective knocks and, when there's still no response, motions to Mrs. Lupito to open the door.

The harsh overhead light exposes a dingy front room. There are dirty dishes and a pan with some kind of burnt-on goop stacked on the counter and in the sink. We walk to the bedroom and discover the one closet there is empty.

"They're gone," I say, returning to the living room. It's then I notice something poking out from under the ripped fabric at the bottom of the couch. Kneeling, I reach for it, but I know what it is even before my fingers make contact. It's Jeffrey, Stephanie's beloved stuffed panda. A shiver starts at the soles of my feet and races up my spine and through my skull until my ears feel like they're vibrating.

"They're gone," I say again. "We need to find them, and soon."

54

Rena

It's really late when Louis picks me up, but it doesn't matter because part of the adventure is that we'll be driving all night. He tells me it's almost a six-hour trip.

At first he doesn't understand why he has to get me at the hotel. I tell Louis that Gary is staying at the hotel around the block from my place while he's in town and that he thought it would be fun for Stephanie to swim in the pool there. I tell him Gary and I had a long talk and that he said he would watch Stephanie. That he would take her to all her medical appointments so Louis and I could get set up in California before sending for her.

"She was so excited about using her new floatie," I say.

"I bet," Louis says, adjusting the rearview mirror.

"And I did send that email to the attorney, but he didn't write back yet."

"Okay, great. Hopefully, you'll hear soon."

"Yeah, I hope so."

The sky is beautiful. The air smells sweet, like a million blossoms are open all around us. We speed down the highway. I feel like I'm in a warm cocoon, just Louis and me, in the black night.

55
Claire

C al talks first.

"Claire, you look funny. Maybe you should sit down." He leads me to the couch and gently settles me onto the ripped cushion.

"Something's very wrong," I say.

"What's wrong? What do you mean?" asks Detective Larson.

"Is it Stephanie? Is she okay?" Gary sits next to me and grabs my arm in a painful grip.

I can hardly talk. My throat feels constricted, but I choke out, "No, she's not okay. She's in serious trouble."

My head pounds, and, strangely, the word *vacation* keeps flashing behind my aching eyes, on and off, like a neon sign.

"Vacation," I say in a voice I hardly recognize. It's

scratchy and at least an octave lower than my normal range. "Vacation. That's all I'm getting. That word, again and again."

Cal sits on the other side of me and tries to get me to unclench my fists, but it's like attempting to unset a mousetrap spring. I feel like I'm about to snap. It's like an electrical charge is zipping throughout my whole body, and now my eyes are burning.

"Vacation, vacation, vacation," I scream.

"Ozzie, look at me," Cal pleads, holding my face in his hands and staring into my eyes. It takes a massive effort, but I finally manage to focus on him. He says, "Good, that's very good. Now, tell me what's going on. This . . . vacation. Do you think Stephanie and Rena went on some kind of vacation?"

"Yes. No. I don't know. It's all messed up. Nothing is clear," I cry, but then the *vacation* neon sign stops all of a sudden and is replaced by a picture of the lobby of the hotel where Cal and I had our brief stay.

Gary says, "Listen, we're wasting time here. Don't we need to search for them? If my daughter is in danger, you need to call some cops or something," he yells at Detective Larson.

"Wait," I shout. "It's a hotel. She's in a hotel, but it's like they're on vacation. No, that doesn't make any sense."

"A vacation? Now? But why would she do that? Why would she move out of here? And in such an obvious hurry?" asks Cal.

Jumping up, I shout, "Because it's not a vacation. It's a hotel that sounds like a vacation. Is there a Holiday Inn nearby?"

Larson leads the way into the lobby of the Holiday Inn, which is only about a mile from Rena's place. There's a clerk on duty watching an episode of *CSI*. He barely turns toward us as we run to the counter.

But when Detective Larson shows him his badge, the kid is ready for action. Yes, he remembers a woman checking in with a small child. Yes, she matches the description Gary provides, and, of course, he's happy to tell us the room number and give us the key.

We take the elevator and make our way down the carpeted hallway, which muffles our footsteps. Outside of room 508, we stop and Larson holds up his hand, gesturing that he'll go in first.

He turns the key, yells, "Phoenix PD," and rushes through the open door. I'm next in, with Cal and then Gary right behind.

"Oh shit, oh shit," I hear Larson say. "Oh Christ."

I run past him to where Stephanie is lying on the floor next to the bed. Above her head, piled on the mattress, are four pillows, on top of which a bag of fluid is perched. A tube from the bag snakes down the side of the bed and over her blond hair until it enters her nostril. She's very still and very white.

Larson's on his phone calling for an ambulance. I can hear but don't quite register that Gary is wailing, like it's coming from far away. I know Cal is trying to hold me back, but it's as if his hands are reaching out to me from another dimension.

All I can feel is Stephanie's skin. How cold it is. All I can see is her tiny body, twisted in an unnatural curve, like a rag doll thrown to the floor, a discarded plaything.

56
Rena

We pull into an all-night truck stop midway. Louis said we need to gas up because there won't be another chance to do that for a while. During the couple of months I've been in Arizona, I never really had a chance to check out the desert. I mean, Phoenix, to me, is like any other city, except much, much hotter. But out here, especially before we came into this town, which is stuck in the middle of nowhere, I begin to understand what I missed.

On the way, Louis got a phone call and pulled over. He asked me to get out of the car. I guess it was a private conversation or something. But I'm glad it happened, because then I could see the desert. His headlights were on a cactus that looked like it was at least twenty feet high. It had these two huge branches, which Louis told me later are called arms and said it took one hundred years to grow just one of them. Then I heard a coyote and got scared and ran back to the car.

At the truck stop, me and him have cereal and a grilled cheese and we talk about California. It's like the weather there is so perfect that anything you want to do, you can do all year-round. Sounds like paradise. I feel like I'm living in a fucking dream.

When Louis goes to the bathroom, I walk outside and look up at all the stars.

I check my cell phone. That psychic left me two texts. I turn it off and drop it on the ground. There's a piece of pipe leaning against the side of the building. I use it to whack the case until it cracks and flattens. Then I walk over to a dumpster by the side of the restaurant, open the top, and toss the phone in.

57

Claire

Twelve Months Later

"They'll be here soon. Hurry up and get your shoes on," I shout to Cal, who is barely paying attention to me. He's preoccupied trying to get a bird feeder to stay attached to the railing on our back porch. Since we moved to Pennsylvania six months ago, he's become an avid bird-watcher. I tease him about the geekiness of this. I have to admit there seem to be hundreds of different bird varieties here compared to the desert, but this feeder—it's been an all-consuming project for the past two weeks. It's good his talents lean toward the human psyche because fix-it-ing is definitely not in his genes.

My mom and Aunt Frannie arrive right on time,

carrying a casserole dish, which smells like my aunt's famous manicotti, along with a plate of cookies covered in foil. It's one of the many wonderful things about moving east—having the two of them within walking distance.

"Mom, are those what I think they are?"

She grins and says, "Macaroons—chocolate covered, of course. Special cookies for a special day." She asks, "When do they get here?"

"Soon. Cal, shoes," I say as he comes through the back door, still barefoot.

"Oh yeah." He goes back outside to retrieve his loafers.

The doorbell rings, and we all freeze in position, our eyes darting back and forth, like children playing that statue game. Mom starts to giggle, which breaks the spell, and I walk to the front door and swing it open.

Stephanie is a completely different child from the one I last saw a year ago. Her cheeks are pink, and her pale blue eyes sparkle. Her hair is thicker and curling in tiny ringlets down her back. She must have grown three inches and put on a good ten pounds. She looks . . . healthy. And so happy.

"Stephanie." I bend down and wrap my arms around her. She hugs back, arms squeezing my neck. I breathe in the sweetness, the realness of her.

"Hi, Auntie Claire." She whispers into my ear, "Guess who's with me?"

I lean back and say, "Who?"

Her grin reveals her two dimples.

"Jeffrey," she shouts and runs to retrieve him from the little pink rolling suitcase she brought with her.

After more hugging and saying hello to (and kissing) Jeffrey, who looks like he's had a bath since I saw him last, I finally stand and embrace Gary. He too looks much better than when I last saw him. The pinched, stressed forehead has disappeared.

"How is she? And how are you?"

"Good—we're both doing great."

Cal comes forward to shake Gary's hand and hug Stephanie. I introduce them to my mom and aunt, and we move to the back porch for dinner.

Stephanie eats a little salad and bread but then is so excited to have spotted our cat, Oliver, who's prowling through my vegetable garden, that she slides from her chair and runs over to make friends. Ollie's a good sort, and I see him roll onto his back to receive her tentative pats on his stomach.

Over the pasta, I finally ask the question we've all been wondering about. "Anyone hear from her?"

Gary wipes the corners of his mouth and says, "She hasn't been in contact at all with her sister or her mother, although I'm really not surprised she hasn't called her mom. They never had a great relationship. But Janet's another thing. She's beside herself with worry. And . . . she's shocked and feels extremely guilty. She said she would never have imagined Rena could do something like that to Stephanie."

"Rena seemed to be amazingly good at impersonating the model mother," says Cal.

Gary says, "Yeah, she fooled me, for sure. When I look back, I realize now she did everything she could to keep me away from Stephanie, I guess so I couldn't catch on to what she was doing. Then I started remembering things. Like how Rena would change doctors, and at least three times, she checked Stephanie out of the hospital against medical advice." He looks down at his plate. "I guess I share a lot of those same guilty feelings Janet has."

"How could you know? All those doctors didn't know," I say, patting his hand.

"These women are really hard to catch," adds Cal. "From what I've read, some mothers with Munchausen by proxy get away with this multiple times, with multiple children. So don't beat yourself up."

Gary nods and reaches for a piece of bread. "It's such a strange name, isn't it?"

"It was named after a German officer who told really

outrageous lies about his life and adventures," says Cal. "Actually, there's an updated name for it: factitious disorder imposed on another."

"Cal's considering writing about it for his master's thesis," I say. "And the police? They haven't been able to find her?"

"Nope. It's like she disappeared off the face of the planet. But then last week I heard from Detective Larson. There might be a small break in the case."

"What? Does he know where she is?" I ask.

"Not yet, but remember the neighbor, Mrs. Lupito? She told Larson that Rena was working at Bert's Pharmacy, which was around the corner from the place where Rena and Stephanie lived. Larson talked to the manager there, Joe something, who said he thought Rena was seeing some guy who came into the pharmacy a lot. In fact, Joe remembered this guy getting a prescription right around the time Rena disappeared, so he checked through his records and identified the prescriptions that were picked up during that time period."

"And he found the guy?" Cal asks, waving to Stephanie, who is now sitting next to Ollie, tickling his whiskers with a piece of parsley.

"Well, Larson's narrowed it down to two possibilities. Some guy named Dean Phillips from Colorado, who was visiting Arizona with his family, and another man, Louis Castle. Turns out this Louis guy recently moved to California—like, just left Arizona one night and never came back."

"How'd Larson find that out?" Cal asks.

"Said he talked to Castle's wife. She didn't have much good to say about him, but did tell Larson that he just disappeared and supposedly was going to California on business, but she's not exactly sure where in California. She couldn't even tell Larson what kind of work Louis did. Said that he was an accountant but had changed jobs and never told her much. Apparently, they're going through a real nasty divorce. He calls to talk to his kids but never from the same phone number, according to her. Anyway, Larson's still checking it out."

"I sure hope they catch her," I say, passing the green bean salad to him. "And Stephanie? She looks wonderful. Is she doing as well as she looks?"

"Thank you. Everything's delicious. She's good, really good. Steph and I are both going to counseling. But it was pretty scary for a while there, as you know."

That night is never far from my conscious thoughts and probably colors more of my unconscious life than I even realize. The picture of that tiny child lying crumpled on the floor, a tube attached to her, filling her with what we found out later was a concentration of salt and water that nearly did its intended job of killing her. It seemed to take forever for the ambulance to arrive. I kept holding Stephanie's limp body and whispering until I was hoarse, "Hang in there, honey. Help's coming. It'll be okay. Stay with us."

Cal told me the EMT had to pry my arms from around her in order to check her vitals.

"When I think of how close I came to losing her, I . . ." Gary can't finish the sentence.

We followed behind the ambulance to the hospital, the same one Rena had taken Stephanie to for her recent ER admission and her appointments with Dr. Norton. The action in the emergency room was frenetic. There were so many white coats around her, we couldn't tell what was going on, or even if Stephanie was still alive.

When they took her away to a private room, Cal, Gary, Detective Larson, and I huddled together in the waiting area. I don't know about them, but I assumed from all the bent heads and closed eyes they were doing exactly what I was: praying hard.

When a young woman entered the room and called out "Mr. Cole," we all stood as a unit. She walked toward us, and Gary held out his hand, introduced himself, and confirmed he was Stephanie's father.

She said, "I'm Dr. Norton. Please, let's all sit down."

She told us Stephanie was still in critical condition.

That she was suffering from hypernatremia, with a serum sodium level of 182. She explained this was the equivalent of almost seventy packs of salt, a life-threatening amount. Stephanie was having trouble breathing, so they'd inserted a tube and also administered medication to stop the seizures.

"We're attempting to equalize the amount of salt in her system through an intravenous drip of normal saline and five percent dextrose. This has to be done very, very slowly so as not to further tax her body." Dr. Norton placed a hand on Gary's arm and said, "We won't know until later whether or not she's suffered neurological damage." I saw him shudder, and then tears rolled down his cheeks.

I was trying hard to concentrate on each of her words, but they only swirled over and around my head, with a notable exception: *life-threatening*. Those landed with the ferocity of a boulder and took up residence on my shoulders for those next torturous hours.

I couldn't say what actually happened during the wait. I remember drinking lukewarm tea that tasted a lot like coffee, probably because the water had been filtered through the same pipe as coffee in the machine. I remember Detective Larson was in and out, having called for an all-points bulletin, which included the picture Gary provided of Rena and Stephanie he had in his wallet. But this seemed like shooting blind. There was no real direction for the search since nobody had a clue where she could have gone and how. Because Rena didn't have a car, Larson told the police to check airports, train stations, and bus depots. Attempts to track her through her cell phone were also unsuccessful.

I know I eventually fell into a fitful sleep. My head was in Cal's lap, and his head was flung back on the top of the small plastic bench. He was snoring loudly. Every now and then, I'd open my eyes to find Gary sitting stiffly in a chair, staring straight ahead, like a seventh grader who'd been given detention. As far as I know, he never closed his eyes at all during that interminable night.

Finally, as the sun was rising and sending a shock of light into the waiting area, Dr. Norton came to see us again, a tentative smile on her face. Collectively, we all breathed, not realizing we'd not been inhaling and exhaling in a normal fashion for many hours.

"She's doing much better," said the doctor. "The sodium levels have finally started to normalize and we were able to remove the breathing tube. Obviously, we'll keep monitoring, but you can see her in another half hour or so."

"Brain damage?" Gary asked, his voice shaking with exhaustion and fear.

Dr. Norton took his hands in hers and said, "I think she's going to be fine. She's a very lucky little girl."

I look at her now, racing up and down the rows of tomatoes and basil, trying to play a game of hide-and-seek with Oliver, whose version is slightly different from hers and amounts to staying completely still while she skips around and over him. The sun glints off her golden hair, and her giggles sound like tinkling glass. She's incandescent.

"Where are you guys living now?" asks Cal.

"We're still in the house Rena and I owned, but I'm thinking we might move down south. Away from the winters here. Fresh start, you know."

My mother nods, looks at me, and smiles.

We know about fresh starts.

After we saw Stephanie and were sure she would recover, Cal and I started our drive back to Sedona from Phoenix. I had a lot of time to think about what had happened. One surprising realization was that I no longer felt guilty about my dad. It was as if the rotations on some giant cosmic Rubik's Cube had snapped into place and, somehow helping to save Stephanie had absolved me. Once that guilt was finally out of the way, I felt myself unburdened, and as a consequence, more willing to become burdened. I actually felt the need to be needed, to be depended upon, to take responsibility for someone other than myself. To be a part of something bigger than myself.

Midway back to Sedona, Cal and I stopped at a tiny chapel along the side of the highway. It's not a formal church at all, only a wooden structure, maybe ten feet square. It's been there for years, and people stop to put their prayers up on its interior walls. The only light is what comes from the two small windows along one side. The surfaces of all four walls are filled with torn scraps of paper, pieces of clothing, remnants of paper towels, and even some toilet paper bits. Some people write directly on the walls in colorful markers, but most of the time, the words are scribbled on whatever someone had handy at the moment. They're affixed with thumbtacks, for those who remembered to bring them, but most often with tape, gum, or toothpaste.

Please help my dog, Trixie. She's having surgery tomorrow.

My mom needs prayers bad. She real sic with the diabetes. Losing her leg.

I pray for the world, for our leaders to keep peace, and for people to love each other.

Make Jeremy ask me to the prom.

I took the receipt from the Taco Bell we stopped at an hour before, wrote on it, and placed it on the wall with the end of a paper clip I had in my purse that I unbent, poked through the paper, and inserted in a knothole. It was wedged between *I'm so scared, please give me strength* and *Dad has to stop drinking. Help now!!!*

Cal walked up behind me and asked, "What are you doing?" and I pointed to my note, which he read out loud.

Please help Stephanie to recover fully, put all this pain behind her, and live happily.

And please, please have Cal marry me, soon and forever.

He turned me to him and kissed me for a long time. We were married the next spring in my mother's backyard, among her blooms and herbs and butterflies. Cal was able to transfer his credits, and his company, not wanting to lose him, offered him a part-time position at one of their stores nearby.

It's taken some time, but my mom and I are slowly building our relationship. She frequently reminds me that I am not the mother, she is. When I see her doing so well, happy and independent, I feel like I'm finally taking full breaths, emotionally speaking.

"Hey, do you think you'll ever work on another case? You know, use your psychic skills to help the police?" Gary asks.

"Who knows? Maybe," I say, but I'm thinking, *No time soon.* I'm still trying to find ways to channel my gift so I can provide the most helpful and accurate information to my clients but not be swept away in the sometimes overwhelming vortex of messages.

I look around the table at my mom, Aunt Frannie, Cal, and Gary and as I watch Stephanie in the garden, I realize how truly happy I am. Right now, I need nothing more. All that happened this past year—it was like white light going into a prism and coming out a gorgeous spectrum of colors.

58

Rena

Another beautiful day in California. Actually, there are only beautiful days here. Not that I'm bitching about it. I'd be very happy to never shovel another flake of snow for the rest of my life. And the weather here has sure helped my knee.

This place isn't exactly the bungalow I dreamed about, but it's okay for now. We're only fifteen miles or so from the beach in an apartment complex with a lot of loud college kids. I keep telling Louis I can't have his children or Stephanie visit us until we get a bigger place. He understands I don't need any extra stress during my pregnancy. It's only temporary, this apartment, just until Louis's divorce is finalized.

Which, he says, should be real soon. Hopefully, before the baby is born. Then we can get married, and he can put me on his health insurance, like pronto.

When we came here that first weekend to find this place, I immediately fell in love with California. I told Louis that Gary and I had been talking about joint custody for a really long time. That he had been begging me to have Stephanie for half the year and I could have her for the other half and that he wanted to start this arrangement right away. Louis put down the deposit on the apartment, and him and me got busy setting up the place.

Louis still has to travel all the time for business. I'm having a blast checking out the area and going to the beach nearly every day. There's a bus stop right outside our apartment. I even joined a gym and have been working out three days a week.

Louis was pretty surprised when I told him I was pregnant, but eventually, he was real happy about it. I rub my stomach. It's a boy. I'm so excited. I even found out that the local library, which isn't too far away from us, has weekly Mommy Loves Baby meetings.

He keeps asking about the settlement. I tell him it's supposed to be decided soon and then we'll get the money. I know once this baby is born, he'll be so excited he'll forget all about that and will even stop talking about going to Arizona to see his kids.

You can really do shit around here since there's no bad weather. And organic products—they're fucking everywhere.

I know I'll be able to feed this child all the right things from the start—like a good mommy should.

Acknowledgments

I t's astounding what it takes to pull a book together. I am incredibly grateful to the legions of passionate partners who championed *The Perfect Fraud* along its path:

To Molly Friedrich, Lucy Carson, Heather Carr, and the team at the Friedrich Agency, for your unfailing advocacy, honesty, and guidance and the fact that my characters and story traveled all the way to Italy with you for Lucy's nuptials. And Molly . . . I will forever be apologizing for not sending the manuscript to you first. Obviously, I'll never make that mistake again. You are magnificent!

To Sara Nelson, Mary Gaule, Leah Wasielewski, Heather Drucker, Stephanie Cooper, and everyone at HarperCollins. What a wonderful, collegial group you are. From our first lunch, I knew Sara was the perfect editor for me. Thank you for your fantastic ideas and support through this exciting process.

To my family, whose enthusiasm made a phenomenal thing even more so. It's a privilege and a joy to be able to share wonderful news with people who care and have always been rooting for you. I'm especially grateful to Dean LaCorte, who reminded me it takes grit to make something happen; to Sophia LaCorte, for alternate endings; and to Summer Segal, for her expertise in genetics.

To Dr. David Nicklin for providing medical background information and to Anna Tobia for helping me uncover and release the stories. To the many psychics and mediums I saw who provided background for this novel, any mistakes in card readings and interpretations are mine.

To my fantastic beta and first readers in the Philadelphia Writer's Group and particularly to Julie Mount, Julie Rea, and Dawn Kane—thank you for reading every word. My love and gratitude to Bobbie Cassano and Lynn Schindel who provided valuable feedback but also, always, their affection, laughter, and encouragement.

Finally, to my husband, Michael, our sons, Chris and

Nick; our daughters-in-law, Roxie and Mags; and to our lovely granddaughter, Amelia. Without you, there are no tales worth telling. I love you all and thank you, thank you, thank you for helping me to believe it was possible.

About the Author

ELLEN LACORTE worked for many years in HR. She now writes full-time from her home in Titusville, New Jersey, where she lives with her husband. They are the parents of two grown sons.

HARPER LUXE

THE NEW LUXURY IN READING

We hope you enjoyed reading
our new, comfortable print size and found it
an experience you would like to repeat.

Well – you're in luck!

HarperLuxe offers the finest in fiction and
nonfiction books in this same larger print size and
paperback format. Light and easy to read, HarperLuxe
paperbacks are for book lovers who want to see
what they are reading without the strain.

For a full listing of titles and
new releases to come, please visit our website:

www.HarperLuxe.com